I0601642

Alan Dale

His Own Image

A Novel

Alan Dale

His Own Image
A Novel

ISBN/EAN: 9783337002282

Printed in Europe, USA, Canada, Australia, Japan

Cover: Foto ©Andreas Hilbeck / pixelio.de

More available books at **www.hansebooks.com**

HIS OWN IMAGE

A NOVEL

BY

Alan Dale

"O, beware, my lord, of jealousy!
It is the green-eyed monster which doth mock
The meat it feeds on.

NEW YORK:

COPYRIGHT, 1898, BY

G. W. Dillingham Co., *Publishers.*

MDCCCXCIX.

[*All rights reserved.*]

CONTENTS

HIS OWN IMAGE

Chapter I

THE ACTOR *en négligé*

REGINALD RELLERICK, actor, of carefully embroidered reputation ; ego-maniac, of almost psychological import, turned in his big blue bed, drew up his feet, and yawned. He was unstudied, and unconsciously human, for even a great actor cannot set nature entirely at defiance.

The dingy sun of London was not allowed full play in Mr. Rellerick's apartment. It fought its way through rosy festooned curtains, and planted an absurd carmine clot on the actor's nose—a nose that had been discussed throughout the land.

Mr. Rellerick " came to " slowly, as though the act were enjoyable—one that he savoured. His marvelously one-toned mind gathered up the threads of its own make-up, and the actor, like a serial story, gradually prepared himself " to be continued in our next." A smile illumined his chaste, yet classic features, as he realized that, after all, he was himself. He rejoiced each morning as he renewed his own acquaintance. This is invariably a pleasant and a goodly thing for an ego-maniac to do.

As he lay there, wallowing in the mere animal warmth of his own well-groomed body, his importance arose in his mind like a mental giant, and filled the room. He saw nothing else. The furniture was all—himself ; the decorations were all—himself ; the big blue bed was all—himself ; the pink adulterated sun was nothing but a useful property designed to agreeably tint it all.

Mr. Rellerick heaved a deep, fat sigh of content. He wondered why the outside world bothered about getting up and fretting around while he was there on his pedestal. For him nobody else existed. The whole non-ego outside was but a feebly defined shadow. Tom, Dick and Harry, in the rush and fever of their pursuits are fully aware of their own subordination to the rest of humanity. Mr. Rellerick was unable to see that anything he did, or might elect to do, was not of vast, of universal importance.

The bottle-washer, who washes bottles for his daily bread, realizes that, necessary as his work may be, the world yet contains men and women who occasionally think of other things than bottles. The actor ego-maniac, on the contrary, preferred to believe that the universe was constructed to lead up to the great act of Himself. Those who thought otherwise were his mortal enemies. Those who coincided were his slaves and his unworthy dupes. The former he hated ; the latter he despised.

As soon as he was thoroughly awake, Reginald cushioned himself artistically in the big blue bed. His perfect profile indented the soft white pillow. He wished that there was somebody there to see him. He was so accustomed to audiences that the solitude of his bed-room seemed almost ludicrous. A large, cool, white statue, supposed to represent the Venus de Medici in the Museum of Florence, arrested his attention momentarily. He amused himself by thinking how envious the outside world would be of this Venus, if she could only manifest one single symptom of living appreciation.

By this time Mr. Rellerick was completely himself. All traces of unconscious humanity had vanished. He had resumed his deleterious occupation of acting a part. The external *brou-haha* of London surged and circled in the streets, but the big blue bed was just then the actor's world, and he was its population—a teeming, tumultuous population of one.

He sat up and leaned his cheek upon his hand, in the attitude of his picture at the National Gallery. All the London art critics had lauded that attitude. He rather liked it himself.

He had " closed his season " at his own theatre, built for him by his own admirers. The night before had been one of much glory. For the final and ornamental event of his season he had produced a new play by a well-known playwright. The playwright's name had figured in tiny type on the programmes—as it deserved to do. His own had been limited only by the size of the bills.

Every thing came back to him in a sweet, swirling rush. He had made a delightful speech, that had cost his hard-worked secretary at least two weeks of earnest, undiluted thought. He had talked blithely of the education of the masses—although he regarded the masses as " supers " in his own seething life-drama. In this world everything is pretense, and he was obliged to pretend that he had some object in view, other than his own self-aggrandisement.

How they had all applauded—those dolts in the audience! The Prince of Wales had been there, with pearl kid gloves, and the Princess. He had led the applause with his own hands, and had remained until the final curtain fell. He had been noticed talking to the Princess with quite unusual vivacity, and when Rellcrick had glanced, in loyal deference, at the royal box, Albert Edward had been positively observed to very nearly smile. The honour of it all! The glory!

" The strain upon the actor is great," Reginald had said. " The constant demands made upon his emotions are bewildering. I am sure you will not grudge me a holiday, ladies and gentlemen. It is hard to leave you, even temporarily. Your favour is sweet; your encouragement is dear and lovely. However, nature needs recuperation. I go from the fevered splendours of this glittering metropolis, to those glad, poetic haunts, where there are rippling brooks, and violet landscapes, and all the gorgeous features of nature unadorned."

That had been his final utterance. Even the

ego-maniac is not completely fenced in from the sublime and healing sense of the ridiculous. Reginald Rellerick choked with suppressed laughter, as he lay there in his big blue bed. Rippling streams! there was nothing that he loathed so utterly. Violet landscapes! They were exceedingly useful for threadbare, velveteen artists and school-girl amateurs. The gorgeous features of nature unadorned! They had always seemed to him to be miserably *kif-kif*. What were all those gorgeous and unencompassed features to the soothing rebellion, the exquisite mutiny, of Piccadilly Circus?

He frowned as he reflected that he should probably be expected to leave London for a time. The odious idea of " taking a holiday " like the butcher, the baker, or the candlestick-maker, oppressed him heavily. The public, however, insists that we shall behave conventionally. We must go to bed when it is night, and rise when it is day, and " take a holiday " once a year, when we are tired. To be successful in the world, we must subscribe to its conventions. That is inevitable. Reginald Rellerick knew it. The fact was perpetually dinned into his ears by his secretary. Great though he might be, there were certain grooves that he would never be permitted to leave. Only the disapppointed and impecunious cynic can afford to do as he likes.

The actor sighed. Could he ever bring himself to leave London—appreciative, wonderful London, where he was known and recognised at all times? A dreadful picture of country barbarians weighed upon him.   The idea of being obliged to introduce himself ; to explain that he was an actor ; to walk through streets where nobody cared whether he was shaven or unshaven ; to pass whole days among people who were absolutely unconvinced of his greatness, frightened him.   The mere notion was self-obliteration.   It would be a gap in his life.   Yet he smiled again as he recalled his words of the preceding night—"the mental strain upon the actor "—" the constant demands made upon his emotions."   Ha! Ha! Ha!   The smile developed into a laugh.   Even the cool, white face of the Venus de Medici seemed to smile.   What nonsense it all was!   Imagine an actor putting aside the balmy favour of a " crowded house," and rushing off, with a valise, to listen to purling, gurgling streams!   The mental strain of pretending to like it all is surely the most arduous task of his life. At least that is what Reginald Rellerick thought.

The actor sat up and touched an electric bell by the side of his bed.   The gentle tintinnabulation was music to him.   It placed him in communication with his sycophants.   Without them, he was like an opium eater destitute of drug.

"Send Mr. Crampton to me," he said to the valet in response.

The menial stood for a moment in well-rehearsed admiration of his master.   He had a part to play, and he played it every morning.   It was a thinking part, but it was one of those " bits " that stand out.   All that he had to do, was to look at the recumbent figure on the bed with a sudden expression of joy, and then draw himself up semi-apologetically, as though the lovely sight had been too much for him and had caused him to forget himself.

Reginald Rellerick smiled indulgently. The valet was always his first sycophant, and he loved this introduction to the obsequious galaxy! Sometimes he called his menial "sirrah," because the word had a haughty, old-time-y sound that was distinctly luxurious.

Mr. Crampton, the secretary, was a mouldy person, with stooping shoulders and a cadaverous face of jaundiced hue. The face was quite devoid of any expression. The shoulders were very respectable. They had acquired their stoop in Reginald Rellerick's service. Mr. Crampton wrote his speeches when he opened bazaars, laid foundation-stones, or addressed students. Mr. Crampton answered all his letters, and was responsible for various learned articles that had appeared above the signature of "Reginald Rellerick" in leading reviews. He was an Oxonian Master of Arts, but he had forgotten the fact. He had forgotten everything, in the service of the great and famous actor.

Mr. Crampton opened the door and entered. In his right hand, he had half a yard of column, clipped from a newspaper. The ruddy hue of the drawn curtains turned his gamboge face to old rose, but imparted no expression to his features. Nothing could do that.

"This," said Mr. Crampton, holding up the half-yard of column, "is a most agreeable and just criti-

cism of your work last night.   It will please you, I
am quite sure."

Mr. Crampton hesitated.   He knew what was
coming.

" Is that the only clipping you have to give me
this morning ?" asked the actor, absurdly anxious,
and carmining slowly.

The secretary shuffled, ungainly as a dromedary.
" I have carefully read every paper," said he, "and
I am sorry to say that many of the notices are flip-
pant, and unworthy of your attention.   You, sir, as
you have told me often, have nothing to learn from
the asses who call themselves critics.   Every great
man has his enemies.   This morning I have noticed
an unusual amount of spite, malice and pettiness.
All these are really tributes to your greatness."

An observer might almost have imagined the
ghost of a smile on Mr. Crampton's corpse-like face.
In reality there was none.   The mouldy secretary
had no illusions.   Only people with illusions know
the bliss of a surreptitious smile.

" Read me your criticism," commanded the great
actor harshly.

It was a magnificent adjectival commendation.
Mr. Reginald Rellerick was world-famous, and he
had produced a new play ; not that the great yet
paying public attached much importance to a play
when Rellerick deigned to appear in it.   He had
been plied with a part that again gave his stupend-
ous genius emotional opportunities.   Far from that
genius being on the wane—as certain malignant
writers professed to believe (Rellerick winced at

this) it had never been more convincingly instanced. The leading lady, Felicia Halstead, had contributed a "reliable" performance, but one that was, of course, unimportant artistically, as compared with the bewildering effort of the actor, who was at present making the history of the English stage. *Et patati. Et patati.*

"It is badly, wretchedly written," said the Oxonian Master of Arts, "but," added the obsequious secretary, "it is very just."

"It is admirably written," cried Reginald, pushing aside the pillow. "Why there is not an unfriendly note in it. It was the work, I believe, of young Winkle—you remember the fellow I recommended to the *Screamer.*"

"I believe that it was, sir," replied the secretary. "He is evidently a very grateful young man."

The eyes of the ego-maniac rounded themselves in surprise. "I don't know what you mean by the word 'grateful,' Crampton," he murmured. "It is not a question of gratitude. Mr. Winkle saw my performance without prejudice, without envy, without spite, without sinister motives, and he told the truth about it. The others are all liars and perjurers. Winkle, I notice, never even mentions the name of the playwright. He is a far-seeing youth. He knows the love of notoriety, and the hankering for publicity, that move the modern playwright. He declines to prostitute himself to that sort of thing. No playwright's name should ever be used in the review of a great actor's work."

"Except, occasionally, Shakespeare's," suggested the secretary.

"You are right, Crampton. Shakespeare's name never does any harm. It rather enhances the actor's value. However, as I was saying, I am quite pleased with Winkle. He is a remarkaby talented young writer. If I had my way, I should have his views set up in all the papers. I must discuss the question in the *Fortnightly*. You can write the article at your leisure, Crampton. Why shouldn't there be but one critic in a big city? Dissenting opinions are really an obstacle in the way of progress. I like Winkle, Crampton. They tell me that he has a wife and nine dear little children. Suppose you send Mrs. Winkle an autograph letter from me——"

"I am afraid that the children won't find it nourishing," interrupted the secretary.

"I am astonished, Crampton. Nobody has ever yet accused me of penuriousness. I was going to say when you so foolishly interrupted, that you may enclose in the autograph letter, a ten-pound note, to buy boots, or comforters, or under-affairs for the olive-branches. I like to encourage merit. You may leave me now. I shall get up, and possibly I may run in to the Garrick for an hour or so."

Crampton shuffled again, in his dromedary-like clumsiness. "You have said good-bye to the public for the present," he said. "You have announced your intention to rest. If you could bring yourself to avoid the club for a few weeks, the effect, I think, would be artistic. Remember you are tired, exhausted, bent upon recuperation."

The mouldy secretary again seemed to suggest the inception of a smile. He knew Mr. Rellerick so well! The great actor lived in the petty adulation of his club, in the unhealthy warmth of its sycophancy, in the mute adoration of Tom, Dick and Harry. It was hard to forsake it all, even temporarily. There was the joy of being gazed at when entering; the bliss of knowing that the Babel of tongues ceased as he took his favourite armchair; the dulcet satisfaction of the triumphal exit. Only the absolutely ego-maniacal actor of diseased personality understands the furious delight of perpetual pose.

Reginald Rellerick bit his lips as he listened to the diplomacy of his secretary. It was wholesome advice. He knew it. Yet to accept it was like voluntarily wooing incarceration. The great actor lived for himself, as the public saw him. Minus that public, every incentive to existence was lacking. The ego-maniac cares little for riches, except for the sycophancy that they purchase; he has scant interest in art, save for the glamour that it may cast over his personality. Friendship is a rung in the ladder of self; love a mere sensual commodity.

Having offered his modicum of advice, the mouldy Crampton withdrew. Before leaving, however, he took from his pocket a budget of newspaper clippings—the adverse criticisms of his master's performance—and placed them ostentatiously on a marble table. This mode of procedure was inevitable. Baleful curiosity might take possession of Mr. Rellerick. He was human, after all. A great actor, like other deluded people, suffers from what is known as the " mania of persecution." He likes to know his enemies. Adverse criticism is to him the ammunition of the enemy.

To the public, Mr. Rellerick never " read newspapers." To Crampton, he perused the " helpful " criticisms—those that " helped " the illumination of his ego. In the solitude of his sanctum, *vis-à-vis* to the voluptuously inert Venus, he mastered the inimical comments of his traducers. Crampton guessed this. He gave him the opportunity to satisfy his craving. After every " first night " the same things happened. The secretary appeared and read aloud all that was laudatory, after which he deposited all that was non-laudatory within the grasp of his master.

Reginald Rellerick dressed slowly. It was an occupation that he savoured. In the silken garments given the honour of immediate acquaintance with his cuticle, the actor surveyed himself in the long cheval-glass. It was an honest admiration that he felt, and there was no need for disguise. His own personality was, to him, a precious gift. The preparation of his own person for contact with a charmingly appreciative world entertained him extremely. Yet the solitude of it all was at times irritating. He would have admitted an audience gladly, without the slightest qualms of modesty. He enjoyed this daily preparation, but it would have been sweeter if the chairs in his room had been occupied by an admiring public.

Reginald Rellerick was not what is known as a "dandy." To have imagined that mere clothes enhanced his glories, that a blue necktie stamped him with individuality, or that a creased trouser betokened refinement, would have been to over-estimate the value of sartorial effect. Clothes are the solace of the squalidly sane. The world said that he was badly clad and that his taste was execrable. These facts made his trademark. He would not have changed his baggily-fitting garments for the sprucest tailor-work he could find. It was all a question of arranged dis-arrangement, of zealously planned slouchiness.

Breakfast was served to him in an alcove that swelled from his bed-chamber. It was a breakfast of substance. There was nothing in it suggestive of rose-leaves and dew-drops. Although Mr. Rellerick posed in public as a genius to whom mere food was distasteful, in private he gratified the longings of a material nature. He ate eggs—the acme of all that is commonplace and sordid. He drank the tea that solaces the unintellectual washer-woman and opens the floodgates of a frivolous eloquence.

The eyes of the Venus de Medici—or so it seemed to this connoisseur of eyes and their glances—watched him reproachfully, as he ate and drank greedily. He felt uncomfortable. His self-consciousness was embarrassing.

When he had finished his meal and lighted an

Egyptian cigarette, the great actor unceremoni-
ously seized the budget of criticisms which had
been placed upon the marble table by the seedy
Crampton.

It was apparently an interminable budget.
Every newspaper in London, with the exception
of that which owned the worshipful Mr. Winkle as
its critic, had a point to make. It was a dreary
and an intolerable point. As it was brought home
to the ego-maniac he flung the Egyptian cigarette
to the ground and stamped it out of existence. As
its full significance dawned upon him, the calm of
his features was dissipated, and in its place appeared an odious expression of rage and hatred.

He arose and stood glaring at the Venus de
Medici as though that white witness of his fury
might have helped the situation. Backward and
forward he paced, his mind in a tumult as the real
force of the catastrophe struck him.

An actor's soliloquy on the stage is generally
considered unreal. A soliloquy in actual life is
uncanny. Mr. Rellerick soliloquized aloud in his
room. What he said was neither poetic nor elevat-
ing.

"The cat!" he cried. "To undermine me in
the minds of those critical vermin. And that is the
woman I have helped and praised and loved!"

He brought his clenched fist down on the breakfast table. The cups shivered in their frail, china
way. A plate fell to the floor, rudely broken.
Once again he picked up the clippings and read

them all anew, his eyes gleaming, his lips quivering, his frame in a paroxysm of anger.

It was all too malevolently true. Felicia Halstead was the name with which these criticisms reeked. The fact that she had deliberately wrested the honours of the play from his stellar grasp, was the story that they told. Enthusiastic praise of her work was the derogatory theme; graphic description of her " magnetic personality " flavoured the whole thing. Felicia Halstead, his leading lady! Felicia Halstead, his automaton ! Felicia Halstead, his plaything and satellite !

The rage of the great actor, like a snowball rolling over snowy ground, gathered weight as it revolved around its own sensations. No such overwhelming calamity had suggested itself to him. There had, perhaps, been indications, but to the ego-maniac, indications rarely indicate. He had never even noticed her work. She had been to him what in the jargon of his over-rated " profession " is termed a " feeder." She was an animated " super "—nothing more. Yet these malignant penny-a-liners, whose lucubrations were permitted full sway, dared to assert that it was she, Felicia Halstead, who had triumphed, and that he, Reginald Rellerick, whose name was a household word throughout the land, had been swamped !

The shock of it all dazed him. As he looked at his Venus he saw it distorted. There was a devilish smile on its icy lips, a sinister arching of its marble brows. A chilly horror of the figure seized him, and with one blow he felled it to the ground. It lay at his feet unbroken, and a slight satisfaction at his manifest power visited him. This satisfaction was short-lived. His perturbation returned in full force. A dismal presentiment of waning happiness took possession of him. After all, his career was his life, his hope, his excuse for existence. She was a thief, an interloper, a menace.

He rang the bell and Crampton appeared. The secretary saw what had happened but was quite undismayed. He picked up the bust of the Venus and set it carefully upon its pedestal. He glanced at the shattered plate and at the demoniac expression on his master's face. Then he shrugged his shoulders, and waited.

"Get a hansom," cried Rellerick, "and go at once to Miss Halstead's house. Bring her here. Don't return without her. If she declines to come, use force. I insist upon seeing her."

Crampton showed surprise. This was an unusual proceeding. He could imagine no circumstances that could induce Felicia Halstead not to respond to her master's bidding. He could as soon have seen the flowers in the garden opposite refusing to turn to the sun.

"Go!" shouted the actor. "Why are you waiting there gaping? Bring her back with you."

Crampton nodded. He could think of nothing to say. Diplomacy seemed to be unnecessary. Advice was out of the question, for what could he advise? Some inkling of the truth probably reached him as he turned to leave. Five minutes later he was on his way to Miss Halstead's apartment. Poor Felicia! The secretary sighed as he thought of her.

Chapter II

FELICIA MAKES A HIT

FELICIA HALSTEAD was one of those neutrally gray, incomplete creatures we used to call woman, before Mme. Sarah Grand's hideous prose had declared war against Tennyson's matchless poetry. She was " as moonlight unto sunlight, and as water unto wine." The pale art of self-obliteration was her chiefest coquetry. She was a plaything, with wires made to be pulled by the dominant sex. In any other of life's walks Felicia Halstead would have played the maternal rôle delightfully. The soft cushions of her being were designed by nature for pillows to the young idea. She might have been a mother of lithe, brave sons, or of sinuous, wholesome daughters. Her life had moulded itself otherwise. Her lovely feminine qualities had been poured into the lap of Reginald Rellerick. All her instincts had been turned in his direction. His was the shrine at which she worshipped, as far as this world was concerned. Her pearls were cast before swine. It is a very usual case.

Felicia's face suggested sunshine. It was bright, imperfect and warm. There was warmth in her eyes; healthy life in her red, wet lips. Her face was shadowed by a tangled growth of thick, picture-book hair. That hair was dyed to the conventional theatrical " shade " of impossible yellow. Mr. Rellerick preferred it so, his own being dark and sinister. Felicia would have crimsoned her tresses had he suggested it. Her tints were matters of the utmost indifference to her. He had told her that she was pretty with her improbable yellow hair, and she was satisfied. . . She cared to be pretty, because she was eminently natural. She was glad that Reginald had indicated the exact way in which to acquire beauty. It was so much easier than thinking it out for herself. If she had been left to her own resources she would probably have had the courage of mud-coloured hair.

Her figure, in an artistic country, would have made the fortune of artists. But Felicia lived in London, where curves are looked upon with distrust, and a straight corset denotes a straight morality. Miss Halstead laced herself into stays supplied by Her Majesty's favourite corset-maker, and did the correct thing unquestioningly. The pretty face of an Englishwoman is supposed to atone for all her defects. It generally does so—in England.

The young actress lived in a quiet little Notting Hill house, with a respectable, black alpaca lady, used as a housekeeper. The housekeeper was propriety itself. She always wore a cameo brooch, with an extinct husband's hair at the back, and a circle of white ruching round her neck. Nobody doubted her. Nobody could doubt her. Any jury in England would have acquitted her of anything on earth, without leaving their seats, with the cameo brooch and the ruching as damning evidence of her virtue.

Mrs. Landington had been selected as the black alpaca associate of Felicia Halstead by Reginald Rellerick himself. Mrs. Landington was there to protect his own reputation, rather than that of the careless Felicia. The housekeeper was amusingly squalid and non-provocative. She could have been the mother of a professional beauty, and have watched her daughter's career, without an inkling of its truth. She could have posed as the parent of a sealskin chorus girl, with princely perquisites and a salary of thirty shillings a week, and have felt no misgivings. Her salient black alpaca bust was comfortable and reliable. Felicia was to her an ordinary working-woman in need of a domestic background. She fed her on chops and boiled potatoes, and affected to misunderstand Miss Halstead's aesthetic longings for more artistic nutriment. She alluded to Mr. Rellerick as Felicia's "employer" and was persistent in her efforts to please him.

It was Mrs. Landington who opened the door for Mr. Crampton, as the mouldy secretary hastened to do his master's bidding. Crampton, in Mrs. Landington's eyes was the lowest grade of servant. She retained her housekeeper's apron, after she had looked through the key-hole of the front door to ascertain the identity of the visitor.

"Miss Halstead is not up," she said unpromisingly. "If you wish to talk to her you had better come again."

"Please tell her," quoth Crampton, "that Mr. Rellerick wants to see her at once. I am to wait for her and take her back with me in the hansom outside." Then he added, in a sort of washed out attempt at easy commonplace: "It's rather early to be here, isn't it?"

Mrs. Landington made no response whatever to the secretary. She motioned to him to enter, and swept him into a reception-room that held wax flowers under shades, and woolen mats on ricketty tables—according to popular suburban dictates of taste. Then the black alpaca lady trotted upstairs, and two minutes later Felicia's voice was heard from aloft.

"I shall be ready in a few minutes," it said, for Mr. Crampton's benefit. "Have you any idea what Mr. Rellerick wants?"

The secretary raised his foggy tones and sent them upstairs as well as he could. He had no idea, he said. But he bit his lips immediately, and sighed. There was no need to play a prelude to the great actor's evil intentions. She would discover them for herself soon enough.

Miss Halstead was not long dressing. There were no mysteries about her toilet. It was a simple and unassuming affair. She appeared before the secretary in a robust dark blue costume that would have been scorned by a cook on her Sunday out. Her face was fresh and rosy. Her gold-dyed hair was exquisitely dishevelled—according to

Reginald's ideas—and it was the only feature of her personality that spoke of the fevered life that she led.

"Good morning, Mr. Crampton," said Miss Halstead. "You are indeed an early bird. I suppose that Mr. Rellerick is going to alter my part in last night's play. I think there was rather too much of it. It conflicted too much with his own, as I thought it would do. The public doesn't want two stars when Reginald is there, does it, Mr. Crampton?"

Felicia's sunshine lightened the room. Poor, mouldy Crampton thought she was the most bewildering picture of a bewildering sex that his pale, platonic eyes had ever seen. The wax flowers seemed to melt in her presence, and Mrs. Landington's evil, suburban ornamentation to acquire an artistic value. He said nothing, however. Felicia knew him so well that she expected his silence.

"I must just drink a cup of coffee and look at a slice of bread and butter," she went on, "or Mrs. Landington will be mortally offended. She is very touchy on the subject of breakfast, and if I went away without eating she would look upon me as a sort of heathen."

As she spoke the alpaca housekeeper appeared with a tray that held so much stodgily wholesome food on its lacquered surface, that Felicia tinkled with laughter.

"I shan't eat at all, dear," she said to the respectable lady, "because Mr. Rellerick must be in a great hurry.   It looks very nice, though."

Then as Mrs. Landington's lips began to purse themselves rather threateningly, she added, " I'll make up for it, Landy, when I come back.   You can give me boiled mutton for dinner, and I'll eat it all.   And—and—do let me have one of your bread puddings, dear.   I shall be as a hungry as a hunter and a half.   Business is business, isn't it, Landy?   You couldn't expect me to eat this nest of eggs, and that aquarium of fish, when my employer sends for me at a moment's notice."

" I never ask the impossible, my dear," was the housekeeper's reply.   "You have a good, indulgent master, and you must obey him."

In the cab, Felicia's glowing matutinal spirits could not be repressed, either by the dingy pictures in the streets or the mouldy secretary's apparently obstinate indifference.

" What do the papers say about last night ?" she asked impetuously ; " I never saw Reginald so completely glorious as he was during my death scene.   It was the most perfect piece of work he has ever done.   I almost forgot to die, I was so engrossed in that splendid farewell utterance he made to me."

" But it was your death scene," muttered Mr. Crampton gloomily.

" And in the second act," went on Felicia, " when he declined to listen to my siren-like blandishments—I am always an utter failure as a siren—

it seemed to me that his voice was sheer, entrancing music. Marvelous—marvelous, I call it."

"But the audience sympathised with you," said Crampton, with a sigh.

"Do you think so? Well, perhaps a few of my superfluous lines might be removed. Such art as Reginald's should stand alone. The trouble was that Pinerville wrote this play for a stock company rather than a star. Still I am sure that Reginald will be able to make changes in it. What did the critics say?"

"Why don't you read the papers?" asked Crampton, with an almost ferocious intonation.

Felicia shrugged her shoulders and laughed. It seemed to her a very absurd question. There was nothing that she wanted to hear but a general verdict. As a rule she relied upon Mr. Rellerick for this. She preferred to abstain from mere technical criticism.

"You are a cross person, Crampton," she said, pinching his arm as though he had been a refractory schoolboy. "I should like very much to be vexed with you, but I haven't time. Tell me this: do the critics rave? I know they do—of course they must—but I should like to hear it from your sedate and unimpressive lips. You are such a sedate person, Crampton! You know you are. If you were a few years older I should engage you to Mrs. Landington. So rejoice in your youth, my dear sir."

The mouldy secretary shivered slightly, in spite of the warmth of the morning, and his face looked

more like parchment than ever. It was not necessary to answer Felicia's question, for she was chattering gaily and volubly, quite forgetful of her
temporary desire for a verdict. She was so certain
of that verdict! She took it for granted. Men were
not blind, and women were not fools to hold themselves aloof from the divinest dramatic powers in the
universe.

"I can't imagine you as Mr. Landington," she
frivoled, "driven to perpetual boiled mutton and
bread pudding. It is bad enough for me. What
would it be for you? Yesterday, Crampton, I stole
away to the Grove—this is distinctly *entre nous*—
and had game pie and a pint of champagne, in
sheer self-defence. The poor old lady would have
cried her eyes out if she had known. But I felt I
couldn't tackle a new play on a boiled mutton
foundation. You see I've confided in you, although
you are so cross. Why are you so cross, Mr.
Crampton? Don't you ever feel, when you see
Reginald act, that life isn't nearly as black as it is
painted? Don't you ever feel that, Mr. Crampton?"

The secretary made no reply. He moved an
inch or two away from Miss Halstead, and murmured something anent the lack of swiftness characteristic of London cab-horses. They fell into a
temporary silence. He, moodily, chewed a bitter
cud that seemed to be the quintessential dregs of
his nature; she was lulled into apathy by one of
those sudden, presentimental gusts that persistently
hover around light, impressionable temperaments.

The hansom rollicked over the neat grey asphalt pavement, and flew through the early street noises and the squalor of London. The mouldy secretary was the first to speak. His voice had a rumbling sound, as though it were not quite sure of itself. His parchment face seemed to mellow faintly, and there was a distinctly human anxiety in his manner as he turned to her.

" Tell me, Miss Halstead," he said, "if you, yourself, never feel an individual ambition ?　Are Reginald's hopes infectious ?　Do you never say to yourself that one of these days you, too, will be the puissant theatrical star, dominating tne masterpieces of pinnacled playwrights, spoken of in all the homes of England, Scotland, and Ireland ?　Are you content to play second fiddle to Mr. Rellerick for ever and for aye ?"

It was a high-falutin utterance, that he attempted to vulgarize by his " second fiddle " allusion. Crampton had grown so accustomed to the writing of ornamental English that occasionally he spoke it.　He looked earnestly at Felicia Halstead as he talked.　He approached her unconsciously and never knew it until the subtle perfume of her uncaught hair spoke fragrantly of her proximity.

" I have no ambition, Crampton," replied Felicia, rather gravely ; " I am a cog—a happy cog—in Reginald's mechanism.　That is all.　I could never be what the world calls 'great,' Crampton.　I have no dominancy, no magnetism, nothing that is unusual.　Why do you ask me such questions ?　They might almost insinuate that I am lacking in loyalty.

Reginald's success is all that interests me. Don't you know, Crampton, that—that—I—love—him ?"

The confession was surprised from her lips. It was an unpleasant and a compromising confession. She felt that, as soon as she had uttered it. It was Reginald whom the words might compromise. The great actor, as she knew, tried to keep himself untainted from the gossip-mongers. For her own reputation, she cared nothing at all. She would willingly have proclaimed her subjection to Reginald from the house-tops.

" When I say I love him, Crampton," she continued hesitantly, " I mean, of course, that I admire his art, and respect his personality. You understand, I am sure."

Yes, the mouldy secretary understood. He sat there, trembling and uneasy. The cab seemed to him like a hideous projectile, shooting them into infernal comprehension. He understood, for the situation was not in the least enigmatical. It was bald and easy. Mr. Crampton bit his lips. There was enigma in that action, at any rate. Why did Mr. Crampton bite his lips ?

Mr. Rellerick's door was opened to the couple by a delightfully theatrical looking " character " person with comedy manners. This gentleman aspired to his master's calling, but was as yet unsatisfied. He played persistent rôles in the kitchen, however, with Reginald's fat cook as a voluntary *ingénue*.

Felicia nodded amicably to the secretary, and ran lightly upstairs to Reginald's study. It was

there that Reginald encountered many other people. Miss Halstead was quite safe in this study.
Even the " interviewer " was permitted to talk to
and to photograph her there. The room contained
a huge bookcase, filled with volumes that the great
actor had never read. These volumes were affronts
to his ego-mania, for they dealt with old, extinct
actors. Easy chairs, a couple of sofas, and an ornamental fire-place were other features of this room.
It was aggressively dark and heavy ; magnificently
ponderous and uncomfortable. It was popular,
however, for in all the pictures portraying " Mr.
Rellerick at home " or " The great actor in his
study " it appeared gracefully. It was distinctly a
room " for the public," glowingly labelled with the
" private " brand. It was part and parcel of Rellerick's colossal lie to the world. It was mendacity,
carpeted and furnished.

Felicia paused at the open door of the sanctum.
She could see Reginald pacing up and down the
Orientally-rugged floor. He wore a dressing-gown,
with affected carelessness, and a large meerschaum
pipe hung from his loose, bulging lips. Much of
his smug complacency seemed to have vanished.
There was action, alert, crafty and vindictive, in his
manner. He saw Felicia at the precise moment
that she saw him. He motioned to her to enter,
then carefully closed the door. The footstep of
Crampton was heard descending the stairs. Then
the outer world was forgotten. Felicia and Reginald were together.

The young actress, after a first performance, felt

her keenest joy in congratulating her idol upon his success. It was a pleasure in which she was graciously permitted to indulge by Reginald himself. He accepted her adulation as a matter of course. Hers was merely a voice in the adulatory harmony in which his sycophants bathed him. With her, it was the luxurious expression of a sincerity that was an almost overwhelming gratification.

On this occasion her words were checked by the saturnine look on the great actor's face. He held up one hand warningly. Then, as a look of blank astonishment crept into Felicia's face, he remarked satirically, " Permit me to congratulate you."

Felicia Halstead decided to smile. Her Reginald's various moods infallibly pleased her. This was a new one, and there was humour in it. Reginald rarely allowed himself a dash of humour.

" As you will, my lord," she said, dropping a mock courtesy, her face radiant with laughter, " Mistress Felicia Halstead is but a woman, and woman is a vain creature. Praise from Sir Hubert, you know,—What is the matter, Reginald?"

She asked the question quickly, impelled suddenly from her frivolity. The lines around the actor's mouth emphasized themselves cruelly. His brows fell, blackly menacing, and the tints of his face grew lead-like. He ceased his aimless parade and folding his arms, stood looking at her gloomily.

" Miss Halstead is playing the usual rôle of the theatrical ingrate," he said sternly. " She is endeavouring surreptitiously to cut herself loose from an enviable position. She is eager to pose before the foolish public as a great actress. She has be-gun war against her benefactor—the man who has given her every opportunity that a woman could ask."

The girl, who had not yet taken a seat, stared at him daftly. She could scarcely credit the mean-ing of what she heard. Then, with a rush, the recollection of Crampton's words in the cab surged through her mind. Still it was all a mystery to her. She sat down quietly in an easy-chair, and began to remove her long, fluffy boa, and to pull the pins from her hat.

" For Heaven's sake say something," groaned the great actor, utterly regardless of her consternation.

" You ask me to say something, Reginald," mur-mured Felicia. " You are ill this morning. I can see that. You have worked too long and too arduously. You must take a holiday. Reginald, let us go to the lakes—where you promised to take me years ago. Nobody will know us. We can live in some little cottage with simple country folks, and we can pretend that we are away on our honeymoon—just as though we had never known what a theatre was, or what London meant. You will do this, dearest, will you not ?"

Reginald's face grew even harder and more ego-maniacal. The " persecution " idea, always preva-lent in the diseased mentality, took possession of him completely. He laughed in an ugly, joyless fashion. Then he came to her, as she waited on her chair, and standing in front of her placed his hands upon her shoulders.

"No," he said harshly, "there will be no lakes for us. There is a plot abroad—a plot for my destruction, and you are in it. The truth has appeared this morning. I won't ask you to deny that you instigated the criticisms that applaud you at my expense. You are a woman. You have made your appeal, and it has been heard. This morning the dolts of the press rave over Miss Felicia Halstead and ignore her star. I might have expected it. Still, remembering the sentimental nature of our attachment, I confess that I looked for other results."

Even as he spoke the never innately perjured human heart realized the infamy of the uttered words. The sentimental attachment between them had been used by the actor as a means of holding the woman in the blind subjection of love. That was all. It was a means to an end. Everything is a means to an end—a selfish end—with the egomaniac.

Still, Felicia failed to understand. " I don't see what you mean, Reginald," she said. " It must be a horrid jest. I don't like it. You know, dear, what you are to me. What do I care for the theatre or for what the critics say ? I am yours, for as much, or as little as you will. I have told you that my dearest hope is to be your wife. How could a wife war against her husband ? Reginald, you are a silly boy. Let us drop the subject. You have not kissed me to-day. You may do so now. Come."

She held up a face in which laughter was struggling with a ferocious battle of tears. If ever sincerity spoke, it could be heard in the sweet, pathetic ring of Felicia's tones. It would have impressed the supremest sceptic with her truth. But the ego-maniac is scepticism diseased—doubt robbed of all logic. Reginald grew infuriated.

"Miss Halstead is acting delightfully, as the critics say she always acts," he retorted viciously. "The fact remains that with the idiots who read the newspapers, it is her name that appeals to-day ; not mine. That is where the mischief comes in. It is ruin for me—an effort to knock down my splendid edifice. Oh, yes, I believe you, Felicia Halstead. How we should enjoy ourselves at the lakes—the famous young actress—with the moribund actor."

He had left her side and resumed his walk. Her fair, ingenuous face angered him now, as it had piquantly convinced him before. He had loved her, and love was the weapon she used.

"You are in earnest ?" she cried at last, rising as it began to dawn upon her that this was tragedy, not comedy. "You are in earnest ? You can really believe that I have tried to rear myself in your place ? You can think that a woman whose only happy moments have been spent in your arms —who has given you her past, her present and her future,—can prefer the theatre, the applause of the mob ? You, who know me, Reginald, can credit this ? No! no! no! It is too monstrous, too absurd. Do I know the critics ? Do I care what they say? Do I ever see them, or read them? Oh, Reginald, I am ashamed of you."

"Spare me your trashy heroics," he exclaimed, cold with indignation. "I have been a fool, and I see it all. I have been an unsuspecting fool, and I am paying the penalty of my criminal blindness."

Felicia Halstead's face was absolutely blood-bereft. Her lips whitely outlined her mouth. She trembled violently.

"Admitting that this were true," she said, in hardly audible tones, " supposing that I were like other women of the stage, anxious for my own self-aggrandisement,—supposing all this, Reginald; there is our love which must make the case different."

He burst into laughter. " Our love! Our love! Ha! ha! ha? And do you suppose that I should allow the love of any one woman to interfere with my career? Our love, forsooth! What is our love? Merely the mutual admiration of a man and a woman. What is my career? That is not usual. That is extraordinary. That is my life. Our love! Ha! ha! ha!"

Felicia sank back, overpowered by this brutality. The ego-maniac stamped his foot to emphasize his vehemence. The overwhelming of the woman before him gave him some slight satisfaction. His nature was sadistic, as well as ego-maniacal. He revelled in his own cruelty.

"I can say no more, Reginald," sobbed Felicia, the slow tears of anguish dripping from her eyes

"Something has happened to you. You see things as they are not. It is hallucination. It must be."

She rose and said more, nevertheless. She could not bear to leave him, afflicted and insane. "You will see how foolish you are, dear, when you think it all over. Try me in any way you like. Make me a 'super.' Give me a part to think, and not to act. Degrade me—and I shall never complain."

The great actor, even in this, saw the germs of conspiracy. "And you would set the gossips talking?" he asked. "You would give my slanderers food for every evil accusation? You would see me charged with deliberately humbling a woman who, the critics say, has risen from the ranks? No, Felicia, you had better say no more. You have thrust your ingratitude right in my face. You have flaunted your vanity in front of the world. You——"

Felicia Halstead stopped his further utterances. She went to him, placing one trembling hand over his mouth, while with the other she held his arm.

"It is not true," she said. "Nothing is true, except that I love you. You do believe this, Reginald. You must believe it. I shall leave you now, but when you send for me, I shall come. If I could suppress those dreadful critics, Reginald, I would do it. I never realized their power before. I never believed that they could cause a man to suspect the woman he has loved, and who loves him."

She turned from him, seized the long fluffy boa and the hat with its pins from the table upon which

she had thrown them, and without another word
opened the door and went out. The mouldy secretary, at the foot of the stairs, mbled away as he
saw her coming. She never noticed him. He
opened the door, and she passed out.

Upstairs, the great actor, walking furiously up
and down, stopped in front of a large porcelain
picture of his late leading lady. With one blow
from his clenched fist he broke it to atoms. That
was, to him, the most satisfactory proceeding of the
morning.

Chapter III

REGINALD DISSIMULATES

THE great actor walked to his club, in order
that he might plunge into the voluptuous luxury of
hatred—one of the most piquant satisfactions of
life. He felt impelled toward the club, as the con-
victed criminal to the verdict that tells him the
worst. He must mingle with the gossip-mongers
and the scandal-brewers. He must drink the very
dregs of this catastrophe, and see what he could do.
He must dissimulate as usual; he must act more
realistically than ever. And to the ego-maniac
there is as much glory in acting off the stage as
there is on it.

He saw Felicia's humid face, as she collapsed
beneath his keen shafts, but he felt no compassion
for her. Tears to him were as valueless as laughter. He had a deep-rooted disbelief in either. She
had wept because she had been detected in her
surreptitious designs. He bit his lips in anger as
he recalled her words: " Make me a super. Give
me a part to think—not to act." How well she
must have known that such a course would be impossible! Though he would have liked to humble
her to the dust, to sink her to the lowest depths of

uselessness, he would not dare to do it. And she was aware of that fact.

How powerless a man is before a woman's wiles! He had selected Felicia as his leading lady for the simple reason that he had faith in the apparent colourlessness of her nature. She would never do anything of any consequence, he had thought. And he had sealed the bargain by loving her—an arrangement in which he thought that body would gradually stamp out the slightest possibility of soul. And now the net-work of his schemes was hopelessly shattered. Far better would it have been for him, if he had chosen some vulgar, arrogant woman, who would have overreached herself at the end of the first season.

The public prefers the woman to the man. This is inevitable in man-governed communities. Great actors cannot be too careful. Mr. Rellerick had taken all precautions—and they were as nothing.

He saw his own name in huge letters on the blank walls, and shivered. How long would that name flaunt itself through the thoroughfares ? And beneath the flaring " Reginald Rellerick," in tiny type, almost illegible to the naked eye, was his leading lady's title. If type means anything, Felicia Halstead had vanquished it completely.

In the celebrity-shows of photographers' windows were his own portraits, in every pose conceivable. There he was leaning on his elbows, standing bolt upright, luxuriously pillowed in a chair, head without body, head with body, head with body and legs. There were no pictures of Miss Halstead.   In the photographers' windows he was the sole sovereign.   He realized this with a sudden flicker of pleasure.   Had he exaggerated the gravity of the situation ?   He stopped in front of the most illustrious photographic display and contemplated himself with a glad sensation.   The intellect in his face had never appealed to him more convincingly. He was not really a handsome man, but his features were distinguished, patrician, cerebrally entertaining.   He had never seen a head as perfect as his own.   What a forehead !   What eyes, in their slightly sunken enclosures !   What a fine tempest of hair !   What a——

He paused.   Two youths of the "Piccadilly Johnnie" type stood by his side.   They were talking.   He clutched at their talk.   He needed some slight consolation from the outer world.

"Did you see the play last night ?" asked one, nodding at Rellerick's portrait, as though further explanation were unnecessary.

"Yes," responded the other, "I saw it and enjoyed it.   But it seemed to me that Rellerick is going off. I never cared much about him, but somehow or other he always managed to be the play.   Last night it was all Felicia Halstead.   Delightful little girl, don't you think ?   I tell you what, old chap, that woman's got a future.   If she will only cut herself away from old Rellerick and start out on her own account, she'll be another Ellen Terry. Mark my words."

"I bet that she will have a dozen offers before the week is out," said the first.   "Good women are at a premium.   There are no more of them.   They go up like rockets, and come down like sticks."

" I say, it wouldn't be a bad idea to——"

They moved gradually away.   The last words were lost.   The dialogue fell like lead on Reginald Rellerick's spirits.   He stood there panting, his breath appearing cloudily on the window pane, his eyes apparently seeking the innermost recesses of the shop.   He had listened, by the merest chance, to a fragment of desultory conversation.   How many similar fragments were being uttered in London at that very moment?   The metropolis had organized a gigantic and devilish conspiracy.   All London was pitted against him.   What had he done?   In what had he been wanting?   What was his crime?   He asked himself these questions, for the ego-maniacal actor never believes in the spontaneity of an adverse opinion.   It has always been bought, or plotted, or manufactured.   You can lie about an actor's merits until you are blue in the face; until you sicken at the nauseating mendacity.   He will fatten on it, and will regard it simply as a necessary tribute to unmistakable genius.   One apparently hostile comment—and you are his enemy for life.   To the actor there is truth in praise only.   Censure is the child of lies —lies, villainous lies.

Every trifle irritated him.   He saw people buying newspapers—simply to read the story of Felicia Halstead's triumph and his own failure.   He noticed on a " sandwich man " a magazine's announcement of " Interviews with prominent actresses," and he writhed at the idea that Felicia might appear in the list. He passed a milliner's shop just in time to see the sudden birth of a new ticket, bearing the legend " The Felicia Halstead hat," and he realized that she was making " capital " out of the very hat that he himself had designed. He heard a *gamin* whistling the " soft music " that had been played during her death scene.

Felicia Halstead was in the air. He had exaggerated nothing. All London was busily singing her praises. How he hated her! He had hated many people in his life—the actor's profession is a sort of manure for the propagation of hatred—but he had never felt the insanity of dislike so keenly as he did at present. He must hide it all .... he must act .... he must act.

He reached his club—a dark-brown institution for actors and literary men. The two classes are invariably confused, although the actor is scarcely closer to the literary men than are the fishmongers and the butchers. The club was not very far from Drury Lane Theatre. The neighbourhood was not exhilarating; nor was the club for the matter of that.

It resembled a mausoleum, rather than the voluntary resort of cheerful temperaments. An obsequious person in dingy lackey-garb took the great actor's hat and coat, and closed the door after him. Reginald entered the smoking-room— an apartment of indescribably dreary aspect. A few of those caked-in monstrosities called " old masters " appeared on the dark, gloomily-papered walls. The furniture was old and heavy, full of lethargic reminiscences—souvenirs of days that had passed—suggestions of days that would pass.

Half-a-dozen men drank brandy-and-soda and smoked pipes in silence. It was a convivial club, without a symptom of conviviality. Each member looked as though he would like to pounce upon a fellow-member's throat and worry the life out of him. They were all pretending to read papers, books or magazines. Through a funereal window dark visions of blackest London appeared—the London of chimney-tops, squalid rear views, and hopeless, uncombed civilization.

A gentleman who wrote book reviews for the *Daily Despair* was glancing at a flimsy novel by "Gyp," and scowling ferociously, as clearly unable to make head or tail of "Gyp's" sallies as she would have been to wade through one of his column reviews. An actor-manager bitterly opposed to Rellerick on general principles, was skimming through an article entitled "The Drama in the Doldrums," and nodding his head approvingly. Of course the drama was in the doldrums—it richly deserved to be in the doldrums—it was always in the doldrums—for had not his season failed?

A "hanger-on" was apathetically watching the inhuman faces of the clubmen, and looking at his watch occasionally as though he were timing the silence. A dramatic critic, who never wrote anything bad of anybody—and was consequently most amiably despised—sat there contemptuously alone. Another, who never wrote anything good of anybody was equally unnoticed, although his presence was felt.

And from one of the London slum-courts came the ironical voice of an urchin, singing " We are a merry family—we are—we are—we are." Nobody laughed. In a London club humour is immoral and suggestive. Few people with a sense of humour would belong to one of those sepia-tinted organizations. And looking at these people, one wondered what they would do in a brilliantly-lighted room, amid a company of wits; how they would take light-hearted badinage; what they would say if you poked them jocosely in the ribs and said " Bah! bah! to you."

It was the home of ego-mania; the grotto of heavy selfishness, the breeding-ground of conceit and pomposity.

Reginald entered, king of the ego-maniacs. They were all feasting on their own innards, but none enjoyed the repast as much as he. They were all wallowing swinily in their own self-consciousness, but he was the prime wallower of all.

As he entered, a concession was made to his greatness. Books and magazines were cast lightly aside. The members nodded, looked at him attentively, sipped their brandy-and-sodas, and prepared to rupture the membranous silence.

The great actor saw them all uneasily. He regarded the magazines and the brandies as pretences. The gentlemen had been discussing him; he felt perfectly convinced of that. If they had sworn to the contrary he would not have credited their words. To the ego-maniac there is but one topic, and in this literary-dramatic club Reginald Rellerick was the great attraction. It never occurred to him that the dreary people before him might, in sheer desperation, be enjoying a holiday and thinking of something else. Of what else was there to think?

However, this dark little room where conviviality parodied itself daily, was merely a stage to the great actor, and he prepared to play his part on it as artistically as possible. His eyes fell upon the dramatic critic who had never been known to write anything bad of anybody. This gentleman was none other than Winkle, whose crescendo family Mr. Rellerick had charged himself with rewarding. But just now Winkle was useless. In their innermost recesses, actors scorn the men who sugar-coat them with praise. They have little interest in them. The praise-slingers are regarded as myrmidons, satellites, flunkeys, and Mr. Rellerick saw poor Winkle without the slightest pang of pleasure. You and I, dear reader, workers in less bewilderingly heralded walks of life than the stage, enjoy a little bit of praise, and beam gratefully upon the beneficent praise-giver. He is a ray of light in our darkness, an ounce of sweetness in our pound of bitter. But to the actor he is a tasteless matter-of-course, unworthy of grateful consideration.

Mr. Rellerick advanced with outstretched hand to Jobberlots, the censorious one, who had incinerated him viciously and had taken particular pains to laud Miss Felicia Halstead to the skies. The great actor's face was wreathed in pleasant smiles ; his manner was cordiality rampant. He was delightfully eager ; his voice was sonorous and crevice-reaching. Jobberlots trembled in his boots and felt about an inch and a half high.

" I want to thank you," said the actor-liar, warmly, " for your splendidly-written review of my poor little production in this morning's paper. No," lifting up his hand playfully, as Jobberlots began to stammer unmeaning words, " do not interrupt me, my dear sir. I am not one of those lamentably blind actors who can see nothing in a critic's work unless it be fulsome commendation. Every man is entitled to his own opinion, Mr. Jobberlots. I have always valued yours. You are so frank, so outspoken, so delightfully just with it all."

As he spoke the pins of keenest hatred were sticking in the vitals of the great actor. If he could have shrivelled up poor Jobberlots instantly, he would have done it, provided that there had been none there to see the deed.

" I don't know what would become of us all," he said, speaking at the assemblage *via* the critic, " if it were not for you gentlemen of the press. How I laughed, how I chuckled—when you likened me to a vulture picking the bones of everyone who approached the centre of the stage. Ha ! Ha ! Ha ! I hope I can enjoy a joke even at my own expense, Mr. Jobberlots. I can always appreciate that which is clever."

Reginald laughed in the most apparently affable manner. He deceived the " hanger-on " who had been timing everything. His contagious humour affected the arid *Daily Despair* reviewer, who had been thinking up adjectives for the demolition of poor "Gyp." Even the actor-manager felt that here was a superior person with a soul above mere selfish considerations. The ego-maniac is the most dangerous maniac of all. If he had guards or keepers—which he should have—he would be quite capable of gulling them all.

"I tried to tell the truth, sir," murmured poor Jobberlots unsteadily. He hated meeting the people he had been forced to criticise, but he bowed to the inevitable.

"And you succeeded admirably," was the magnanimous retort; "I want to thank you particularly," here he raised his voice so that even the menials outside could hear him, " for your splendid tribute to my dear friend and associate, Felicia Halstead. Ah, Mr. Jobberlots, there is a girl who richly deserves to be encouraged. I have recognized her abilities for some time, and I was determined that they should have an opportunity this time. That is why I selected Pinerville's play. My judgment was evidently good, you will allow me to say it, my dear Mr. Jobberlots—for I am quite sure that Miss Halstead impressed the public very favourably. Am I not right?"

Poor Jobberlots fell. He was gulled into enthusiasm.

"You are right, Mr. Rellerick," he said. "Everybody to whom I spoke seemed to think that there was was a splendid future for her. She surprised the audience.   All London is talking of her to-day."

There are some feats that are impossible even to the most accomplished actor-liars.   Even an Irving or a Bernhardt meets limitations.   Mr. Rellerick met his at this moment.   Jobberlots' ready enthusiasm overwhelmed him.   For a moment he was dumb, paralyzed by the horror of the Damoclesian sword that seemed suddenly to have fallen on his head.

It was Winkle who brought him to his senses— Winkle with the crescendo family and the miserable pittance of a salary.   " Miss Halstead has better opportunities in this play," said Winkle, " and it seems to me that a dummy could have made an impression under such very favourable circumstances."

The great actor made a mental note of further instructions to Mr. Crampton on the subject of this promising person.   Outwardly, however, he cast glances of serene contempt upon poor Winkle, and declined to address him.

" Don't you think," he continued pointedly to Jobberlots, " that my dear friend and associate, Felicia, would be quite justified in ' starring ' on the top of this unprecedented success?   I do. Not for the world would I interfere with her pro-. gress.   Only this morning I said to her, ' My dear Miss Halstead, if I were you I should organize a company of my own ; I will give you the pecuniary backing that is necessary.'   I quoted to her the hackneyed but always appropriate lines about the

' tide in the affairs of men.'   Ah, Shakespeare was a genius, my dear Jobberlots.   He addressed you and me, and our children and our grandchildren."

"And what did she say ?" asked Jobberlots, scenting a " paragraph " for his Saturday's "amusement " column.

" I am sorry to tell you that she disagreed with me," continued the actor-liar, puckering his brows as though in pain.   " She says—like our friend Winkle " (here he acknowledged the luckless praise-thrower with an uplifted, dramatic hand), " that her success was simply chance.   And I positively believe that she looked upon me as the impetus to that success.   Silly girl !   Foolish Felicia ! Women are such odd creatures, Mr. Jobberlots.   You can argue with them until you choke, without convincing them in the least.   I told her plainly that there was positive genius in her work, but she laughed in my face.   That is my conviction, however.   And I may add that I was scarcely myself last night, for I was simply lost in admiration of her perfect performance."

" My dear Rellerick," said the *Daily Despair* reviewer, deluded into cordial sympathy, " your sentiments do you credit.   I only wish that some of the fools who are always crying out about stage jealousies and all that sort of thing, were present.   It does me good to hear an actor of your prominence so warmly advocating the merits of a leading lady."

" What is the use of being unjust ?" asked the great actor with a shrug of his shoulders.   " The public judges. Besides, an artist is in love with art wherever he finds it. If I had seen Miss Halstead act in any one's else company I should have immediately engaged her. I can't afford to have mediocrities in my support, my dear Twiston. By-the-by, did you see the play last night? I told Smithson to send you a couple of stalls. I shall be very vexed if I hear that he didn't."

"Oh, I was there," remarked Twiston, "and I enjoyed it immensely."

"And you agree of course,"—Reginald tried to keep the flood of anxiety from pouring into his voice, "that Felicia distinguished herself very signally? However there can be no two opinions." (The anxiety conquered. It swept itself in billows over Reginald's tones, and he waited, fervently interrogative).

"Most certainly," was Twiston's verdict. "If there ever was a clever girl, her name is Felicia Halstead. Admirable, my dear Rellerick, admirable. I should like to see her in some of the old comedies. What a magnificent Lady Teazle she would make. Think of her as Miss Hardcastle. And I don't believe that Shakespeare is beyond her. She is young enough to make a most sympathetic Juliet or Rosalind. In fact, in my opinion, she is a budding genius."

The "hanger-on" put up his watch and joined the discussion. Said he: "Felicia Halstead is one of those women who,—like murder—will out. You couldn't down her. You couldn't keep her in the background. With women of that sort it is only a question of time and opportunity. I wonder if you could arrange an interview with her for me? I believe that the *Weekly Lampoon* would be glad to take it. And it would be doing the girl a good turn, don't you think?"

Reginald Rellerick winced. The "hanger-on" had one specialty, and that was "interviewing." He could make a fool interesting. He had a cer·tain bright and readable "style" that gave force to the most banal subjects. What could he not do with Felicia Halstead, already pinnacling herself in London? What fame might not she win with the aid of a leisurely and enthusiastic pen such as that wielded by the "hanger-on?" The .great actor's cup of bitterness had been filled to the point of overflowing. The "hanger-on" had supplied the one drop too much. It was cruelty. It was tor-ture. And in Reginald's heart his hatred for the offending leading lady swelled and rankled more oppressively than ever. He had no fixed policy in his mind, as he entered the club. His sole object was to hear the truth—the horrible truth. And he had hoped desperately that things would not be as bad as he had imagined. He had clutched at this thin wisp of hope, and behold it had given way in his hands. His mind was in a chaos of emotion. If his policy had been unsettled that morning, it was even more disastrously confused at the present. There was no longer a redeeming doubt. Cold, deliberate minds had sanctioned Felicia's success. She had been applauded not only by the fools in an audience, but by his grave, disinterested club·

fellows. He had played his part and the effort had left him exhausted. He had nothing further to learn. The ugly knowledge of the worst had come easily, even gracefully. He ordered a brandy-and-soda, and ensconced himself in a corner with a newspaper containing an article headed " London has an actress at last."

It will afford me great pleasure," he said, dismally, to the " hanger-on " before plunging into the atrocious newspaper, " to mention you to Miss Halstead. I should very much like you to see her and talk with her. I will do all that I can. Felicia is a strange girl, however, and she is very afraid of journalists. She may dislike the sudden prominence of an ' interview.' But rest assured, my dear sir, that I shall try to talk her out of her foolish scruples."

Reginald invited no further words! He sank behind his newspaper and relaxed the tension of his face. How changed he was from the *riant*, courtly, interested actor, acting so vigorously a few moments before! His face was hidden. He was almost afraid that the devilish look of hatred, with its accompanying outlines and eye-contortions, would pierce through the flimsy sheet. His jaw dropped and he sat there unable to read an intelligible word of " London has an actress at last."

The club gentlemen resumed their occupations. The book reviewer made another attack upon " Gyp." The actor-manager, who had been a silent but interested auditor, took another plunge into the doldrums which surrounded the drama. The

' hanger-on " began to time things again, and the critics drank more brandy-and-soda in nonchalant enjoyment.

Others came in, but Reginald forgot to greet them. There he sat, watching the afternoon shadows creep over the mud-colored carpet ; surveying the crusty old masters in their saturnine decay on the walls, but still apparently reading that fateful, " London has an actress at last."

The voluptuous luxury of hatred ceased to be luxury, and twisted itself into agony. He stood it as long as he could, until the beads of anguish forced themselves from his forehead, each opening pore hurting like a newly-made puncture.

Then he went away through darkening London, and walked through the dim, gray streets in a tumult of pain such as a sane man never knows—one of those tumults that are reserved exclusively for the abnormal type we call the ego-maniac.

Chapter IV

MRS. LANDINGTON sat at the little round table in the Notting Hill dining-room awaiting the arrival of Felicia. The muslin ruching round her neck stood bolt upright, as though prepared to resist any attacks. At the top of the fleshly toboggan-slide that began under her chin, glistened the cameo brooch that had the extinct husband's hair at the back. Mrs. Landington was a picture of lower-class righteousness. Her black alpaca dress " made at home," fitted her closely, and on her head she wore a respectable cap that seemed to sit there defiantly.

On the table was a particularly venomous looking mutton stew—very thick and aggressively nourishing, while on the adjacent sideboard reigned an evil bread pudding of poultice-like consistency and generally unpromising aspect. Felicia was late, and Mrs. Landington was cross. The lower classes in London may be morally lax, grotesquely uncultured, and severely inartistic, but they are always punctual at meal-time. Meals are the great regulators of existence, in their minds, and to keep

[58]

a dinner waiting shows a criminally disarranged organisation.

So she sat there, Nemesis-like, as she heard Felicia's latch-key fumbling at the outside lock. Nothing would induce her to stir from her seat. Her almost pneumatic bust tightened itself, and she was quite prepared to say uncharitable things, as she saw Felicia enter.

She changed her mind rapidly, however. Miss Halstead's eyes were inflamed as though with weeping ; her nose was purple (Mrs. Landington wondered why she hadn't used the powder which every well-regulated woman carries in her handkerchief), and as she flung aside her boa and tossed her hat upon the sofa, it was very easy to see that something had happened.

Mrs. Landington waited. She forgot the sinister stew and the morbid pudding. Something had occurred between the girl and her " employer," and perhaps the situation was grave. Mrs. Landington had an easy job—as the saying is—and she lived in mortal dread of events that might jeopardize it.

"I can't eat any dinner to-day, Landy," said Felicia, sitting down and plunging her head into her hands. " I'm too much upset. Mr. Rellerick has been very unkind—and—and—"

She burst into tears and kept her face well hidden in her hands. Mrs. Landington looked at her in amazement. A dreary dread of something that might send her out into the cold, cold world, the world in which there were no mutton stews and bread puddings, arose within her. She waited a few minutes longer, hoping that Felicia's tears would cease and that an explanation would be forthcoming. Then curiosity, urged on by the instinct of self-preservation, took bodily possession of her.

"I do 'ope," she said, " that nothing has 'appened of a serious nature, my dear. You aren't in danger of losing your situation, are you ? You 'ave a nice post, you know. When I think of the girls that 'as to stand be'ind counters all day, until their very legs are dropping under them—and not even allowed a glass of stimulants, such as we all need—when I think of them, I hoften says to myself that you should be grateful. You 'aven't been riling 'im, 'ave you ? Employers are tantalizing persons —Oh, I know—but they must 'ave their way. And it's right they should. They pay the salaries and foot the bills. And I will say for Mr. Rellerick that he grudges you nothing. 'Give her the fat of the land, Mrs. Landington,' he's told me time and again. And I try to do it, my dear. Nothing is saved. Every penny—every ha'penny he gives me—goes for the table."

Felicia scarcely heard Mrs. Landington's squalid remarks. They buzzed in her ears ; that is all. She was too completely overwhelmed by the force of the double catastrophe that had fallen upon herself and upon her actor.

"I'm sure he's a kind gentleman," continued the housekeeper, "and means well. You musn't mind 'im if 'e's been cross. Business is business, my dear. It's 'ard on the men. Don't I know it ? Why, my poor Thomas was often beside 'imself, when we 'ad that little butcher's shop down Dalston way. Many a night 'ave I cried myself to sleep, when 'e 's gone out, and called me a chattering old cat, and other 'orrid names.   And if a man with a butcher's shop takes on so, why it's no more than natural that a gentleman with a big theatre on his 'ands, should be out o' sorts occasionally—what with sceneries, and hactors, and all the expenses to pay, not forgetting 'eat and gas."

Felicia gave no heed to the querulous suggestions. She heard indistinct sounds of "butcher's shop" and "big theatre" but they could not wean her from the topic of her mind.

"It's silly crying like that," persisted Mrs. Landington, losing her temper.   "Perhaps some folks wants something to cry about.   Three meals a day, and a nice salary paid regular every Toosdy, isn't to be sneezed at.   I'm surprised at you.   It's ungrateful, and you a-sending money every week to your sisters in Lancashire—all out of Mr. Rellerick. And there you sit snivelling like a booby, just because he has said 'Boo.'   I'm ashamed of you. And 'ere's dinner cold as ice, and me a-getting faint for want of a bit or bite."

But the housekeeper was uneasy in spite of her brave words.   She helped herself to a dish of the glutinous stew, but she failed to eat it.   She sat watching Felicia.   Suddenly her fear assumed shape. She struck the table with her knife and fork, and her face changed colour.

"I know what it is," she exclaimed, "I know it.

You've been and given 'im notice, all on account of a little fuss. You 'ave. You know you 'ave. And if it's true, where am I? I ask: where am I, with nothing to me name but me clothes, and a pound or two in the saving's bank?"

Felicia withdrew her hands from her face and looked wearily at the flabby creature in front of her. Was all the world selfish? Did the universe revolve around one single self-pivot?

"I can't forget it, Landy, I can't forget it," she said, the tears still splashing down her cheeks, and an urgent desire for sympathy manifesting itself, strangely and unusually. "He says that I am trying to supplant him, and—and—I can't endure it. I love him so."

Mrs. Landington clutched the cameo brooch at her breast, as though her extinct husband's hair at its back had suddenly tickled her.

"You love 'im!" she gasped, "You love 'im! Well, I like that. Did I hear you say you love 'im? Oh, tell me I've made a mistake. I can't believe it. You love your employer? And perhaps you've told 'im so? Oh, it's all as clear as a pikestaff. Miss Felicia 'Alstead, you're a fool for your pains, and I tell you so, as p'r'aps shouldn't."

Felicia laughed at last. It was a bitter, defiant laugh, but it was a relief from the abjectly wet sensation of tears. She heard Mrs. Landington's remarks on "love," and they gave a piquant zest to the situation. And she laughed again—still more defiantly. The allusion to love had acted as a sort of red flag waved in front of a bewildered bull.

" Yes, I love him," she said, her eyes aglow, "and he knows it, and if you were not as blind as a bat, you silly old thing, you would know it, too. And I would just as soon that you did. I wish all the world knew it. I'd like to publish it in the papers. If I were his wife he wouldn't dare to think such horrid things about me. And I ought to be his wife. Yes, Landy, I ought to be his wife, and you can be as shocked as you like about it. I don't care. Sit there and gape at me. That's right— gape—gape—gape. Landy, I shall throw a spoon at you in a minute. I know I shall. I can't help it."

The housekeeper might have had a paralytic stroke. Her jaw had dropped until it evinced an inclination to career down the toboggan slide that began at her chin. Her eyes were rounded and bulging. Her bosom threatened to burst its way through the black alpaca that was stretched tensely from shoulder to shoulder. She made one or two ineffectual efforts to speak. She was tongue-tied.

Felicia looked at her in amusement. It was a satisfaction to spray the painful situation at this typical lower-class matron.

Mrs. Landington laboured and brought forth words. They were characteristic of her class. Ninety-nine out of a hundred lower-class London matrons would have said precisely the same thing.

" I know, I know," she managed to cry hoarsely, " I see it all. You ought to be married, you say. That means one thing. You want him—your good kind employer—to be the father of your child. Oh, the 'orrid scheme that we read of in the papers every day of our lives."

Felicia blushed. A wave of pink blood tinged her face, neck and ears. She was used to the lower classes, which, in cases of this kind, look for one result only, and that very immediate. Mrs. Landington could sit still no longer. She heaved herself from her chair, and went and stood like a monument in front of the girl. And through her lower-class brain surged all the vulgar possibilities, all the sordid aspects of the question, all its flamboyant immorality, unrelieved by a solitary wisp of humanity.

"Landy, don't be foolish," said Felicia stupidly, a trifle upset by the storm that she had raised. "You don't understand. You don't understand. Reginald loves me and I love him. There is no other question. He was very cruel to me this morning, and I was very, very grieved. If we were married it would be different, because nothing could take him away from me. As it is—as it is— he will never believe that I am the most unambitious girl in the world, and that I want nothing but his love."

"And more shame of you to say it "—the housekeeper spat out the words—" you, with a batch of good sensible sisters in Lancashire. A pretty kettle of fish, and no mistake ! No wonder he was cross, poor fellow. I 'ates designing girls. No good ever comes to 'em. Such goings-on I've never heard of, except in the newspapers. A nice look-out for you, with a baby on your 'ands. And

I suppose I shall be expected to look after you both and—"

"Oh, no, no, Landy," cried poor Felicia in genuine distress. "It isn't so. It isn't so. I wish it were, for Regiuald is so good, and so kind, and—and—"

She rose from her seat and in sheer helplessness threw her arms around the fat housekeeper and sobbed on the monumental bosom that began at the cameo brooch. There is a good deal of comfort in a black alpaca bust. It is always a grateful cushion for grief.

Felicia sobbed in continuous despair, with the persistent picture of Reginald's contempt in her eyes, and the unceasing remembrance of Reginald's words, phonographically monotonous, in her ears. Not for an instant did a tinge of triumph at her unsought success, stain her thoughts. She looked upon it as a calamity, because it tore from her the sympathies of her actor. And as she sobbed, she thought of the very different sensations with which other girls would have surveyed the situation. Women steal, and sin, and sell themselves, for just such "honours" as had come to her, unasked. It was the irony of a "fearful concatenation of circumstances." Why was she unlike other women? Why was she unable to revel in the barren joy of what the world calls success? Why was there no voluptuous bliss in the knowledge that a mob of unkempt, middle-class, mutton-eating Londoners was at her feet? Was not this the goal for which humanity strives? Was she not well aware that man slaves his life away and casts off the creature comforts just to secure that pinnacle of egotism which the mob alone can crown ?

And Felicia wept on, as she realized her own old-fashioned femininity. She knew that she was weak and behind the times and unpractical and unpardonable. She saw her own clinging nature as an infirmity—which, of course, it was, for the clinging woman to-day is ridiculous to our new-fangled ideas. It was true, as the squalid house-keeper had remarked, that her Lancashire relatives hung upon her earnings, and tugged at her purse. The larger her pecuniary gains the more exultant grew her relatives. Yet she could find but feeble pleasure in this thought. The mere fact that she owned sisters—as to whose appearance in this troublesome world she had not been consulted—was not one to influence her largely. The tender fibres of her being cried out for the sympathy of Reginald Rellerick, the man to whom she had given her girlhood, the being for whose approval she would have dispensed with the cheap, mad plaudits of hungry London.

It was the first time that there had ever been a difference between them. She had aimed for success in order to reach it with him, and in an endeavour to please him. He was bound for that goal, and it was not her intention to lag behind. But the goal in itself was as useless and as despicable to her, as it was necessary and adorable to him. She had tried to be his shadow—the dark, inseparable duplicate that the light throws out in keen relief. What horror of fate was it that tried to bring her forward as the substance ? Poor Felicia ! I say " poor Felicia " although I am not at all sure she will win anybody's sympathy. The one clinging woman among a hundred frenzied bread-winners, may perhaps understand her sorry plight. The others will call her a fool for her pains. According to the worldly estimate of to-day she was undoubtedly a fool.

Through Mrs. Landington's heavy embonpoint, gaudily vulgar sensations surged. Felicia wept, and Mrs. Landington thought. Mrs. Landington, nursed in the canny lap of Whitechapelism, knew that two and two invariably made four. The rude logic of her greasy temperament was infallible. She had been deeply chagrined, for personal reasons, by Miss Halstead's revelation, but as she watched the weeping girl and felt her tears as they dripped through the black alpaca to the rigid, righteous corset beneath, she was convinced that this force could be utilized just as well as any other. Mrs. Landington gradually grew to perceive that all was not lost. Things might be " rotten in the state of Denmark " but they could be patched into a semblance of integrity.

The housekeeper in Notting Hill was a philosopher in her way. She had been in contact with the rough edges of the world. That fact brews a philosopher very readily.

She made no effort to shake Felicia's gilded tresses from the sable fortifications upon which they rested. Miss Halstead should cry to her heart's content, and then, when the intensity of her emotion had become relaxed, she would be all the more likely to listen to that logic which is the logic of pounds, shillings and pence. There were no fine sensations in Mrs. Landington's make-up. She was spectacularly sordid, picturesquely squalid, overwhelmingly lower-class. While Felicia cried, she carefully matured her plans.

The young actress' tears were at last exhausted, and she paused, pale and debilitated. The housekeeper plied her with a glass of that lower-London luxury, known as "ginger wine," invaluable alike for pains in the stomach and heart. Then she opened fire.

"I do 'ope," she said, "that you are not angry with me, Miss 'Alstead. I want you to understand that although I'm a woman I'm not a prude. Oh, no, I'm not a prude. While I'm sorry to 'ear what you've just told me, I won't allow any prudery to interfere with my wish to 'elp you."

"Thank you, Landy," murmured poor Felicia, her tearful eyelashes quivering.

"As I have said before," she went on, "I don't believe, and never can believe in those artful schemes we read of in the newspapers. Girls are fools when they try 'em on, unless they are clever enough to carry 'em out without going to the courts. I 'ates the courts. Oh, 'ow I 'ates 'em, Miss 'Alstead. Now, it seems to me that you don't need 'em. A breach of promise wouldn't pay you anything at all, because Mr. Rellerick is powerful and popular, and every jury likes a powerful and popular man."

A flush of mortification reddened Felicia's ears and throat, but she was too limp and lax to attempt argument or protestation. Did it matter anyway, what this stupid old creature said? Felicia sighed and listened—because she couldn't help hearing.

" It seems to me," plodded on the Landington, " that if, as you say—and I've read it, too, in the papers to-day, although I didn't quite understand it until you explained—if, as you say, you made the success last night, then, my dear, it's very evident that Mr. Rellerick is afraid of you. He is frightened that he is going to lose his applause, and that you'll get it. That makes him quite willing to listen to reason."

Mrs. Landington screwed up her eyes tightly and allowed her double chin to rest negligently upon the barricade of white ruching round her neck. She looked like a Hecate, done up in grease and London.

" Now, we all know," said she, " that, in this world, the saying is ' Every man for himself and the devil take the 'indmost.' And if a man, why not a woman? We all 'as to look after ourselves, my dear. Why, when my poor Thomas had his butcher's shop in Dalston, a canny young fellow, who used to take out the meat,—he only got ten bob a week—threatened one day to leave and set up for 'imself if my Thomas didn't double his salary. And my Thomas wouldn't do it—not he.

And I being something of a fool in those days, advised 'im to let the fellow go. The fellow went, and in a month we had another butcher's shop to contend with. And he knew all the tricks of Thomas' trade, my dear, also all Thomas' customers. He dared to sell our shilling a pound steaks at tenpence ha'penny, and so I may as well say, we was 'opelessly injured."

Felicia smiled, although as yet she could detect no logic in these remarks.

"Well, my dear," Mrs. Landington went on, "acting's like meat, I take it, and business is business. Mr. Rellerick 'as a fine trade in the West end, and no opposition. Here 'you are, however, in the field, and the public says as 'ow your steaks are quite as prime and juicy as 'is. That's so, isn't it? He's been very angry with you to-day—not because you gave 'im notice, as I at first thought—but because you're coming into demand and that he's a-going out of it. What follows?" (Logically she held up a hand and checked off a thumb.) "He's afraid that you intend to set up in business for yourself, and sell your acting at one corner of the street, while he sells his at the other. He doesn't want you to do this. He'd prevent it in any way."

A gleam of interest illuminated Felicia's dejected features. Yet even now she could scarcely see any satisfaction in Reginald's fear.

"You tell me that you love him," said Landington, "and I'm sure that I 'opes you do, under the circumstances. He's taken advantage of you, evidently. Oh, 'ow I 'ates that kind of thing. You want 'im to marry you, and as I thinks it over, I find that it is the proper thing for 'im to do. He was a good employer, but, after all, my dear, a girl 'as to look after 'erself, with all the neighbours ready to turn on her and give 'er the black looks. There's only one way for 'im to prevent your setting up in business for yourself, and that way is marriage. A man's not frightened of his own wife. They eats the same bread-and-butter. If he provides it, she eats it, and if she provides it, he eats it—and ain't ashamed to do it, either. Don't I know that my poor Thomas ate mine, when the shop was sold up and I forced to take in washing. So, says you to Mr. Rellerick, ' Reginald, dear,' (or perhaps you calls 'im Reggie, for short) ' marry me, and I'll stay in your shop. Refuse, and I opens in business for myself and takes away your customers.' "

Poor Felicia quailed beneath the quarry-like effect of this crushing logic, which came home to her overwhelmingly.

"I 'ates scheming," insisted Mrs. Landington, " because it gets into the papers and the courts. But if a woman can get the better of a man in a thoroughly ladylike way, why, let her do it. A girl can be quite the lady when she says to a man who is afraid of her , ' Marry me, or I'll set up in opposition.' There is nothing common or unrefined in that, my dear. Nobody 'ears of it. It's between 'im and you and the four walls. And poor old Landy would never leave you, my dear."

(Here she pressed a dry eye with a finger-tip, and caused her pneumatic bosom to lift itself in a sigh.) "She may feel sorry to find this peaceful little 'ome in Notting 'Ill all broken up, but she'll go with you, wherever you goes. Even if he starts a big establishment in a swell street, Landy'll find no fault. She'll look after you married, as she has looked after you single. So cheer up, Miss 'Alstead, all isn't lost. The prospect is encouraging —most encouraging. Suppose we 'as a glass of fine old gin, and drinks to the 'ealth of Mr. and Mrs. Reginald Rellerick, the famous actor, and the more famous—yes, my dear—the more famous actress. The point lies in the 'more famous.' That's our little game."

Non-acquiescent as she was in the grimy details of Mrs. Landington's campaign, a singular repose, nevertheless, crept into the young actress's mind. Perhaps, as the housekeeper said, the situation was amenable to reason. Supposing that marriage was the method that suggested itself to Reginald Rellerick, as the solution of this problem, would she be unwilling to accept it ? Would not his love be as grateful to her if it came through a menace as through spontaneous sources? Poor hungry Felicia was bound to answer herself in the affirmative. Without marriage he was lost to her. The loyal London public would see to it that she was pinnacled and worshipped. Each new success would mean a step away from Reginald. As his wife there would be a plausible reason for her retirement from the stage. As the mother of his children, the footlights need never claim her as their own. It would be best for him, and oh, how infinitely best for her.

"If this plan is such a good one," she murmured —and her voice sounded cavernously unnatural— "he will think of it. If he is afraid of me, he will ask me to marry him. That is quite sure. He is wiser than I am, Landy, and wiser than you are."

She did not "recoil" from the idea, as a noble girl in a play or a novel would have done. She did not cry "Never! Unless he loves me for myself, I will not consent to be his." Heroines of that sort are always popular—perhaps because they rarely exist in real life, and real life is frequently what we struggle to get away from in our books and our plays. Felicia was hopelessly and irretrievably addicted to Reginald Rellerick, and as his wife she saw the only happiness that life held in store for her. Willingly would she have continued as his unmarried slave for the rest of her days—colourless, effaced, obliterated. But the demon of publicity was after her. A horror of success had been forced upon her without a contest—a success that was his god and her bugbear. Nothing succeeds like success—the French proverb says—but Felicia felt that failure would have given her keener happiness. It would not have stepped in the way of the absorbing femininity of her nature.

Mrs. Landington had poured out 'two glasses of rare old gin, the odour of which caused her vivid, lower-class nostrils to dilate in ecstasy. Gin is the champagne of the London mob, and Felicia's housekeeper was an arch believer in its merits. She handed a glass to Miss Halstead, and holding the other to her lips, she drained it to the dregs, crying " 'Ere's long life and prosperity to Mr. and Mrs. Rellerick. May they live long and be 'appy."

This toast had such a benevolent effect upon Mrs. Landington as she smacked her lips until the stiff ruching around her neck cracked, that she looked thirstily around for more. Seeing Felicia's untouched glass, and noting the fact that Miss Halstead had no intention of using it, she drained that as well, repeating the toast in hilarious tones.

Felicia was too confused to give her troubles any further consideration. The housekeeper, moreover, started ginwards, was ogling the fat bottle very insinuatingly. The young actress moved slowly away, slightly comforted, but sufficiently despondent to have satisfied the most rigid stickler for the theory that virtue is its own reward—and viceversa.

Chapter V

REGINALD RELLERICK did not leave London. He remained in the metropolis, to stew in his sensations. He made no excuses for this change of programme, and took no pains to invent a plausible lie for the benefit of the public. A fig for the public, that had shown every disposition to oust him from his unique empire ! Purling brooks and gurgling streams could be endured when the mind was at rest and the outlook attractive. Just at present, however, Mr. Rellerick felt that his presence was needed in London. There were diabolical schemes to thwart, diplomatic measures to pursue, a Macchiavellian policy to carry out to the bitter end. So Reginald remained in London, and tossed about on his big blue bed in all the agonies of insomnia. In the meantime, he carefully " sounded " the situation. It was even worse than he had at first thought. Miss Halstead's success was sung throughout London in pæans of praise. They are always waiting for something, in London. The feverish population hangs upon the expectation of novelty. Miss Halstead had furnished it. Her name was served up hot, with afternoon tea, Mayfair dinner, and the unsanctioned supper. She had taken the town by storm at the very time when Mr. Rellerick was firing upon it from another direction. The fact that she was a woman was a damning fact for him. The actor, pitted against the actress, generally gets the worst of it—for the stage is constructed to please men, and woman is its primest object. It is by means of an Ellen Terry that a wily Irving prolongs his reign. It is with her name that he fills his hypnotic speeches. It is a Sarah Bernhardt, who wins by sensational means what a Mounet-Sully loses by too much art. The names of Kendal and Bancroft, in the sugar of petticoats, have been enabled to make history. The stage is the platform for women, and the great actors fight their way against terrific odds.

Offers poured in to Felicia Halstead, and the great actor knew it. Theatrical "speculators" appeared, and begged her to suggest her own terms. They would "star" her. She should have a theatre "in the West End." There should be unlimited money in the arrangement of her career. It should be built upon the rocks of pecuniary responsibility. A triumphant tour of America was mooted—cruellest blow of all to fall upon the great actor. He had been contemplating this tour for some time and the indefatigable Crampton had written innumerable "anecdotes" of Rellerick for the American papers. The New York journals had teemed with stories of the big blue bed, of the famous man's eccentricity, charity, temperament, resources, past, present and future.

Success rushed upon Felicia like an avalanche.

If she had wanted to enjoy it it would have been impossible. It came so quickly that she was unable to savour its ineffable delicacy. . The London "weeklies" devoted columns to the young actress. Unable to "interview" her—for nothing would induce her to consent to the ignominy of her own laudation—they dressed up the "reminiscences" of associate actresses and actors Miss Snooks, the *ingénue* of the Rellerick company, was induced to bear testimony to Felicia's sweetness and to the purity of her home life. Mr. Kafips, the leading juvenile, contributed some delightful notes upon Felicia's amiability to inferiors. And so it went—in the regular cut-and-dried grooves of stage fame—grooves in which there is never a suspicion of originality. Fame is measured out in carefully tested scales, and each lion gets a stereotyped share. There is nothing more banal than success—the success awarded by the mob.

It was all intolerable to Reginald Rellerick. He had digested just that sort of applause for so long, that his physical and mental apparatus could assimilate nothing else. He could not bear that this printed adulation should be thrust upon another—especially when that other was his own little mechanical toy—his doll that said "Mamma" and "Papa"—his untinted and anaemic Felicia Halstead. His ego-mania, thwarted, grew inward, until his entire brain was filled with diseased pictures of his own martyrdom, and odious "groupings" of persecutors, ready to knife him at every step. A sane man would have made the best of such conditions and would have bowed to the inevitable as gracefully as possible. Moreover, in the sane man's mind, there would have been an inclination to side with the mob and to realize that, for once, his efforts had been surpassed. But the ego-maniac is not a sane man. For him there is nothing but an " I " in the world, and when that " I " is under a cloud, the world grows suddenly dark, and its progress is stayed.

After a night of aggressive sleeplessness—after one of those vibrant self-agonies that are the un-erring symptoms of the diseased ego—the great actor sat up in his big blue bed, with his plans matured. There was a look of defiance in his face, and the calmness of the diplomatic criminal in his eye. He had determined to end all this in the eas-iest and most plausible manner. As he dressed himself slowly, he gloated over his own mental deft-ness. There was a way out of it all. It was a heavy, and eternal way, but it must be followed, and it would bring the slipping land once more beneath his persistent feet.

As he entered his study where his own personal-ity seemed to greet him from the four walls, his faithful Crampton met him with the usual immov-able features. The secretary, during the past few days, had been obliged to conceal his knowledge of Mr. Rellerick's misfortune. He had behaved as though nothing whatsoever had happened, and had not dared to vouchsafe a sympathy which—even if he had felt it—would have enlisted him in the ranks of Reginald's persecutors.

The great actor deliberately extended himself over a long chair, arranged his classic face in the lines of that marble perfection which it was his aim to copy, and motioned Crampton to a seat. Then he began.

"Crampton," he said, in his slowest and most archly affected tones, " You have wondered why I remained in town after the close of my season " (Crampton hadn't), "when my public expects me to be climbing blue mountains and gazing into green streams—to say nothing of studying red sun-sets and other pretty freaks of nature. I will tell you. Crampton, I find that this life of solitude and celibacy palls upon me. I intend to get mar-ried."

The mouldy secretary, impermeable to ordinary sensations, drilled in all the arts of self-effacement, was unable to master himself as the actor's words reached his ear. Into his tawny, parchment skin crept the red flush of shock; while the film that seemed to cover his eyes was dissipated, as they burned in a light that was turned nervously upon Mr. Rellerick.

" Don't show your surprise in such an ill-bred way, Crampton," remarked the inimitable Reginald, lackadaisically. "Why shouldn't I marry? I am not too young, and most assuredly, I am not too old. It is an eminently respectable proceeding, Crampton. My only fear is that it is too respecta-ble. What say you ?"

Crampton moistened his dry lips, upon which the skin stood out in crisp and ugly edges. He murmured something unintelligible, in which the words "proper" and "precedent" seemed to have a place. Reginald was perfectly satisfied with the murmur. He was not particularly anxious to hear another speak. Crampton's gurgle indicated, at any rate, that he was listening ; also that he heard.

"I have thought of it for some time," said the great man, the blithe lie rising to his lips almost poetically. "You may have noticed my affection for little Miss Felicia Halstead, Crampton. Ah! a man cannot conceal his sentiments for a woman, even though he be an actor, and accustomed to dissemble for a living. The little girl is young, bright, pretty, and, I am inclined to think—clever. She is fond of me, Crampton, very fond of me—unworthy and repellent though I undoubtedly am ; and just now it seems to me that she needs a protector. They tell me, Crampton, that she has been pestered by managers and actors who are trying to turn the poor little thing's head. That is true, is it not, Crampton ?"

Poor mouldy secretary! He bowed in acquiescence. Not a word could he find to utter. Something rumbled inside him. It was probably a remark that he intended to voice. But the rumbling died away and he was silent.

"It is my duty to protect Felicia," Mr. Rellerick asserted, averting his profile so that his clear-cut nose lay, whitely triangular, upon the crimson cushions of the chair, "So far, her career has been in my charge. What she is to-day I have made her." (This, with a tinge of irrepressible asperity.) "And now they are trying to take her from me—to launch her upon a sea of trouble, the waves of which she is not strong enough to buffet with. I have decided to marry her, Crampton. Then she can swim with me—sail along placidly by my side, share my popularity and be irrevocably a part of it."

Well schooled as he was, Reginald Rellerick could not subdue the sensation of nauseating hatred that came suddenly over him. It altered the expression of his face and imparted a harshness to his final words. The mouldy secretary, who had never moved his eyes from his master's face, saw it. It was not totally unexpected. Crampton was too well accustomed to the lights and shades of Rellerick's nature to be deceived by mere words.

" If she be really so great, Crampton," Reginald laughed easily, and the world would have said that it was an amiable laugh without a tinge of irony in its texture, " why should I not avail myself of her genius ? Why should I not undertake to place it before the world ? And how can I do this better than by marrying her, when I know that she loves me, and have long been aware that I love her ?"

Then the mouldy secretary recovered his speech. It came with an outburst—a singularly energetic outburst for one so repressed and careful. Still, in spite of all, Crampton's words were deferential— almost obsequious.

"You will make a mistake, Mr. Rellerick," said he. "You are not destined for domesticity. Your hold upon the public has been due to some extent to your quite unfathomed life. The world has said that you are so devoted to art that you need no other mistress; that your success has been due to a life led alone, without domestic influences. The ordinary actor marries and has children, and the world says that he acts for bread-and-butter. They have never said that of you. They have wondered at you, admired you, regarded you as an enigma. You want to change that by marrying—and by marrying a mere chit of an actress " (Mr. Crampton hesitated a moment before uttering the words " chit of an actress " and jumped them out as though they would not bear considering) " who is scarcely fitted to you. Pardon me if I say this, Mr. Rellerick. I do so in all humility. How will it seem to you to find your name invariably associated with that of a wife—' Mr. and Mrs. Rellerick ' instead of ' Reginald Rellerick, the great actor?' The world will talk of the ' Rellericks ' and you will be obliged to entertain, to parade your domesticity before the world. You will have children, and they will conflict with your life labours. Why marry—and why marry an actress ?"

Crampton paused. It had been years since he had spoken so much—years since in his voice there had been the ring of a sincerity that had sounded there in the old Oxford days.

Reginald Rellerick winced. Every reason set forth by Crampton was a reason the truth of which stung him. Marriage! It had always been his idea of cheap and tinsel uselessness. How he loathed the idea of it ! How dismal to think of that perpetual tie, of that extravagantly foolish *solitude à deux !*   Ah, he knew that every word his secretary had uttered was too feeble to convey the full discomfort of what wedded life would mean to him. Suddenly he drove the vexation from his face.   He must act.   Crampton was not aware that he was acting.   How could Crampton know it ?   The secretary was merely giving him advice, which under normal conditions would be wise advice.   This marriage was not to be lightly undertaken for happiness ; it was a marriage of diplomacy.   It was a marriage destined to avert ruin.   Still it was very annoying to listen to Crampton, who was telling him what he knew so well and had known all his life.

" Actors have married without losing their prestige, my good man," he said in his usual bland voice. " It is a noble institution and the world respects it.   All that you say is selfish and cruel.   Why should the happiness of two human beings be sacrificed for such unworthy reasons as you suggest ?"

" Perhaps I am wrong," declared the secretary still vehement, " but if you marry why not choose a woman who could help you—a woman with a position in the world, a woman with money ? You, Mr. Rellerick, could select your own wife. Only last year," how quickly the slow and mouldy secretary made his points—" it was rumoured that the Countess of Dwight was hopelessly in love with you and would be your wife for the asking. That lady has a million at her command.   You knew this, and laughed at the idea—and now—and now—you talk of marrying that poor little girl, that penniless child."

The great actor cast a suspicious glance—one that asked some peculiar question—at his secretary. There seemed to a sympathetic quality to his remarks that was not keeping with their tenor. " That poor little girl, that penniless child."   What did Crampton mean by that?   Reginald swallowed a lump that arose in his throat at the mere idea of the secretary's perspicacity. But Crampton had fired his parting shot and his face had returned to its everyday apathy.   The cheeks were sunken and yellow, the eyes filmed, and the mouth as inexpressive as it was its duty to be.   And again a biting vexation took possession of Mr. Rellerick.   Crampton spoke like an oracle.   Marriage was bad enough, but it was worse when it fed upon such non-nourishing material as Felicia Halstead.   Yes, he remembered the case of the silly Countess of Dwight, with her well-filled pockets.   How he had laughed at it, and enjoyed the newspaper stories it had called forth!   How he had revelled in the knowledge of the foolish creature's discomfiture, and used it as an additional means to add to his own fame !   How the clubs had chattered and the weeklies held forth !   He had refused a countess, and now he was going to wed " a chit of an actress," with a dependent family in Lancashire. Bah ! Then once more he recalled his reasons.   It was not a question of choice.   It was a matter of grim necessity.   He could not tread upon Felicia and stamp her out of his path.   But he could marry her, and —boiled mutton would do the rest.

So he said simply, laughing inwardly at his own

canny plan: "Crampton, you are worldly. I did not love the Countess of Dwight. I could have married her and have built theatres with her millions. But you don't know me, my good fellow. I am not quite mercenary. I have a few human sentiments, thank goodness. In marrying Felicia Halstead—the 'chit of an actress' as you call her, and I hope, Crampton, that you will not think of my future wife in such terms—I am responding to the dictates of my nature—ahem! I am very fond of her, and I have no doubt but that we shall be very happy."

"She will give up her success for such happiness," chanted the secretary. It might have been an ecclesiastical utterance that came sing-ily from his lips.

"Of course."

And then the certain Rellerick, unable to weed from anybody's nature the ego-idea that dominated his own, was suddenly confronted with the thought that this Felicia—this girl of whom he was so sure—might choose the spectacular career that had been offered her. He had not seen her since the morning when she had come to him in all her girlish enthusiasm, and he had insulted her and turned from her. What might not have happened since then? What woman could resist the temptations that had been hers? The idea was horrible, He intended to marry Felicia Halstead, but was it so positive that she would still be willing? This revolutionary notion filled him with fear. He had no more confidence in Felicia than he had in himself. The ego-maniac judges everybody by his own standard.

Unable to endure the possibility that had just wedged itself into his consciousness, he sat upright in his chair and with eyes full of dread, said to his secretary, " Crampton, this woman may refuse me. There is a career for her, in which I have nothing to do. What do you think she will say ? What do you think she will say ?"

And Crampton, who was not an ego-maniac, but who was able to judge poor Felicia Halstead, or any other woman, by the light of his own honest human understanding, shuffled uneasily with his awkward feet.

"She will say yes," he said in a voice so low that it was almost inaudible. " Of course she will say yes. Women are fools. I mean that a woman in love will sacrifice anything for it."

A new train of thought, however, had been started in Reginald's mind. The possibility of Felicia's refusal to link her budding name with his moribund faculties, occurred to him with renewed force. This marriage was now the one redeeming hope in his life. It must take place, and it must take place as soon as possible. Even while he had been luxuriously talking to Crampton, and cosily surveying the situation as though it were something established and certain, he should have been with Felicia, pleading his cause with the fresher and bitterer insults of professed love.

A few minutes later, as though the crisis were bound to work itself out, with or without his intervention, a telegram was brought to Mr. Rellerick, by a salaaming lackey in uniform. The great actor's usual method was to leave all correspondence to be opened and attended to by his Crampton. On this occasion he broke the seal of the telegram himself and read as follows :

"Am leaving for Liverpool five o'clock to-night. Shall stay with my sisters.   Return in three weeks.
                                        FELICIA."

Leaving London and to be away for three weeks! Evidently Felicia had made her plans and—according to the methods of the conventional actress—was going home with a contract in her pocket. He must know all. He must see her, talk with her, and convince her. Mr. Rellerick made up his mind to an undignified interview with the "chit of an actress" at Euston. He would sink his pride, forget his "position," and hurry matters to the ending he had mapped out, even if by so doing he were forced to make a fool of himself in a railway station.

Chapter VI

"MARRY ME, FELICIA"

"THE fix'd events of Fate's remote decree" took Reginald Rellerick to Euston Station—a resort that has vivacity, but no very conspicuous romance. The great actor told himself that this little trip was the result of the diplomatic determination set forth in the preceding chapter. Reginald, however—like the rest of us—was merely Fate's little mechanical toy, the string of which was being pulled in order that the doll might work.

It was a new experience for Mr. Rellerick, and he spared himself none of its flavour. He walked along the dishevelled Euston Road as though it were a new and undesirable hemisphere into which he had been suddenly plunged. It was all so very odd, and so exceedingly revolutionary, that he could scarcely enjoy it. Still, as a new epoch in his life was undoubtedly about to begin, and the whirligig of time evidently contemplated ousting him from his groove, it was perhaps just as well that he should accustom himself to novelty.

It was very disgusting to the great actor—was this Euston Road, so far removed from his own walk in life. Nobody knew him; nobody paid any

attention to him !   It was almost as bad as a holiday among the purling brooks and rippling streams.
The ego-maniac saw the vulgarity of the thoroughfare flaunted in his very eyes.   It affected him un-
pleasantly—as an evil odour would have done.
His features were puckered up into the expression
worn by a person who suddenly and unexpectedly
finds a ripe Camembert cheese beneath his nose.
You know the expression.   It is unique.   It should
find a place in the category of expressions.   I
have not coined it for this occasion.   The Camembert cheese expression is one that has lived, and
will live, in the annals of facial history.

The ego-maniac found himself confronted by
cheap and ignominious hotels in which a temporary
matrimony is tolerated for ready money ; by frugal
and non-luxurious Turkish Bath establishments in
which each Euston-roader can stew for a shilling
apiece ; by colossal, gaudy houses in which “ac-
cordeon-pleating ” is done for the high-life of the
West end, and by “ homes ” that laugh at the
word.   The noisy “ busses ” rushed past : the pov-
erty-thin sidewalk artists sketched impossible pictures in chalk on the sidewalks ; grimy children
played at dreary games, sorrowfully parodying
“ childhood’s happy hour,” and carriages heavily
laden with luggage passed on their way to the station.   All these things were foisted upon Reginald
Rellerick’s attention.   He was not interested in
them.   He would have played a part on the stage
with these sights as “ properties,” but in real life
they were devoid of all significance to him.   A

scene in a melodrama setting forth all these facts to beguile an audience's attention before he made his supreme and engrossing entrance, might have captured his approval. How could this ego-maniac feel a spark of curiosity in the real thing, when it went on undisturbed, uninterrupted, even while he passed through its midst? The great Rellerick made no impression whatsoever upon the Euston Road. The people did not flock to the sides of the thoroughfare and form a lane through which he might pass. The sidewalk artists did not cease to labour; the children made no pretence of stopping their games, and the men in the hotels never noticed his presence. This galled the ego-maniac, and the Camembert cheese contempt puckered up his features more hideously than ever.

Into Euston Station he turned rather wearily. It was a very rude place—all shrieks, and noise, and smoke, and endurance. He had been there before, *en route* for the provinces—for fêted weeks, in Birmingham and Manchester and Liverpool. Then there had been groups of sycophants to wish him Godspeed; now, there was nothing. He was there to intercept a woman whom his soul hated; to ask her to allow the law to sanction his hatred for ever-more; to beg her to wear his name, and to cling to him as he knew that she would be only too willing to cling.

"Out of the way," cried an odious person in green corduroys, as the great actor almost fell over a wheelbarrow of luggage. And Mr. Rellerick obeyed the crude command in disgust. The odious person had no regard for him at all, but went on his way with the wheelbarrow freight, whistling and unconcerned.

He inquired the number of the platform from which the Liverpool train started, and was treated with ill-disguised contempt. With these menials it was a crime not to know every detail of this Euston Station's business. He should have been able to check off every train on his fingers, and state at a moment's notice the exact minute of departure and arrival. The actor felt that this world of the non-footlights was a cold and a cheerless affair.

He reached the Liverpool platform through a labyrinth of clanking pavements. The train was there, snorting and impatient. He had fifteen minutes in which to mould his refractory career. Twenty minutes from now, Felicia Halstead would be on her way to Liverpool, his affianced wife, and he would be free to mature his subsequent plans. She was not yet here. The platform was filled with the usual crowd of London-leavers,—juvenile business men with satchels and travelling caps, casting their bundles into the least uncomfortable corners of the least uncomfortable carriages ; old men leaving the metropolis, with families and homes in the provinces ; matrons all perturbed and anxious ; maidens all giggle and illustrated papers and sandwiches.

Mr. Rellerick went to the book-stall and tried to read the titles of the books. He saw one illustrated weekly, from the front page of which the picture of Felicia Halstead stared him in the face. Quickly he turned away his head. Those large, wide eyes and that soft-lipped mouth caused him a pang of distress, and after a moment he left the book-stall hurriedly. He was just in time. A hansom drove up quickly; a porter rushed forward obsequiously; a portmanteau was flung to the ground recklessly, and an instant later Felicia Halstead, accompanied by Mrs. Landington, was in the station. The housekeeper went to buy the ticket and attend to other details, leaving the young actress standing alone on the platform. His opportunity had come at last.

Felicia looked pale and ill. Never had he seen her so carelessly prepared for public gaze. She wore an old travelling ulster that was slightly frayed at the edges, and a hat that contained straight and dejected feathers, gone astray. He could even notice that her gilded hair began to look less gold at the roots. It was carelessly twisted into an inartistic knot at the back of the head. Yet Miss Halstead, in her unconsidered attire, was delightful to look upon, and the people in the station looked upon her. He could even hear the boy behind the book-stall say to a customer, " That's Miss Halstead, the actress, whose picture you see in this paper." The remark was bitterest wormwood to him. She was recognized —she, the novice and the upstart ; while he, London's favourite, had escaped attention of any kind.

Mr. Rellerick rushed instantly to his plans. He had twelve minutes. Felicia was there alone, pensive, thinking perhaps—of him. The sun was not shining, but the sort of hay he intended to make could be bleached in any weather. He approached her slowly, drilling from his features the detestation that he felt for her, disciplining himself into the effort to act. Never had acting been more necessary. It was before an audience of one—but upon that one depended the applause of audiences of thousands.

She looked up, just before he reached her, attracted by the subtle magnetism that exudes from the person in one's thoughts. As she saw him she started, the blood rushed to her face, her lips trembled, and she sat helplessly upon a wooden bench near her. The great actor advanced with an admirable expression of remorse upon his face, then quickened his steps as though suddenly impelled by sheer gladness.

"Felicia!" he said, and was silent. He thought that her name, with an exclamation mark, sounded very well. The utterance was distinctly non-committal, but it could be construed—and he meant that it should—into meaning a great deal.

She tried to speak, all the sincerity of her nature in the attempt. Her lips moved helplessly. She could only look at him—and wait.

"You were running away from me, Felicia," he said, mournfully. "You were going to Lancashire without a single word of farewell. You were treasuring up against me those foolish words I spoke some time ago. Ah, Felicia, I never thought that you were so unforgiving, so vindictive, so ready to forget your—your—old friend!"

He stood there, convincing enough to have satisfied any audience. Into his voice furtive tears had seemed to drip. His tones were low and admirably dismal. He appeared to be uncertain of himself and of her. The lines of his attitude suggested utter depression and melancholy. Not a sign of the raging discontent that steamed in his entrails, was visible to the naked eye.

Felicia Halstead was instantly aroused, first—as was natural to her sweet temperament—to sympathy for him ; then to a joy and satisfaction for herself.

"I did not think you would come," she said, "but —but—I hoped it. That is why I sent the telegram. I could not come to see you again, Reginald, for I felt that you did not want me ; that you looked upon me for the first time as an enemy. It was impossible for me to stay in London without seeing you, so I wrote to my sisters and told them to expect me in Liverpool. You have forgiven me, Reginald? I can see that you have. You realize now that no disloyal thought has ever entered my head, and that the stage—the horrible stage that separated us—is a nightmare, in my eyes."

How very easy it was, after all, thought Reginald. And for an instant he felt the need of breaking once more into a storm of abuse and of overwhelming her again with fierce invective. For he did not believe a word that she uttered—he could not. To him, it was quite impossible that a woman whom the little bookmonger in the station had recognized as the actress of the hour, could lightly disregard such adulation. He checked himself, however, and forced himself to sit by Felicia's side.

"I was wrong, Felicia," he said, after a pause that was necessary to him. "I was terribly shocked by my——" (he stumbled and could not utter the word at first. Then he forced himself, and managed to murmur it) " my failure. It was a bitter blow to me, Felicia. I have been ill since I saw you last—unable to leave the house. I have suffered agonies, both physical and mental."

The ego-maniac, unable to indulge in brutality, seeks to awaken sympathy for himself as a last resource. Reginald Rellerick felt a genuine distress as he talked of his imaginary ailments. It was almost a pleasure to depict them. But his words told upon Felicia, and through her leaden dejection the first ray of sunshine crept.

"You are a silly boy," she said, lightly, in the tones of the sympathetic woman attempting to administer comfort, " and I can't understand you. Every actor has his ups and downs " (Reginald shivered) " and because you were less successful in this new play than you have been in others you worry yourself sick. I am angry with myself for not having been with you, for I see that perhaps I exaggerated our last interview. I am selfish, Reginald, but—but—I really thought that—that— you had begun to hate me."

Now for an ounce of pity in the actor's breast for this fond, dependent girl, you will say. Surely, even his nature must be impressed by these weakly, silly words. But, perhaps, you do not know the ego-maniac, the man with the " I " abnormally enlarged. There was no pity for Felicia Halstead from Reginald Rellerick—nothing but a sensation of relief at the facility with which this game could be played. By the station clock he saw that the train would leave for Liverpool in eight minutes. The men were still standing outside the carriages ; the matrons were inside, plunged in the illustrated papers ; the giggles of the girls were silenced in the discussion of sandwiches.

" They tell me that you have had wonderful offers, Felicia," said Reginald—he placed one hand before his eyes and knew that this was very effective—" I hear that managers have tried to rob me of my little actress ; that they have promised to 'star' her, to take her to America, to build a theatre for her. It is true, is it not ? And has she listened to all these persuasive voices ?"

He touched her arm and noticed the little gold bracelet with the padlock that he had given her. That was still there, at any rate.

" What do I care for managers and theatres and America ?" she asked, so genuinely indignant that her truth was unmistakable. " What do I want with them ? It seems strange, Reginald, that you should know me so little. How can I prove to you —what I told you the other day—that it is you, and you only, that I care for ? These offers came to me unsought, and I scarcely listened to them. The managers whom I saw retired very quickly. I told them, one and all, that their inducements were absolutely useless.'

"Ah!" Reginald's exclamation of utter, glad relief could not be suppressed. It sounded loud and forbidding in the echoing, vaulted station, but, great actor though he was, he could not keep it back. He did the most advisable thing under the circumstances. He glossed it over and lied about it.

"Thank you for that, Felicia," he said, "you have taken a weight from my mind. I could not bear to think that you contemplated abandoning me. After all, we have worked together for a long time. Your methods are my methods. I have helped you, as " (with a great effort) "you have helped me. You will never leave me, Felicia. Promise me that."

The young actress made no feint at reluctance. It was all so very vital to her. She declined to hesitate a moment. "Of course I promise it, Reginald," she said. "You know it, even without such a promise—or, at least you would know it, if you were not such a foolish, blind old bat, that can't see and won't see, and has to be taught to see."

He looked once more at the big, round face of the station clock. Four minutes remained—less than four minutes, for Mrs. Landington would hurry up with the tickets and her interminable small-talk. The train was beginning to tremble uneasily.

"Felicia," he said—he must really get it over, for all this sentimental nonsense was unendurable —"what has happened this time, may happen again.

Each time it occurs my heart will suffer as it has suffered during the past week. I shall live in perpetual dread of your leaving me. You really might be induced to do it, you know. Don't protest, for human nature—the best of it—is unreliable. Marry me, Felicia. Be my wife. Then nothing can ever separate us. My enemies may do their worst; they will be your enemies, as well. That is the only thing to do." (Then feeling that this parchment-like declaration might cause a sensation of revolt in Felicia's heart, he added a flavouring of sentiment.) "You know that I love you, dear. You must have known that. You will consent, I am sure."

The young actress, even after having listened to the diplomatic, sordid words of Mrs. Landington, was unable to link them with this heaven-sent declaration, even though it happened to be the very thing that the housekeeper had foreseen. The sun seemed to have suddenly appeared in a glory of red and gold. Her heart leaped joyfully within her. She tore the glove from her hand and gave him her cool, bare fingers. For a moment she could not speak, and Reginald glanced uneasily at the clock. Two minutes.

"I will be your wife whenever you like," she said simply. "It doesn't matter to me when. I shall stay in Lancashire for three weeks. When I return, if you so will it, I will marry you. Reginald, do not doubt me any more. Tell me that this time you believe in me fully, irrevocably, eternally."

Her eyes were wet. The tears sparkled on her

lashes. There was no lovelier picture in all London than this overjoyed Lancashire lassie, whose nature the metropolis had been powerless to spoil.

"I will doubt you no more," he promised, genuinely pleased at his own victory. Then—for the sake of colour—he forced himself to add (and it was with difficulty he succeeded) " my dearest."

One minute more. "Take your seats," cried the porters. Mrs. Landington, all out of breath and perspiring copiously, hove into sight with the tickets. Reginald Rellerick hastened to secure a compartment for Felicia—a dreadful fear that she might miss her train seizing him and causing him to wonder what he could do with her, in the new position she held toward him. A carriage occupied by a couple of bicyclists was the only available one. He pushed her in and caught the ticket from the housekeeper's outstretched hand.

Mrs. Landington, in all her hurry and excitement, was unable to prevent a triumphant " I-told-you-so " look from creeping into her face, as she saw Reginald Rellerick and noted the change in Felicia Halstead's expression.

" I nearly lost myself," she shouted into the carriage "in this beastly station. Such uncivil people, such boors I've never met. Good-bye, my dear. Write me from Liverpool. If any more managers call, I'll let you know, and——"

There was a snort and a whistle. The train steamed out of Euston. Felicia's gold head hung from the window. She kissed her ungloved hand to the great actor. Reginald Rellerick turned away, the contempt and hatred in his face once more holding sway there. He had forgotten the fat, alpaca housekeeper. She stood there, pantingly radiant, having uttered her last words to Felicia for his especial benefit.

Mrs. Landington's views had changed within the last week. The influence of the kind and necessary "employer" had grown smaller. She had seen that Felicia could be richer, more powerful and more popular without him, if she chose   Her own position, at any rate, was certain, however matters turned out. She was a trifle more independent than usual, therefore, as she spoke to him.

"I'm glad she's gone," were her words, "she's been a-worrying herself sick, poor thing. And the managers a-rushing to the house as though crazy. She's feathered her nest, Mr. Rellerick. Felicia Halstead won't starve. That's sure."

"Of course it is," assented the great actor, bowing in the most courtly manner to the stout lady. "It is very sure   I'm going to marry Miss Felicia Halstead—and I don't think I am going to starve just yet."

Mrs. Landington instantly adjusted herself to the new situation. If Felicia had decided to leave her good, kind "employer," Mrs. Landington, aware of her young charge's growing power, would have ruthlessly snubbed him, in the most graceful, East-London manner. The girl had accepted him as her huband, however. The relative position of the three was virtually unchanged. Before one new minute had been marked on the round station-clock, the housekeeper had returned to her former abjectly obsequious manner.

"Well, and I'm sure and I wish you joy," she said " Miss 'Alstead's a nice, respectable lady, and she's wrapt up in you. I 'ope to be with you both as I've been with 'er, and I shall always endeavour to do my best, I'm sure."

Mr. Rellerick called a hansom and urged her into it, feeling that if he didn't, there were some cruel and uncomfortable moments in store for him. It was not until he had seen the tired horse pulling her out of Euston, that he slowly followed.

The air seemed keen and bracing. The Euston Road looked less formidable and ugly. He walked along its turbulent, kaleidoscopic length, and emerged, still according to "the fix'd events of fate's remote decrees," into the Marylebone Road.

Chapter VII

THE Marylebone Road is the great goal of the sight-seeing picnic-mongers that infest London; for it contains the crimsonly ornate edifice known as "Madame Tussaud's,"—an edifice devoted to what the late George Augustus Sala called "a world-wide display of ceroplastic art.'" Abominably accessible and dreadfully "convenient" to everything in London or outside of it, this large and hectic building cannot be avoided. Omnibuses rush at it from Baker Street, and the metropolitan underground railway vomits forth crowds that clamour for a mixed shilling's worth of history, biography, sensation and horrors. The juvenile Londoner sees "Madame Tussaud's" before his teens have set in—never afterward if he can help it. At that age, the boiled queens, meltable kings, plastic criminals and adjustable celebrities, appeal to him with all the vivid illusion of corpses. The years bring him no desire to revive those illusions. Most Londoners have seen "Madame Tussaud's." They rejoice in that fact, for no fantastic duty compels them to see it again. But the sight-seers go to the Marylebone Road, in all ages and conditions, led there by guidebooks, and kept there by cunning catalogues. The effects of colour and costume upon cheap minds is invariable. The picnicking sight-seers who would vote a collection of marvellous sculpture cut by famous artists in imperishable marble, as "slow" and unimpressive, hasten to Madame Tussaud's for the palatable and easily-digested entertainment of almost libellous figures, with the yellow of death on their faces; the decay of months in their clothes, and a lack of all photographic veracity in their careless contours.

As Reginald Rellerick stepped in front of Madame Tussaud's Exhibition, he noticed a large poster setting forth the vivacious fact that a brand-new figure of Déjazet, the notorious murderer, who had expiated his crime on the guillotine at Paris, three days ago, had been added to the collection. "Lifelike," said the poster, "and absolutely true to nature; the face was modelled from a cast taken after death."

The great actor knew nothing whatsoever about Déjazet. He had been too engrossingly absorbed in the details of his own drooping career, to pay any attention to the published accounts of a criminal *cause célèbre*. Moreover, Mr. Rellerick rarely read the daily papers. Crampton supplied him with all those points in the world's daily history that it was necessary for him to assimilate. He was not vulgarly curious. He liked to read his own history in a nation's eyes occasionally. That of other people was not particularly stimulating.

He viewed the poster before him with a silly and unintelligible feeling of semi-envy. The ego-maniac is jealous of every human thing that temporarily monopolizes the world's attention. Rellerick felt just a momentary sensation of anger, as he noted the gaping crowd devoted to Déjazet's name. The line that separates notoriety from fame is after all very feebly defined. For some minds it is not defined at all, as the students of medical jurisprudence will testify.

Reginald's pang passed quickly away. He himself was ignorant of its ephemeral existence. A whimsical idea to enter this flushed and impudent "exhibition" occurred to him. He had seen it twice—once, when he was a boy for whom the effigies of Anne Boleyn, Katharine of Arragon, Jane Seymour, Anne of Cleves and Catherine Parr had adequately illustrated the sensational history of Henry VIII; and, again, when the Tussaud people had invited him to view a ridiculous waxen monument dedicated to his own greatness. The actor felt lighter and happier than he had felt since the fatal performance that had closed his theatrical season. His interview with Felicia at Euston Station had been so eminently satisfactory that his spirits were volatile and his mind at rest.

The crowd filed in to gape through the various halls and seek a temporary self-forgetfulness in the contemplation of extinct and famous others. Reginald paid his silver tribute with the rest and entered the building. He smiled rather wanly as he contemplated this climax to a plebeian day that had begun in the Euston Road and had paused in the Euston Station.

The exhibition was lighted up and a fitful Hungarian band was squeezing out " popular " music—music that might have convulsed the waxen congress of kings and queens if anything on earth could have affected their immutability. Reginald bought a catalogue in order to insult the lifeless figures, as the mob insulted them, by labelling them with the names of the illustrious. Half the joy that attends a visit to Madame Tussaud's is due to the human ecstasy of insult—the ferocious idea of dubbing a calm and helpless mound of yellow wax George III, or the Grand Duke Nicholas of Russia.

The actor's spirits sank as he found himself surrounded by these staring, ghostly, tallowy dolls. How sinister and how silent they were ! How utterly regardless of the hushed voices of the catalogue-reading throng they seemed to be ; and yet what a tribute the involuntarily lowered tones of the multitude were to their bloodless and unreasoning power!

They overpowered him as they stood there on their pedestals, waiting to be insulted by the sightseers—so dead, and sere, and boiled, and sensationless. To the trained imagination of the actor they did not seem like real men and women, suddenly mesmerized, or robbed of life. They appealed to him as intangible phantoms, and a chill went down his spine as he forced himself to contemplate them. They unnerved him as their open, glassy, meaningless eyes met his own, and he could not believe

that they stood there merely for the easy delecta-
tion of these groups of hungry sight-seers. The
massive breasts that neither rose nor fell, oppressed
him with a heavy sense of melancholy, and he
shuddered at the hatefully smooth and nailless
fingers, that were moulded into a wicked semblance
of life.   For a moment he thought of turning back
and going out again into the Marylebone Road,
where things moved and pulsated. This chamber of
death that had never been life, seemed to be singularly distressing. He wondered why. He asked
himself if his actor's imagination were more suscep-
tible to impressions than that of the healthy,
thoughtless crowd.

He tried to recall his early historical, school-boy
delight in the halls of royalty. He looked at his
catalogue and learnt that the jaundiced atrocity at
which he was gazing was Matilda of Flanders, wife
of King William I. " She was celebrated for her
beauty, and she greatly encouraged her husband
to attempt the conquest of England."   How cruel,
how irrelevant these words sounded ! Was this the
reward of Matilda's beauty and wifely encouragement—this ignominious reign on a platform in a
cheap museum, in the midst of an unappreciative
and irreverent city ? How much better it would
have been for Matilda if she had been hideous, and
had left her husband to his own devices !

Some youths were gazing in rapt attention at
the effigy of " Berengaria, Consort of Richard I,"
and many of the remarks they made were neither
chaste nor elegant. They called the queen of their

remote ancestors "the old girl," and they laughed at her soundless lips and her mouldy attire. "She lies buried in the Abbey of L'Espan, near Le Mans," said the catalogue. Reginald could have smitten the gibing boys as they stood there—insects of to-day, jeering at the phantoms of the past.

It was exhausting and he began to loathe it all. Why had he entered this sarcophagus? What unknown force had induced him to slip from his habits of exclusiveness and join this collection of unsympathetic men, preying like vampires on the waxen bodies of Tussaud's exhibition? Why did it affect him so strangely?

Still he wandered around among the kings and queens, and attempted by a supreme mental effort to feel a cold and respectable interest in the imagined forms of Isabella of Valois, Joan of Navarre, the Georges and the Edwards and the Richards. They sickened him, and lowered his vitality. They made him creep, and filled him with genuine gusts of horror. It was absurd ; it was childish ; it was laughable but—but he could not laugh. He could not smile or even relax the hard and painful tension of his features. The fitful Hungarian band continued to squeeze out tunes, each of which went through him like a knife. Surely even this careless orange-peel mob must feel the impropriety of waltzes and polkas, rung out among these cadaverous effigies. Was the English public utterly devoid of imagination?

Sandwiched in between Martin Luther and Col-

onel Fred Burnaby, he saw his own waxen repre-
sentation, attired in the costume of Hamlet. If it
had really looked like him! A *frisson* of horror
raised his hair as he thought of that improbability.
The figure labelled " Reginald Rellerick " was
simply inane. In no line or feature did it resemble
him. The mob that looked at it with him, never
even guessed that the living Rellerick was in their
midst. The face was ugly, expressionless and old.
But these facts did not affect him at all, for he felt
that he was looking at anybody else. Probably
this waxen Rellerick was some unpopular knight
or fading celebrity, stewed down to meet the exi-
gencies of his own case. It was a ragout of unused
figures, flavoured with the Hamlet garbs that he
had once popularized. Yes, the clothes were correct. They were neatly copied from those that he
had worn ten years ago, when his name first
stamped itself upon London. Irving, Ellen Terry
and the Bancrofts were there, in his vicinity—portraits that their own mothers would never recog-
nize, but waxy, vacant, corpse-like and uncanny as
the rest.

He heard somebody suggest a visit to the Chamber of Horrors, where the " brand-new figure of
Déjazet, the French murderer," was on view. The
Chamber of Horrors ! He could imagine nothing
more horrible than those chambers through which
his unwilling feet had already pushed him. Possibly the Chamber of Horrors was less detestable
because its detestability was blazoned forth and
the public was invited there to be thrilled and

amazed. He had seen enough of this exhibition, however. A cowardly dread of more gaunt and tongueless people induced him to retrace his steps. The incoming crowd was thick and furious. He could not get back without wedging himself into a mass of uncivil men and women bent on getting what they are pleased to call their "money's worth." He must move with the tide and the tide was flowing into the Chamber of Horrors.

So to the Chamber of Horrors he went, mentally protesting against his own weakness. What would Crampton say if he could see his famous master, struggling to gaze at the saffron monsters of Marylebone Road—struggling with the Toms and the Dicks and the Harry's for a good position from which to view the repulsive objects? Felicia Halstead, in the panting train bound for Liverpool, would probably ascribe his action to the common impetus of curiosity. Madame Tussaud's was exactly her style. He could almost see her with the heated odour-reeking women around him, ah-ing and oh-ing before each figure, admiring the beauties and the celebrities, and expressing dismay at the criminals and the outcasts. This, to her provincial mind, would be "entertainment." How she would enjoy a day in this odious vault with him! He could hear her volunteering quite unnecessary explanations. He could almost smell the bag of chocolate-drops that she invariably carried for refreshment to just such places. Felicia was cheap and happy; he was rare and miserable.

The Chamber of Horrors was appropriately

gloomy and cavernous. He could scarcely hear the Hungarian band or see the gay illumination of the other halls. Deeper became his sensation of oppression. Lead seemed to clog his footsteps and to hold him back. The voices of the mob grew even lower than they had been previously. Men and women were bent upon seeing the whole ghastly show, and paid their additional sixpence for the Chamber of Horrors with almost picturesque alacrity.

Reginald Rellerick felt damp and unstrung. His life seemed to be an uncertain quantity, as it does in the eerie hours before sunrise. Yet he forced himself to look about him, and fingered his catalogue nervously. His fingers left wet marks upon the pages. The impression of his thumb was distinctly visible.

The waxen murderers, however, looked no whit more terrible than did the collection of kings and queens and patriots and orators. " James Lee, the Romford murderer,"—he saw him vaguely and stupidly ; " Marguerite Diblanc, the murderess of Madame Riel in Park Lane,"—he noticed her with awe in his eyes. She had been a cook and she looked it. " Michael Eyraud, a strangler executed in the Place de la Roquette, Paris,"—Reginald's eyes were dim as he gazed at this waxen memorial.

The mob read everything that the grudging catalogue vouchsafed, and hungered for more. The meagre details were insufficient. What of the childhood, the later history, and the personal characteristics of these wretches ? The 'Arries and the

'Arriets clamoured for these, and nothing of the sort was forthcoming. They could imagine nothing. For London sight-seers every " i " must be dotted and every " t " crossed.

There was a huge stationary crowd in front of the new figure—that of Déjazet, who had died three days ago, and to whom the London papers had devoted columns of space. Reginald followed the procession, but Déjazet was invisible. He would be obliged to wait his turn—to stand there until the people had satiated themselves with the details of Déjazet's personality.

His elbows, pushed by the crowd behind him, were forced into a wide expanse of serge-covered back, the owner of which, inconvenienced in his open-mouthed study of the dead Déjazet, turned upon the great actor, instantly insolent.

"No pushing, mister," said he, rudely. "Your turn'll come. You'll 'ave to wait with the——"

The sentence was unfinished. The country lout suddenly paused, and stared at the great actor with eyes in which a sort of puzzled astonishment was visible. Then he nudged the woman at his side and whispered a few words in her ear. She immediately moved her head and looked over her shoulder at Mr. Rellerick. In her eyes was the same expression of curious amazement. The masculine and feminine louts were soon whispering and tittering, quite oblivious of the waxen brute that they had just studied in silent awe. They were urged on by the crowd, however, and passed out of sight.

Reginald was weak from the varied sensations that this hideous wax-work show had called forth. Now he grew physically weary, as he stood waiting before the hidden effigy of the murderer, unable to turn either backward or forward. He was dependent upon the caprices of the people in front of him—people who had paid out their "good money" and intended to realize its value as much as possible. Nearly ten minutes passed before the strata of perspiring humanity had given to Mr. Rellerick a position in the front ranks.

By that time he was scarcely able to stand. Listlessly he took his catalogue, opened it, and read the "synopsis" of Déjazet's career, before he studied the figure itself. The Frenchman had been an artist in Paris—an artist of renown. He had lived a wild and untrammelled life, and he was known in the Quartier Latin as the most reckless of an aggressively reckless set. He had a mistress —the beautiful Geneviève Delaunay. For years the two had indulged in an irregular "*ménage*," that the entire Quartier had visited. Geneviève, however, was the daughter of a noble and almost classic family living near Lyons. Her relatives had hunted for her without success. When they found her, she was discovered living a Bohemian life as the mistress of Déjazet. Thereupon the father insisted that Déjazet should marry the girl, for the sake of her name, which was illustrious. Déjazet declined, but suggested that he should fight a duel with Geneviève's brother. If he were victorious, Geneviève should go back to her relatives near Lyons. If he were vanquished, he would marry her. The duel was fought, and Déjazet was slightly wounded. Geneviève's brother was master of the situation. Déjazet redeemed his promise grudgingly. A bitter hatred of Geneviève had taken possession of him—a horror of her seemed to have arisen within him. He was forced to the marriage almost at the point of the sword. On the wedding night, unable to overcome his loathing for his former mistress, he strangled her and tried to escape to London. Her body was found with four black finger-marks on the throat. Déjazet was captured, and, without any reluctance whatsoever, confessed his crime, the result of which was—death by the guillotine, and Madame Tussaud's in wax. And the catalogue, in a burst of confidence, added: "And these are the last clothes that he wore."

Reginald read it all in a sort of dreamy stupor. Then he looked up at the gruesome yellow figure before him. The distant strains of the Hungarian band throbbed in his ears. The sombre vault with its galaxy of monsters seemed to close around him. It was Déjazet he was looking at—it must have been Déjazet, for all the people said so—but the tawny, glass-eyed, soulless image before him was in every line and feature—himself. There he stood, fixed to the ground, gazing at his own waxen double, an indescribable terror rendering him stationary. Fascinated, he peered at the repulsive thing. Those were his own eyes set forth in glass; those were his own features moulded in the filthy

wax.   The smooth and nailless hands were counter-
parts of his own; the grim, unyielding, selfish,
unsympathetic mouth was a copy of his own.   The
hair, the moustache, the eyelashes were unmistakable.   For the first time in his life Reginald Rel.
lerick beheld his own likeness with a sensation of
such bitter repugnance, that he was appalled.

He could not move; he was glued there.   He
heard the people around him, vigorously commenting on the face of the criminal.   The sound of
their voices discussing the details of his infamy
reached him.   How could a girl like this Geneviève
Delaunay have possibly been under his influence?
How could she have lived with him as his mistress
and have been willing to become his wife?   Why
were women so foolish and so unreasoning?
Really, it almost served her right.   Surely with a
face like that she should have known—and so on,
in balefully querulous logic.

And still the great actor stared as though hyp-
notized.   The glass eyes seemed to return his look
in a sort of cynical sympathy.   The saffron-tinted,
waxen mouth appeared almost to twist itself into a
smile, as he stared—and stared—and stared.

The people looked at him and noticed the resemblance, laughingly and good-naturedly.   To them,
this was an unexpected relaxation from the oppression of this funereal grotto.   They whispered
about it, and alluded to it, as to the merriest coincidence.   Such coincidences were not rare.   The
clothes worn by the mimic Déjazet were the stum.
bling-block to this audience's complete apprecia-

tion of the likeness to Rellerick.   Clothes mean so much to vulgar and uneducated minds.   Had this yellow ceroplastic horror aped the polite frock-coat, the shining, bulging silk hat, and the irre-proachable neck ribbon that the great actor wore, these men and women would have been riddled with awe and curiosity.   As it was there was a striking resemblance, and they were quite good-humoured about it.

"Say, Mister," remarked one old person with whiskers, "next time you sit for these Tussauds don't choose a murderer.   Be a king, or a prince, or a prime-minister.   He ! he ! he !"

"Makes you feel as though you was small pota-toes, eh ?" asked one of those friendly London matrons to be met at all the " exhibitions."

They went away, and were soon absorbed in other abominations—in Mary Ann Cotton, the poisoner ; in Kemmler, the wretch who was the first to be killed by electricity in New York, and Dumollard and his wife, " fiends who decoyed young women into a wood."

Reginald Rellerick stood there, lost to all sur-rounding influences, numb and magnetized by the counterfeit presentment of his own personality—the personality that had been the joy of his life ; the great solace of his leisure hours ; his early mornings' care ; his daily encouragement to re-newed labour.   What a loathsome personality it was—that dual arrangement shared by Déjazet, the guillotined criminal, and Reginald Rellerick, the celebrated English actor.

He awoke slowly from his stupor and read once more the black legend of the girl-killer. " He was forced to marry her, almost at the point of the sword. On the wedding-night, unable to overcome his loathing for his former mistress, he strangled her and tried to escape to London. Her body was found with four black finger-marks on the throat. Déjazet was captured, and without any reluctance whatsoever, confessed his crime."

Perhaps—perhaps this waxen atrocity looked no more like the Paris artist than the figures of the Royal Family resembled their living inspirations. Reginald thought of this, but there was little consolation in the idea. The face had been modelled from a cast taken after death. It was no whim of the modeller's fancy. He had read the poster outside. Why had he read the poster outside ? Why had he wandered into this marrow-disturbing resort ? What evil fate had led his footsteps in this ghastly direction ?

He would go at once and speak to the " authorities." The figure, merciless and libellous, must be removed. He would not rest while this odious counterpart of a criminal was held up to public gaze in his own likeness. They would laugh at him. They would—for the sake of a profitable advertisement—revel in ·his wrath and heroics. The affair would be paraded in the newspapers and his persecutors would hail a new field for contempt and vituperation. No, he would utter no word. He would not call the attention of the metropolis to a foolish coincidence—yes, it was a coincidence, of course; even the mob had laughed at it as such. He would laugh at it as well. He certainly would laugh. Ha! ha! ha! These waxen figures were really very amusing, extremely——

His waxen double was looking at him. He felt the cold, glassy eyes fixed upon him. The coloured lips were smiling; the figure seemed to bend in order that it might study him more closely. He knew that this was absurd. He realized that his imagination was unduly affected by this episode. And then the surroundings—the place itself—the ugly crowd—the dark, lowering atmosphere—all combined to add to his terror.

He would go at once and never set his foot within these precincts again. He would forget it all until it occurred to his consciousness as a joke,—one of those jokes, the humour of which never convinces at the time of perpetration. He closed his catalogue with one more glance at the words, "On the wedding night, unable to overcome his loathing for his former mistress, he strangled her." These words seemed to appear before him, even after he had put the miserable pamphlet into his pocket.

He looked straight in front of him. There they were on the walls. They towered over him on the ceiling. He made an intense effort and drew himself together. This was folly, idiocy, more than puerility.

He turned on his way out, and took a last look at his waxen double. It was grinning at him. There could be no doubt of it. It was not his imagination that was playing him a trick.

"Déjazet!" he murmured, as he passed the outer portal, "Déjazet! Déjazet! Déjazet!"

He hailed a hansom, and told the driver—much to that bleary-faced individual's bewilderment, to drive him to "Déjazet." The air fanned his humid forehead and dried the wisps of his wet and straggling hair. It revived him. He lay there and closed his eyes in an attempt to think of other subjects. But he thought "Déjazet;" in his mind he saw "Déjazet." He felt that his entity was merged in the wax of the monster at Tussaud's.

Chapter VIII

IT was scarcely nine o'clock when Reginald dismissed his hansom cab, at the door of his club. He
had intended to drive home, and plunge his exhausted body into his big, blue, restful bed, but he
felt that his mind might, perhaps, be easier, after
an hour spent in his massive, dark-brown club—
that clearing-house for all cheques drawn upon the
gossip, malice, and *petits potins* of the metropolis.
His face was haggard, and drawn, and he was
ashamed of it—he, Reginald Rellerick was positively ashamed of his own usually luminous appearance, as the obsequious person in the dingy lackey-
garb let him in, and took away his hat and coat.

They were all there, in the " convivial " smoking-
room.   Apparently they had not stirred from their
seats since he had last seen them there.   Silent as
owls, they sat drinking the incessant brandy-and-
soda, while the clock ticked away the club's life.
The book-reviewer who had killed and buried poor
" Gyp " within the last week, was now exercising
his mental scowl upon the latest D'Annunzio novel,
which he considered (of course) " morbid " and
" unwholesome "—utterly inferior in every way, to

the English health and spirits of the exuberant Anthony Hope. The "hanger-on," with his legs crossed, was on hand, looking at his watch and timing everything, while the dramatic critic who was addicted to unalloyed praise rested, cheek-by-jowl, with the dramatic critic wedded to unadulterated censure.

For a moment the great actor could hardly believe that he had left Madame Tussaud's. This dark, little sepia-tinted room might be another Chamber of Horrors. For an instant, he felt inclined to refer to his catalogue, and "look out" the description of the fat scowler with the D'Annunzio novel. He might have been labelled: "An English book-reviewer of the nineteenth century, notorious for his mutilations of popular authors."

Pinerville, the dramatist, author of the luckless play that had blazoned forth Felicia Halstead, sat in a corner of the room, silent and meditative. Perhaps he was contrasting this morgue, with his own theatrical version of club scenes—rollicking, glass-tinkling, chattering episodes, that always went well with the public, because they were so "true to life." If he had dramatized this sodden assemblage of London "wits," he would have been accused of drawing upon his imagination.

This time, Reginald entered his club almost unnoticed. The dreary men bowed slightly, but declined to disturb themselves. They had been dining, and the process of digestion was achieving itself slowly. The actor was greatly relieved to find that his entrance was not emphasized. At any other time, he would have considered this apathy in the light of an insult. Now, it gratified him, for —try as he would—he could not get rid of a guilty and skulking sensation that his wax-work visit had foisted upon him. Even while he sat in this room, there were crowds in the Marylebone Road, staring at his glassy double, referring to him in the catalogue, ogling him vulgarly, and uttering comments upon his appearance. He hated to think that he stood in that exhibition among the murderers, powerless to move away from the collection—yellow and hideous, in that sombre cavern of public "entertainment." He could not divest himself of the idea that he had no right to be at large in these haunts of unrestricted life. It seemed to him as though he had a ticket-of-leave, and must return to the Marylebone Road later, to stand and watch his own image ; to see that it was properly cared for, and that the mob did not insult it, or do it bodily harm.

He stretched himself, and yawned. He could move and pulsate as readily as ever. That was a consolation. Yet his hands looked ignobly smooth and nailless, and he hated to see them. They annoyed him ; he felt that his " convivial " brothers in this club must be watching him. He hid them in his pockets, and drew them forth from time to time to see if the warmth had robbed them of their cold and yellow hue.

Pinerville, the dramatist, approached him, and took a chair by his side. He hated this man who had been responsible for the first halt in his career.

The eyes of the dramatist seemed to be fixed upon him mockingly, so thoroughly wrought-up was his imagination. Poor little, harmless, plodding Pinerville, who had never owned a sinister motive in his life, was meeker than usual on this occasion. He was wise enough to know that a play, however good it might be, that had caused the discomfiture of a popular "star" was doomed to the misfortune of "innocuous desuetude."

"I do not despair, Mr. Rellerick," he said, amiably, "and I always persevere. I know that my last play will never find a place in your repertoire next season, but I should like to submit to you the scenario of a new one—one that will give you, I feel sure, the best opportunity you have had for years. Nowadays, I do not care to write for the actor—for any particular actor that is to say—but in this case I have a story that is so eminently fitted to your—ahem! genius, that I cannot avoid submitting it to you, and asking your permission to go ahead."

Pinerville was bland and excessively polite. His suave, soft tones fell pleasantly upon Reginald Rellerick's ear. The actor felt once again that he was his own inimitable self. He clasped his hands expectantly around his knee. They looked warm, and pink, and the white, carefully manicured nails were there as conspicuously as ever. Thank Heaven that this nightmare seemed to be vanishing! If he could only forget! Yet even as he tried to do so, there arose before his mind's eye a picture of a thick and aromatic mob gazing intently at a yellow waxen figure, standing erect among a group of corpse-like horrors in the Marylebone Road Exhibition. He called for a bottle of champagne—champagne was the stuff that cleared the mental vision, and penetrated the films of imagination. He poured out a glass for Pinerville, and another for himself, which he drained feverishly. He felt better. After all, he was Reginald Rellerick. He had been Reginald Rellerick for years. Every man in the club, every menial in its kitchen, could swear, under oath, that he was Reginald Rellerick.

"Of course I want a new play, Mr. Pinerville," he said, pompously—he could be pompous again. "Your last play was good—very good—but somehow or other I did not feel that I could do myself justice in the leading character. The interest seemed to centre——"

"Yes," interrupted the dramatist, anxious to finish with his dead-and-gone creation, "The interest centred in the leading-lady. It was a good part for Miss Halstead only. A clever girl—a very clever girl. She——"

"My dear Pinerville," said Mr. Rellerick, making a sickly effort to smile with his usual nonchalance, "My time is very limited. I have promised myself a good night's rest, for I am tired, and a trifle indisposed. If you will proceed with the story of your new play which is so suited to me" (he was able to inject a dash of appropriately incredulous sarcasm into his tones), "I can then tell you if I agree with you."

"You will, I am sure," remarked the dramatist.

" What do you say, Mr. Rellerick, to a part that runs the gamut of the emotions—one that will portray you as loving, and hating, and dissembling, and scheming—one that will give you a final scene which, I am quite convinced, will be as strong as anything that has been acted upon the modern stage ?"

He paused. His eloquence was running away with him. Reginald smiled ; he was so used to that sort of thing. Every failure was heralded upon his notice in that way. An indulgent expression stole into his face. Even the popular Pinerville was a victim to the conventional playwright's mania. He sat there and permitted the dramatist to proceed. All his haughty, up-in-the-sky manners were returning to him, and he felt temporarily happy. The champagne was perhaps responsible for the change. It is an admirable stimulant.

" I won't say that I have captured a precisely original idea," continued Pinerville, affably. " After all, originality is a myth. I read the papers, Mr. Rellerick. I find in those penny records of daily life most of my inspirations. They are human documents, you know, written in flesh and blood. In my new play, my idea is to dramatize as closely as possible, with a few theatrical improvements, the story with which all the London papers have been teeming of late. You are, of course, familiar with it. Every actor must be. I am referring to the recent history of that clever, artistic, and dramatic criminal, Déjazet."

Every muscle in Reginald Rellerick's body

seemed to stretch tensely, as though an electric current had been sent through it. Then came the relaxation, and he sat there drooping and limp. This man—this Pinerville—knew of the ignominy to which he had been subjected. He was there to scoff at him, and to add to his humiliation. Yet Reginald could not look him in the face, with his Déjazet eyes and his Déjazet expression. He felt as though he were being hunted down, and cornered. The men around were still silently attentive to their brandy-and-sodas. The only voice in the room was that of Pinerville, who was there to subject him to the anguish of the earlier evening. He would not submit to such cruelty. His anger swept everything before it.

"This is an insult, Mr. Pinerville," he said, thickly; "one which I will not tolerate. How dare you sit there and suggest to me—to Reginald Rellerick—for I am Reginald Rellerick—such a scheme? Do I look like a man who could impersonate a vulgar criminal? I ask you that. Do I look like it, Mr. Pinerville? I insist upon an answer."

The little dramatist seemed to be lost in absolute amaze. The violence of the great actor's words overpowered him. He blushed; he paled; he looked around in astonished distress. Then he glanced at Rellerick to see if he had heard aright. Possibly the champagne had affected him. The actor was but slightly addicted to wine.

"You are not in earnest, Mr. Rellerick," he murmured. "Why, I do not understand you. Of course—of course—you do not look, in your private life, like a man who could play a criminal. But—but—you are not well; you cannot be yourself. Look at Irving. Why, his best successes have been in such plays as 'The Bells' and 'The Lyons Mail.' With this story of Déjazet I can make a play quite as powerful as either of those dramas. The history is a perfect one. All London will flock to see you as the famous Déjazet, with Felicia Halstead as Geneviève Delaunay."

"Stop!" cried Reginald, glowing with rage, sweeping his arm across the table that held the champagne glasses, and dashing them to the ground. "I will not listen to you. You came here to-night to tell me this horrible plan of yours. You shall not succeed. I will not sit and listen to you. You couldn't write this play. I say you couldn't. Your last was a hopeless failure. You will never write another play. You are cheap and vulgar, and you appeal to the gallery. Send your horrid drama to the provinces. Keep it away from London and from me."

His voice was loud and excited. The gloomy creatures in the club arose, and joined the two at the table, kicking aside the fragments of the champagne glasses, and alive for once, with the knowledge that something real was happening.

"This is an affront, Mr. Rellerick," remarked the little dramatist, emerging from his overpowering astonishment, "an affront for which you shall pay dearly. Gentlemen," turning to the parchment faces of his associates, "I was merely suggesting the scheme of a new play to this actor—suggesting it in all humility, and in the legitimate pursuit of my profession—when he turned upon me in this unseemly manner."

Quick as lightning, through Reginald's mind were flashed the prospects of publicity. Sanely it occurred to him that these men would hear of his aversion to the hated name of Déjazet, and would laugh at it. The journalists present would paragraph it, and perhaps even weave it into some sort of penny-dreadful, psychological story. He had aroused Pinerville's ire, and the thing to do was to allay it before further damage was done.

"I was quite in the wrong, Mr. Pinerville," he said, spectacularly humble, "and before these gentlemen I apologize. Mr. Pinerville,"—turning to the members—"was telling me his idea for a new play. I had heard the story, and it had impressed me so vividly, that I could not quite reconcile to myself the idea of its dramatization. That is all. Mr. Pinerville, I quite agree with you that it would make a good drama—one that I should like to produce. Promise me that you will not mention the story to anybody—I must insist upon that, for it would be instantly.seized upon and used —and I will discuss it with you later, with a view to next season. You forgive my little incomprehensible— " (he paused and looked at the faces before him. Was it incomprehensible ?)—" outburst. I can say no more."

The little dramatist—the most peaceful and inoffensive of men—held out his hand. The great

actor took it, and wrung it fervently. He was
saved—temporarily saved, and he would avoid the
club henceforth, and deny himself persistently to
Pinerville. He would never see that dramatist
again, if he could help it.

The club-members, robbed of their tit-bit, went
back to their seats, like dogs that had looked upon
a bone which had mysteriously been torn away
from their teeth. Reginald Rellerick forced himself to talk indifferently upon the topics of the day,
until he saw that Pinerville had left. Then he followed, and jumping into a cab, was driven home.

He was admitted to his own apartments by his
comedy-butler. Apparently the domestics were
giving a party downstairs. He heard them laughing,
and talking, and the mellow tones of his cook's
voice were wafted up to him. The sounds grated
upon his ear, but he said nothing. He went upstairs to his study. Crampton was there arranging
his scrap-books, mouldier than usual. He nodded
to his secretary, threw off his coat and waistcoat,
and flung himself into an arm-chair in front of the fire-
place. The secretary continued to paste the newspaper clippings into the book. The room was
horribly silent, except for the distant sounds of the
servants' laughter below stairs. Why was Crampton such a mummy? Why had he engaged a
secretary who had no more animation than an
oyster?

Thomas, the comedy-butler, brought in a tray
bearing soda-water and spirits. As he opened the
door, the exuberance downstairs came flowing into

the room. It was irritating to the great actor, and he turned pettishly to the butler.

"Send the servants to bed," he said, "and tell them that I won't have this noise. It is most disrespectful. What are they laughing at, Thomas?"

The staid butler paused at the door, and straightened his upper lip into the usual semblance of discreet solemnity.

"Oh, it's nothing, sir," he replied, reverently. "Cook and Jane went out to-night and were at Madame Tussore's Wax-works. They say they saw there a new figure that looked so much like you that cook declares she almost dropped, and Jane says she went all of a tremble. They're silly things, but they're laughing so much about it now, that they don't feel like going to bed. The figure—"

Reginald jumped from his chair and pointed his quivering hand at the butler.

"Send them to bed at once, and tell them to behave themselves. If they can find nothing better to do than discuss such nonsense, they had better go elsewhere and find work."

The door closed behind the butler, and Reginald sank into his chair again. The mouldy secretary, pasting the slips into the scrapbook, might have been deaf and dumb, so completely was he absorbed in his work. Reginald lay there in a tumult. His cook and his Jane had been merry at his expense. They had seen the loathsome image, standing to be gazed at for a few coins. Perhaps they had been in the building at the very time that he was there—menials and master, staring at the waxen counterpart of a notorious criminal. It was intolerable. He could not endure that these servants should remain in his employ. He could not meet them, day after day, in the knowledge that they had been impressed by the fact that he was duplicated in the Marylebone Road, by a lifeless form, labelled " Murderer."

" Discharge the servants to-morrow, Crampton," he said, huskily. "I must have a quieter set. My home is a pandemonium."

Crampton nodded in his usual apathetic manner. If Rellerick had told him to ask the Queen to abdicate her throne, he would have nodded in the same remotely human way.

The silence was almost tangible. If only Crampton would talk, and break this intolerable spell! But the secretary plodded on with his task, and the great actor stifled by the side of the redly burning fire.

" Crampton," he said at last—he could endure it no longer. " You heard what Thomas said just now."

"Yes, sir."

'Well, I am told that at this wax-work exhibition there is a figure that resembles me very strongly. It is meant to portray a criminal who was executed a few days ago in Paris. I never read the papers, Crampton. Do you remember the name of the criminal ?"

He could see it luminously around him. Every letter in its composition was seared into his brain Yet he wanted to hear Crampton pronounce the word, as he was anxious to know if it were possible that his well-newspapered secretary could possibly have avoided hearing it.

"I suppose," said Crampton deliberately, "that you mean Déjazet."

"Yes—yes—that is it.   Déjazet."

There it was again, ringing in his ears, this time uttered by the slow-voiced, monotonous Crampton. How dismal it sounded!   What a hideous name it was!

"Déjazet," sang Crampton, in chant-like syllables, "was the person who murdered his mistress. It was a sensational case, but I did not tell you of it, because there were other more important matters to discuss.   The story might make a good play, Mr. Rellerick.   You could get a clever dramatist to put a few theatre touches to Déjazet himself, and to that poor little girl, Geneviève Delaunay."

"That poor little girl!"

The words seemed to smite Reginald Rellerick. Where had he heard them before, recently uttered? He cudgelled his brains to investigate this stupid trifle of a coincidence.   "That poor little. girl!" Why, it was Crampton himself who had used the words, that very morning, in discussing Felicia Halstead.   He recalled them very well.   "That poor little girl, that penniless child."   That had been Crampton's own phrase, when Reginald had told him that he intended to marry Felicia Halstead. He laughed aloud.   This new idea of making mountain out of molehills was genuinely entertaining. Poor Crampton's vocabulary was very limited.   It was bounded on the north and the south by " That poor little girl."

" Talking of poor little girls, Crampton," he said harshly, as though some of his inner strings had broken, " and you like to talk about them, Crampton, don't you ?—I must tell you that Miss Halstead has accepted me, and that as soon as she returns from Lancashire, we are to be married. ' For we're to be married to-day, to-day—for we're to be married to-day,'" he sang stridently.

The secretary looked at him, a trifle paler than usual—more like bleached parchment than anything else. His fingers trembled with the wet slip of paper that they held, ready for transference to the scrap-book. He looked at Reginald with the eyes of a dumb animal. He knew him so well ! He was so completely initiated into the mysteries of that complicated ego-maniacal mind. But he could not speak. He pasted the moist clipping in the book, shut it up, and after carefully putting away the details of his work, left the great actor alone for the night.

Yes, he was alone for the night, in his redly curtained room, with its unread books, and its lounging chairs. He lay there, still looking at the fire, and finding no comfort in his surroundings. He was alone for the night, shut off from the dimly lighted streets, and removed from the reach of man or woman. He was there—and his double ? His awful counterpart was alone for the night in the wax-work exhibition of the Marylebone Road, surrounded by other waxen terrors, murderers, poisoners and outcasts. He shuddered as he thought of it. He could see the black, impenetrable Chamber of Horrors, robbed of all its illumination, free from the noise of the gaping, sight-seeing crowd. They stood there—those monsters—just as silent and just as ghastly as they had been when he had viewed them. They would never stir, nor move, nor utter sound, and yet the detestable tragedy would begin again on the morrow.

The big blue bed was yawning for him, but he could not seek it, with the knowledge that the atrocity which had been perpetrated in his image, was standing up there alone, in the dark of the wax-work collection. Perhaps it was grinning with no eyes other than those glass imitations to look upon it. Perhaps the defiance of its attitude had changed to one of pleading and of pity. At any rate it was there. It must be there. It was an awful thought. He could not bear the idea of staying alone in his own room all night, with the remembrance of this silent monument, linking itself with him in the Marylebone Road. It haunted him. He looked at himself in the glass, and his face was yellow and bloodless ; his attitude seemed unreal and moulded, and his hands—always those hands—were as smooth and as nailless as those of of any of the kings and queens and wretches he had gazed upon.

The silence of his room could scarcely be greater than that in the scarlet edifice devoted to the monuments. He looked around him fearfully, half expecting to see a galaxy of poisoners and decoyers rearing itself about him.

He went into the hall, and opened the door of Crampton's room. The mouldy secretary was asleep, but his breast rose and fell, and he breathed. It was such a relief to see those signs of life. As he gazed at the sleeping man, Crampton's lips moved, and he distinctly heard the word " Felicia " emerge therefrom. And as he continued to watch— startled into a momentary sensation of genuine, eavesdropping curiosity—the secretary's lips bubbled again, and this time the word " Déjazet " issued forth.

He left the room hurriedly. Everything was conspiring against him. There was a plot—a coldly-laid plot—to affect his mental health by these uncanny coincidences. He went downstairs, put on his hat and overcoat, and let himself quietly into the streets. He walked quickly and unthinkingly along, as though impelled by some hidden mechanism. The policemen on their beat looked at him curiously. The night-owls slunk away at his approach. The roysterers called ribaldly after him, but on he went—on—on—on.

He never paused, until, miles away from his starting point, he had reached that hectic building in the Marylebone Road, where his double stood up, king among the evil-doers; newest of all the detestabilities; latest addition to the criminals of the century. The poster was still there, flaunting its blueness unseen. Even in the badly lighted street he could still read the words, "The face was modelled from a cast taken after death."

How gloomy it all looked, without its sight-seers and its inane, laughing mob. This was the place where they amused themselves in the day-time. This was a sort of vile hereafter for all who distinguished themselves from their fellow-men, either by good or by evil—it didn't matter which. Famous and infamous were both stationed here, separated by nothing more than a compartment.

He would not go home. He would remain as near to his double as possible. He wondered if Déjazet were at the window, looking out and grinning at him, as he stood there nervelessly, outside the cage, pacing backwards and forwards. If some of those laughing sight-seers should pass by, they would think that the new waxen figure had escaped from its prison, and was haunting the Marylebone Road. It was a fantastic idea, but it was not a pleasant one. A night watchman stared at him seriously. He averted his face and moved away. A policeman stood by him and looked at him suspiciously. He asked the peace-guardian what time it was, more for the sake of hearing his own voice than to secure the information.

At day-break the edifice looked lighter, and more cheerful. In a few hours the doors would be opened once more, and if he chose, he could look at Déjazet again for one-and-sixpence. In a few hours! He could wait.

Chapter IX

"LIVERPOOL, *May 3, 1898.*

"MY DEAR REGINALD: Doesn't it seem odd to reflect that I have never yet written you a letter? You can ransack your desks; you can ask your dreadful, seedy Crampton to rummage through your correspondence; no letter from your Felicia has a place there. Consequently, my dear, dear Reginald, I am going to try to do justice to myself to-day. Oh, the joy of writing to you! You don't know what it means to me. All morning I have been nervous and excited at the mere idea of addressing you by pen and ink. And now that I have started—well, I have a trembling hand and a palpitating heart. I don't intend to write to you often, my dear, because I have a sort of horror of establishing a volume for 'Letters from Felicia.' Such a title always sounds to me so cheap and penny-dreadful-y, and I hate women who write diaries and letters—yes, even Glory Quayle and Marie Bashkirtseff. These words are destined— not for publication—but for the waste-paper basket. However, I don't insist upon the basket. If you should happen to be in a Felicia mood when you get this—well, you can put it next to your heart; I shan't mind, and you needn't confess, Reginald; you really needn't.

"I can't tell you how I got to Liverpool, because I don't know. I believe I sat on cushions and was propelled swiftly through sweet, warm air, but I am not quite sure. You see, I couldn't worry myself about such details. In my mind were words that had been spoken at Euston Station by a certain stern and merciless knight, and they sang themselves to me until I was in a very ecstasy of reverie. Dear old Euston Station! Little did I think that my happiness would come to me in that vaulted, noisy, going-away place. How often have I cried there, and despaired there, and rebelled there! Euston was to me a sort of devils' rendezvous. And now, you original, reckless boy, you have suddenly transformed it into an Elysium.

"The bicyclist-boys in the train with me were very polite. They insisted upon pulling down the window when it was warm, and putting it up again when it grew cool. They gave me funny papers to read, and plied me with chicken sandwiches. They were very young, and talked bicycle to me by the hour. They introduced me to sprocket-wheels, and gear-cases, and it is absolutely my own fault that I don't know how to darn a tire, under any condition of puncture. Reginald, these youthful bicyclists recognized me. They had with them a magazine containing my picture. Such is fame— which I never have wanted, don't want, and shan't want! I told you the truth, dear boy, when I said that I hated the theatre and everything connected with it—except one ' star ' actor, in whose halo I I long to participate, for his sake only. I can't understand the joys that fame is supposed to yield. Certainly it can't make one happy to be thought of and noticed by a lot of strangers. If fame could render one more entrancing to one's own selected circle—then I should like to be famous. But does it ? I think not. Fame is a bait for the outsiders, for the Toms, and the Dicks, and the Harrys, and I don't want it. (I have just read this over, and it sounds rather nice—really book-y, and breezy. Don't you think so ?)

" Floss and Edna met me at Lime Street, and took me home to mamma, as though I were the prodigal returned. What a fuss they made of me, these three good, and unreasonably affectionate women. Somehow or other, Reginald, I felt that I was a sort of blot upon the purity of their picture —a fraud, as it were. It was not until I told them that I was engaged, that I could feel at my ease. You should have heard their exclamations of pleasure and their questions. They had been longing for such news, and mamma—dear, innocent mamma—said, ' Well, my dear Felicia, I am glad it has ended so nicely. I have heard of young actresses who fall in love with actors, and who are lured to their ruin.' Dear mamma ! I love that expression, ' lured to their ruin.' It is so picturesque, and so exquisitely middle-class. How middle-ciass we are! Really, I never knew it so vividly as I know it now. Floss and Edna are typical middle-class girls, addicted to doting upon beardless curates and afternoon tea, and mamma is one of those easily satisfied matrons to whom watercress and shrimps—to say nothing of periwinkles—are the acme of joy. The metropolis has had its effect upon me, though I thought I was still narrow and provincial. These dear, beloved people—flesh of my flesh—run so persistently in one groove. They all discuss the fact that I am going ' to marry well,' —just as though you were a butcher with a big bank account. I am quite sure that mamma thinks we shall live in a brick terrace in the suburbs, and keep chickens and rabbits. She has warned me that actors are very fond of divorces—in fact, mamma believes that it is an incentive to them to marry— and I am to be very careful and prudent.

" Reginald, I hate myself for writing so lightly of my family. It seems so graceless, and so unlike the Felicia of other days. Alas! I am afraid that the Felicia of other days is no more. In her place has arisen a new, pert, and frivolous creature with but one object in her life, and one desire to get away from everything that is not connected with that object. Floss wanted to know why I hadn't an engagement ring, and when I told her that there was no jeweller's shop in Euston Station, she nearly fainted. Floss and Edna think that a proposal in Euston Station is most ignominious. Edna wondered what on earth the people thought of you when they saw you on your knees on the platform, begging the radiant Felicia to be yours for ever and for aye. They are very ingenuous girls, Reginald,

Was I ingenuous when you first knew me? You used to tell me that I was, but seriously I can hardly believe it. I feel so abnormally wise, and sensible, and worldly—in this unpoetic, yet secluded Liverpool.

"At an afternoon tea, yesterday, I met a spinster with ringlets, who told me that she had seen you in London some years ago, and thought that you looked like a dreadful person, capable of anything. You were playing in 'Richard III,' and she was quite unable to disentangle you from your part. She asked me if something couldn't be done for the hump, and when I told her that you were trying to remove it with caustic—like a wart—she seemed to be quite pleased. I should hate you to come to Liverpool, and see the people whom I meet daily. They would be so exactly the folks that you would despise—you lordly, regal and peerless thing! So, if you should feel that you can't possibly exist a day longer without your Felicia—well, my dear, bid her come to you, but prithee, go not to her.

"How my pen is flying on, and what nonsense I am writing. Verily, I believe that even the waste-paper basket would reject me. However, I am not always as light-hearted as I feel at this moment. Sometimes I ask myself if really, in your heart of hearts, you love this foolish, flighty Felicia? And the answer is not satisfactory. If it were, it would be too good—too consummately blissful. I don't believe that you would die of anguish if she positively declined to see you again. I cannot imagine you suiciding on account of hopeless love for Felicia Halstead. If I were only proud, and correct! If I only were! I would force you to woo me violently, and would revel in coyness, and woman's pretty defensiveness. But alas! I am so desperate, and so very much in earnest. I have no pride, and I am not coy. I would marry you, even if you hated me, and trust to fate for better things afterwards. In fact, Reginald, I was quite willing to be your wife, even when I thought that you might ask me just for the sake of—but no, I will not tell you of that contemplated conspiracy until we have been married five years. Married five years! I can scarcely realize what it means. Perhaps by that time I shall have grown to think of nothing but boiled mutton, and roly-poly puddings. I am afraid I am not artistic—merely feminine.

"You will laugh when I tell you that I almost expected to find a telegram from you awaiting me in Liverpool, begging me to dismiss the Euston interview from my mind. My first words when I entered the sitting-room were: 'Is there any message for me?' What a relief it was when I heard that there was not. You see, I am uncertain and unsettled. But nothing can alter the fact that you have asked me to be your wife, and that I have accepted. It was, as mamma says, a happy ending. There are episodes in our past that we may think of in mental solitude. How much better that there should be no more of them. Yet, I would have been your slave—your willing satellite forever—if I could not have been your wife. Never, to my dying day, shall I forget my agony when you accused me of trying to supplant you—never, never, never. And yet, in some way or other, I can't help thinking that this incident is connected with my present happiness. How wretched I was when you saw me at Euston! Positively, Reginald, I had even neglected to dye my hair. I was going to forsake my colours, not caring whether I was blonde or brunette. Poor old Landy was in despair, but I could not do otherwise.

" By-the-by, Reginald, mamma, who is a most voracious newspaper reader, and frightfully addicted to horrors, which are to her as the salt of the earth, has been telling me about a wonderful case that occurred recently in París. It concerned a person called Déjazet, who murdered a girl named Geneviève Delaunay, rather than marry her. Mamma gave me all the details in a very vivid manner, and I couldn't help thinking, after I had heard them, what a very admirable play it would make. I could almost see you as Déjazet—made up with a pomaded, spiky moustache, and I am sure that it would be a magnificent rôle for you. And then, my dear, I think I could be Geneviève to perfection—just my style. She must have been just such another un-coy, un-proud thing as I am. It served her almost right for insisting upon marrying the poor fellow when she knew that he hated her. I am afraid that I should do precisely the same thing, my poor, entangled Reginald. Consequently, who could be a better Geneviève Delaunay than Felicia Halstead ?

"I read in a local paper that they have just added a picture of Déjazet to the wax-work collection at Madame Tussaud's, and that the face is modelled from a cast made after death. So, my dear, if you should ever play Déjazet, you won't have to worry yourself with the British Museum, where you always go for inspiration, but you can have a cheap shilling's-worth of Madame Tussaud. Wait until I come back and we will go together. I adore the wax-works. Landy and I have spent hours there. In fact, my idea of happiness is a morning at Madame Tussaud's, with a nice catalogue and sixpenny-worth of chocolate creams in a bag. My grave and artistic lord, how you must despise me for this confession. Yet I make it, because I am so anxious to confess everything—or nearly everything—to you. Dear old Madame Tussaud's! I am always so desperately anxious to examine the petticoats and lingerie worn by all the queens and princesses, that it is hard work for me to conform to the rules and regulations of the place.

"I must be thinking of closing. I imagine that the only lines in this letter that you will really care for are those connected with Déjazet, and a possible play. They were really the point of this letter, and I felt so jealous of them that I tried to get even with them by all this flimsy Felicia talk. I wonder if mamma's chatter has really given you an idea. I know that you never read the papers. Perhaps you have never heard of Déjazet, before you receive this. I had not. Landy never discusses horrors, and never tells me of newspaper topics. Consequently, if I am responsible for any new plans that you may make, let me know. I should love to believe that I was really useful to you at last. And if you do play Déjazet, remember that I must be the Geneviève—even if I never play another part, and retire immediately afterwards. I could feel like Geneviève without the slightest difficulty! I could put myself in her place, without the faintest effort. And you—you clever, versatile boy—you could put yourself with equal ease in anybody's place. You can be an angel as readily as a devil.

"Forgive me all this frivolous outburst. I have waited until I could wait no longer. I did not expect to hear from you. I do not expect to do so. I tell mamma and Floss and Edna that you are too busy to write. Perhaps you are. How I should appreciate a letter, but—but—I am not hinting for one. If it came, I should not return it unopened. But, I am not hinting for one, Reginald; oh dear, no.

"I shall return to London at the end of my third week, and then—and then—well, since you insist, I will be yours. Mamma talks such a lot about trouseau and bridesmaids, and a wedding-cake with sugar on it, and—all the usual things that you know nothing about. I have ventured to hint that we may be married by the registrar, and that my wedding dress will probably be whatever I happen to be wearing at that moment. She is very much horrified. I have tried to break it gently to Floss and Edna that there will be no bridesmaids. Poor girls, they had already mapped out for themselves

blue silk dresses with white tulle veils.   Sometimes
I sigh, and just for one moment—only one—I wish
that you were a provincial person, who went every
morning to business at nine o'clock, and came back
to tea at six; that we were going to settle down to
humdrum life; and that you would like a supply
of doilies, knitted mats, clocks and sugar-spoons for
wedding presents.   For one moment only!   The
next—and I see you superior to it all—soaring
above the provincialism of the thing—my own regal,
peerless, and irrevocable Reginald.   Good-bye,
dear.   One word from you to the effect that I must
not stay away three weeks, and back I come, regardless of etiquette, of reason, of mamma, or of
Floss and Edna.   I may be all wrong, but then
you know I can't help being

" FELICIA."

" What will be the fate of this letter?   Somehow
or other, I can picture you reading it, and frowning
upon everything but that little business matter
concerning Déjazet.   I can see the sheets left on
your desk, for Crampton to file away in the H's.
Shall you put me in the F's or the H's?   Do you
think of me as Felicia or as Halstead?   I have a
dreadful idea that Crampton will pigeon-hole me
in the H's.   O Reginald, save me from this fate.
Tear me up, and scatter my bits over the waste-
paper basket.   Burn me, but don't put me away
with demands for engagements, offers to read plays,
and—other professional matter.   What will be my
fate?

" F. H."

This was the letter that Reginald Rellerick found waiting for him after another mentally exhausting evening spent in the Marylebone Road. The address upon the envelope gave him no clue to the identity of the writer. He had never before seen a specimen of Felicia's handwriting. Before he read it, he dried his humid brow and drank deeply of the ever-welcome champagne-cup prepared for him by the obeisant Thomas. What an evening he had passed! He had stood for two hours before the image of Déjazet, greedily listening to the comments of the throng. Every scathing criticism of the murderer stung him as though it referred to his veritable self. He felt humiliated, disgraced, prostrated. He found himself eagerly awaiting some extenuating comment from some extraordinarily charitable person. He scanned the features of the crowd as though to analyze the sentiments expressed therein. He recalled one graphic utterance that had been balm to his bleeding soul. It came from a stout labourer, who remarked: " Women are the devil. This isn't the first victim, and it won't be the last." It had been difficult for him to restrain himself from shaking the hand of that humble and lenient philosopher. But he could not forget that the crowd had growled at the rude philosophy, and had even hissed, as London crowds consider it their privilege to do. The sympathies of the herd were not with Déjazet—the evil, yellow thing with the glassy eyes and the nail-less hands, that stood there recklessly, as though wallowing in its own unholy powers of attraction.

Every man in that crowd was a critic, to the wrought-up, nerve-tightened actor. It was as though he were listening to his own judgment; as if his future life depended upon the whims and caprices of this gathering of 'Arries and 'Arriets.

He had taken the precaution to don a soft felt hat, which he pressed down over his eyes, so that his panoramic expression, and that odious resemblance, might both be kept from the curious men and women at the exhibition. He skulked, when chance brought him into closer contact with the visitors, and once when a confidential countryman spoke to him, he moved quickly away, without attempting to utter a word.

And now he had returned to his own apartments. Crampton was out. The house was still. He opened the letter carelessly, and read it derisively. His lips curled at poor Felicia's exuberance of expression, and he laughed aloud at the words that told him she had expected a telegram. It was not until he reached her " point "—the allusions to Déjazet—that he was aroused to any sort of demonstration. He arose from his seat, and pounded round the room, speaking aloud, as very few sane people do—off the stage.

"She would like to see me play Déjazet," he foamed. " She, too! She can ' almost see me ' as Déjazet ' made up with a pomaded, spiky moustache.' And she would like to play Geneviève! Devils! They are all conspiring against me! If I am not crazy, I shall be soon. What have I done to be cursed like this?"

He was engaged to be married to the woman who had lacerated his career. Marry her he would, and then—and then he could retire her to oblivion, and seek forgetfulness of this morbid horror in his stage work. Yet how loathsome it seemed! Already she began to speak as though she owned him, body and soul—the matrimonial condition at which his ego-maniacal soul rebelled. Would he ever be able to endure her exactions? Could he ever calmly resign himself to those insistently expressed endearments, which, destitute of passion, were cold and clumsy in his ears. What a detestable fate! How she would " dear " him and " darling " him in public, and look after his health, and see that he changed his stockings if his feet were wet! What a prospect! He was paying a big price for the adulation that the public offers. His ego-mania—he called it fame—was an expensive luxury, to be obtained at the risk of all personal happiness.

A normal man—even a normal man with a heart of ice—would have been touched at the gentle femininity of this clinging Felicia's letter. A normal man might even have become coxcombical, as he read her adoring words. But this ego-maniac hated her as the one obstacle in his glittering, self-laudatory path. If he could only have married her, and shipped her next day to Australia.

Sitting down again, he tried to conjure up some plan by which he could resume his career without marrying Felicia. There was no harm in thinking up a plan. If he could find one, the telegram that she had expected should be hers without further delay.

But there was no way out of the tangle. Felicia left alone—resourceless as she was, with a family dependent upon her—must earn her living. All London was discussing her at present. There was not the faintest shadow of doubt but that she would succumb to managerial persuasion. Moreover, she was a woman, and women were vindictive. If he withdrew his offer, she would oppose him out of sheer revenge. Even the gentle, pliant, lamb-like Felicia had a woman's foibles.

No, matters had been arranged. He had even blessed the arrangement, and thanked his lucky stars at its success. It was marriage, or the downward path. Marriage it should be.

Henceforth, he would never again seek for any pretext to break the bonds.

So he forced himself to write a few words of hypocritical affection to the Lancashire lass of his reluctant bosom. No need to chronicle them. There are some tasks at which even the student of humanity quails. Suffice it to say that he lied as valiantly as possible, and wrote what it would have been impossible for him to speak. He made no reference to the Déjazet topic. Fate was linking him with it. He would let fate work its own way unaided.

He went out and posted the letter himself. He felt relieved when he had consigned it to the pillar. For two days at any rate he could forget Felicia and his engagement.

Once more he felt it impossible to retire. Crampton came in, mouldily uninteresting, sedate as usual.

Was there anything he could do for Mr. Rellerick before going to bed ?   No, there was nothing.

The great actor waited until his secretary was quiet, and stole noiselessly out of the house, bound for the Marylebone Road.   He promised himself that this should be the last time he indulged in such folly.   His mind must be recovering its tone, for he began to realize the ludicrous side of this nocturnal promenade.   Imagine a man in his sane senses, gazing at a closed exhibition, in the dead of the night, more especially when he had spent the major part of his day there.   Reginald laughed and felt better.   He would end this farce with to-night. But even as he said this he hurried his footsteps, and arrived panting at the Marylebone Road.   How could he sleep, after all, with the knowledge that his own image—the image which all London had worshipped, and for the adulation of which he lived and breathed—was standing alone, in the dark, in the Tussaud sarcophagus ?

Chapter X

THE rusty Crampton was quiet, but the rusty Crampton was not asleep. The nerves of the man, whom you may have regarded as an automaton, were on the alert. Crampton was growing suspicious. He felt that some strange forces were at work within the masterful Reginald Rellerick. So far, he had been completely able to understand all the motives that actuated the ego-maniac's life. He had read his Nordau, and in the old Oxford days he had studied the psychological authorities from which the astutely advertised author of " Paradoxes " derived so many of his facts. Rellerick was quite intelligible to him, and he had led the self-dazzled actor into many harbours, from the depths in which his blindness would have sunk him. But now, something else was at work, and Crampton was puzzled.

He lay awake in his bed as Reginald prepared to leave the house. He heard the creaking of the floors, his master's step in the hall, the opening of the door, and its closing. The rusty Crampton, with an amount of energy quite surprising in one so sere and yellow, leaped from his couch, and hastily trousering himself, resolved to follow Mr. Rellerick. Quick thoughts coursed through his brain. At another time he might have analyzed them; now he simply thought them, without wondering. He was impelled to remember that hour in the cab with Felicia Halstead, when he had brought her from Notting Hill to his master's sanctum. She had sat beside him, and had talked in such sweet frivolity that his mission had been hateful to him. He recalled her departure from Reginald's house, bewildered and miserable, and following that, like a flash of disaster-bringing lightning, came the news of her engagement to the actor. He thought of all this involuntarily, without attempting to ask himself why these old subjects came to him at midnight, as he was about to follow Reginald Rellerick on some unknown adventure. Crampton had once had as much colour as you and I are proud to own. It had simply worn off. Colour is a perishable quality, heightened by contact with the world, destroyed by stagnation. Crampton had been colourless for a long time, but in spite of that fact, he is the only irreproachable character in these records, and I insist upon your liking him. It is your duty to like him, because he was a good man, with no vices worth speaking of, and no virtues to worry about lauding. It is the absence of vice, rather than the presence of virtue, that dishes up to the world what the world calls a a good man.

Crampton passed into Reginald's sanctum. The lamp was burning low, and the unoccupied room still reeked of the intense vitality of its owner. Crampton glanced hastily around.   Time was precious.   He must see on what fool's errand the egomaniac had started.   Under the desk he saw a crumpled letter.   The sheets had evidently been squeezed together by a vindictive hand.   They were twisted into most uncomplimentary contortions.   Crampton read a few words of the postscript : " What will be the fate of this letter? . . . I can see the sheets left on your desk for Crampton to file away in the H's. . . . I have a dreadful idea that Crampton will pigeon-hole me in the H's. "

The mouldy secretary looked around him with— what the old-fangled novelists called—" the eyes of the hunted antelope."   A dash of the colour that had tinged his character in the old University days returned to him like a whiff of youth.   The hour was certainly propitious for everything unusual and unexpected.   Crampton took up the sheet containing the words he had just read, and kissed it.   It crackled against his frayed-out white-ended moustache.   Then, as though ashamed of himself, he tore open his shirt and placed Felicia's writing next to his heart.   " Pigeon-holed in the H's," he thought, and this eerie person actually smiled at what he considered an excellent *jeu de mot*.

All this had taken place so quickly, that by the time Crampton was in the open air, he was able to see the figure of Rellerick at the end of the road, about to turn into a street at the right.   He followed swiftly.   He had heard of somnambulists performing strange feats with which they were un-familiar when awake, but he could not suppose that Rellerick was sleep-walking. Could the actor be in pursuit of some sordid adventure with the street-walkers that infested the vicinity? He did not believe it, for the actor had a tinge of refine-ment, and his sexuality had never seemed protru-sive.

Crampton kept about two hundred yards behind his master. The chase was a somewhat exhaust-ing one. The secretary noticed the soft felt hat that the actor had donned, and realized the fact that his mission was evidently one that rendered recognition undesirable. By the time that the huge brick pile in the Marylebone Road was reached, Crampton was out of breath. Reginald's hurried steps had suggested impulsion by electri-city. Such violent exercise was fatiguing to the secretary.

He stood still and watched his master, who stopped, in an attitude of almost reverent study, before Madame Tussaud's landmark. He remem-bered Reginald's anger with the servants who had visited the exhibition, and he recalled his master's inquiries on the subject of Déjazet, whose image, it appeared, strongly resembled him. Crampton's fatigue soon left him. His brain set to work with remarkable facility, and it made out an astonish-ingly accurate case in a very short time.

Reginald walked backwards and forwards with his hands in his pockets, and his head bowed. Occasionally he glanced at the windows of the building and stood still peering through the darkness. Crampton's eyes never left him. At the end of a half hour the secretary's mind was made up. He approached the actor, as though meeting him in an opposite direction, and when a few yards away from him, coughed and came to a standstill.

Reginald looked up, and Crampton noted the haggard, anxious expression that he wore. His eyes were sunken and lustreless; his face gray in the dull midnight street. The secretary felt a sensation of pity sweeping over him. He was rather sorry that he had broken in upon him so suddenly. The great actor's ego however, asserted itself almost instantaneously. No sooner had he recognized this intruder, than his listless demeanour vanished. The life came back to his eyes, and the vitality to his expression. His imperial impudence asserted itself rapidly.

"So you have dared to follow me, sirrah," he said, blazing forth into anger, and feeling a sensation of relief in the mere change of sensation. "You have presumed to spy upon my actions. I choose, for personal reasons, to walk in this neighbourhood with my thoughts, but I find myself confronted by my paid servant, wearing a puzzled look, and behaving like a missionary attempting to rescue a heathen."

Crampton, usually so limp and dejected, did not wither beneath this scathimg rebuke. His logical mind, scenting complications the significance of which he could not over-estimate, was not to be imposed upon. Moreover, he was genuinely alarmed at the expression that he had noticed upon his master's face—an expression of nervous exaltation that the most exacting " first night " had failed to induce.

He looked the great actor calmly in the eye, and said quietly, " If I were you, Mr. Rellerick, I should not brood over a fancied resemblance to a waxen figure. You will disturb your mind, and ruin your mental constitution. It is absurd. It is illogical. If you read it in a book, you would say, ' How vastly improbable.' Forget it—for your own sake, and for that of—" Crampton's voice sank—" of the girl who has promised to be your wife."

Reginald was conscious of a sense of consolation at the beginning of his secretary's remarks. They soothed him as " some sweet oblivious antidote " destined to " raze out the written troubles of the brain." But the allusion to Felicia was unfortunate. Impossible as it must always be for him to forget his loathsome double in this museum, it must be equally out of the question peacefully to consider his necessary entanglement with Felicia. His anger gushed forth.

"Forget ! Forget !" he cried wrathfully. " Could you go quietly to bed, and sleep calmly through the night, knowing that a jaundiced but frightfully accurate model of yourself was standing, reared up among an army of murderers, girl-decoyers, and obnoxious criminals ? I ask you—could you feel comfortable—you, a man without nerves, a healthy type of British stolidity, addicted to regular habits and stagnation ?"

Crampton saw him shudder, and pondered carefully over the question. Yes, he was a man without nerves, one of those happy go-to-bed-at-ten-and-get-up-at-six specimens of English health. He was a college man, an Oxford M. A., a distinctly normal person. He was bound to admit to himself that Reginald's predicament was a trying one, and he realized that this actor, diseased with ego-mania, and living persistently the hothouse, malarial life of the stage, was a magnificent target for these arrows of the imagination. But Crampton resolved to lie rather than cater to such imaginings. What would become of little Felicia Halstead, linked to such a character ?

So he answered cautiously. " It is all folly. If I heard of a waxen Crampton in Madame Tussaud's wax-works, I should laugh at it as a ludicrous coincidence. You, with your fame, could work this up into a magnificent advertisement for yourself. Think of it."

He tried, in this way, to lure him from the miasma of his thoughts. It was quite useless. A shock went through Reginald's system, as he even contemplated the odious idea of publicity. An actor will submit to a great deal for the sake of notoriety's will-of-the-wisp, but the real ego-maniac will not endure abject humiliation, because he has never yet discovered a public that is worth winning at such a cost.

" No," he said, ferociously. " No, no. It is bad enough to know that this unfortunate creature —— this yellow waxen horror—is there, without publishing it to the world. And he stands there with the vilest of the earth."

Crampton thought for a moment, before he retorted. "Undoubtedly. Would you see him with the kings and queens—a murderer of the most noxious type—a brute who, after having ruined a girl, deliberately took her life ?"

They were walking slowly towards the end of the railings surrounding the Marylebone edifice. As Reginald heard Crampton's words, he stood still, and—just for one second—he wondered at himself. He was instantly conscious of a deep-rooted resentment as he listened to his secretary's criticism of Déjazet. He forgot his original horror at the knowledge that Déjazet was a murderer. It seemed to him at the present time that such accusations were hideous. Pangs shot through him as Crampton spoke of the ruin and murder of a girl. Then he gazed indignantly at the prosaic Oxonian, and lost all sense of restraint.

"That's hitting a man when he's down," he declared savagely. " It is insulting and unworthy. Déjazet cannot speak for himself, but I am thankful to say that there is one who will not listen to such one-sided charges. How do we know what amount of provocation he endured? Women are the devil. The horrid feminine idea of owning a man's body and soul forever has been the cause of untold misery. Déjazet may have had justification for his act, such as the world knows nothing of. Why call a man a murderer because the mob insists that he is one? The mob is always wrong. The mob has injured me. I hate it. I hate it."

His excitement was painful to see. His overwhelming ego-mania, that was reaching out to include his waxen presentment, filled the poor secretary with amazement. The actor glanced at the windows of the exhibition, as though he expected to see his double looking out to applaud him for this defense—to applaud him with those smooth and nailless hands.

" The mob could not be wrong in this instance," Crampton murmured, almost wishing himself back in his bed. " The case was as clear as a pikestaff. He murdered his mistress on their wedding-night, and was captured red-handed. Moreover, he confessed his crime. What court of justice could hope for anything more? It was a horror in the annals of crime."

" How dare you talk like this?" the furious actor cried, the volume of his augmented voice reaching a distant policeman, and causing that individual to shake off his lethargy. " I will not be argued with. I will not permit it. You are my satellite, and I will not allow you to thrust me into the wrong." Then, changing his tone to one of almost supplicating import, " Crampton, you are uncharitable. You believe in the conventions too fully. Can you not, as a man, imagine a condition of things so hideous that what we call crime would be justifiable in order to remove it. Can you not believe in an obstacle so monstrous that a man may be pardoned for his anxiety to rid himself of it?

Suppose Déjazet—poor Déjazet—felt that his whole artistic career was imperilled by this woman, this clinging, stupid Geneviève Delaunay. Suppose he felt that future generations, which might possibly be delighted with his work, would lose everything, if he lived with this millstone round his neck—this daily meal of hatred constantly before him. Suppose all this, Crampton. Why, why should he be placed in this detestable mausoleum to be gazed at day after day by vulgar men and women with catalogues ?"

Crampton had never seen his master in such a plight—with all his soul let loose, as it were. The man might have been pleading for the jewel of his own reputation. The agony of his recent theatre failure was no keener than this. In each case there was an injury to the personality, for the egomaniac's defense of Déjazet was due solely to the fact that the murderer was flaunting before the public in his image. The actor's hair was damp and the perspiration ran in drops from his forehead. His ego was endangered, and he had nothing else to live for. There was nothing else in the world, as a matter of fact. All other men and women were mere automata. The secretary scarcely knew what to do or say. He felt that the situation was far more serious than he had supposed it to be. It was psychological—beyond the reach of medicine and cheap words.

"There may have been provocation, as you suggest," the embarrassed Crampton remarked, " but for the sake of society—for the sake of organized decency, we dare not consider it.   Probably all the figures in Madame Tussaud's Chamber of Horrors had some sort of provocation.   Mr. Rellerick, you must not dwell on that matter.   It is the feeble excuse of most crime.   Adam ate the apple because Eve provoked him to do so.   Eve's provocation came from the serpent.   Even the serpent—if tried in court—could find a lawyer willing to prove that he was innately bad and suffering from hereditary taint.   We must conquer our provocation."

"Ha! ha! ha!" laughed Reginald, hysterically. "Crampton, you talk like the 'Child's Stepping-Stone to Knowledge' or 'Mangnall's Questions.' I don't care what the world thinks of provocation. There is something in the knowledge that it has existed.   If I could only know—and I feel certain of it—that this unfortunate artist was more sinned against than sinning, I should feel easier in my mind.   I must know it.   I must know it," he repeated, grinding his teeth.   "Poor Déjazet."

They had left the Marylebone Road and were walking quickly to the west.   The actor's pallid face and sunken cheeks looked as lifeless in the darkness as those of the wax-works they were leaving behind them.   It was a gloomy and marrow-chilling night.   Each person they met seemed to be abroad for some sinister motive.   The sleeping houses appeared to enclose tightly all that was light and virtuous and spiritual in the tortuous and interminable metropolis.   Women spoke to them as they walked through the clanking thoroughfares, but Reginald, held up by Crampton's arm, was pushed rapidly along.

They reached Piccadilly Circus, bound for nowhere at all. The actor was anxious for movement and sensation of any sort. The secretary had sunk into a sort of comatose condition of dread foreboding. It was so much worse than he had thought. It was a farce turning into a tragedy, as so often happens in this world, where extremes meet, and laughter and grief overlap. He could imagine this wax-work notion that was weighing him down, as the theme of a merry, tripping opera, with waxen nymphs coming to life, and the bogie-man subjected to the ever-enjoyable insults of the modern stage. But no laugh could he coax to his lips at the present time.

Piccadilly Circus had concluded another of its infamous nights, and was comparatively deserted. The ghastly galaxy of creatures that come forth like beetles was no longer apparent. The traffic was over, and the vampires had fled, with but few exceptions. Occasionally the occupant of a cab looked from the windows to see if anything was "going on." A few women chatted hopelessly with some maudlin boys, who were on their way home. The curved expanse of Regent Street looked forbidding enough, but Crampton knew that in the morning it would be gay and busy once more, and that the virtuousest matrons would stand on the very spot that had just been pressed by the women of the pavement. Messalina and Lucretia share the "modern conveniences" of London together.

It is a very ingenious sort of Box and Cox arrangement.

Reginald and Crampton were just about to cross the Circus in the direction of the Criterion Theatre, when two highly illuminated women coming from the Leicester Square vicinity attracted their attention. The women were undoubtedly French. They had very large, loose, bulging bodies, tiny compressed waists, and sinuously padded hips. They were laughing and talking loudly, and they soon noticed the two men, hesitant at the curbstone.

As the largest and loudest of the Frenchwomen approached Reginald, with ribald words on her lips, she suddenly stopped, as though paralyzed, and clutched at the arm of her companion. An electric light that stood near showed that even beneath the kalsomine on her cheeks she had grown white and bloodless. Reginald heard her say '*Grand Ciel!*' and a moment later, in response to the query of the other, she cried, "*Mais, ma cherie, c'est Déjazet lui-même!*

Crampton scarcely noticed the words, embedded in French, and Parisianly pronounced, but to Reginald the remark came like a bolt from the skies. He was instantly alert, and keenly attentive to the protection of his ego. He pulled his hat over his eyes, and started to cross the street. The siren from Leicester Square was not in the least nonplussed. She followed him, deliberately plucked his hat from his head, and standing before him, arms akimbo, gazed at him relentlessly.

" *Sacre bleu !*" she cried—and there was awe in her tones, "'*C'est Déjazet revenu à la vie.*" Then in excellent English, "My little gentleman, you remind me of a friend of mine who is dead—gathered by force to his ancestors. Ah, you are so like him. The same eyes, the same chin, the same hair, the same expression. *Tiens ! Tiens ! Tiens ! Ma mouchoir, Cerisette, que je pleure.*"

Cerisette had joined the group. She immediately handed a handkerchief to the large lady, who forthwith dissolved into tears. Reginald was so agitated that he could scarcely speak. Crampton, upon whose duller brain the meaning of it all had suddenly dawned, tried by brute strength to drag his master away. He was quite powerless.

"I will not go," the actor said, hoarsely. "I will not go."

"No, no, do not go," cried the large lady excitedly, "I must look at you again. *Ah, Déjazet, mon pauvre bon homme ! Te voilà encore. Tu ne pourrais pas rester mort. Sapristi !*"

Again she wept, and Reginald watched her, a wild hope rising in his breast. He waited until her sobs had ceased.

"You knew Déjazet ?" he said. "And you remember him pleasantly in spite of what he did ?"

"I knew him. I loved him. If he had remained with me, he would have been alive to-day, and I would have been true to him. Then there would have been no martyred Geneviève. The martyred Geneviève ! What a martyr ! Ha ! ha ! ha !"

"I will come with you," said Reginald excitedly, "and you shall tell me all about it."

The woman looked at him suspiciously, and then glanced at Crampton in the background, and at Cerisette, who had just waved a farewell and departed in quest of livelier scenes, with a thorough French horror of the tearful.

"This is no investigation ?" she asked. "I have had enough of that sort of thing. You are in earnest, and are interested in Déjazet's story ?"

"I am in earnest, before heaven," replied the actor solemnly. "And I will pay you well for your trouble."

"They have him at Tussaud's—my poor Déjazet," she whined. "And I would willingly go to him there, if I could. But, Monsieur—Monsieur is Déjazet. The same eyes, the same chin, the same hair, the same expression. *C'est épatant.*"

"For heaven's sake," said Crampton, coming quickly forward, "I implore you, Mr. Rellcrick, to leave this woman. Think of your reputation. What would London say if it saw a man like you parading Leicester Square with a creature like this ? Think of the danger of what you are doing. Think of the scandal. What would Miss Halstead say ? For her sake come home with me."

"For her sake," cried Reginald contemptuously. "For my own sake, I will clear Déjazet if I can, and this woman will help me, I am sure. At present, Crampton, I am the yellow murderer you can see for one-and-sixpence in the Marylebone Road. I cannot rest under the charge. The mob may always believe that he is an atrocity, but if I can think otherwise, I may once again be happy. Write and tell Felicia that you left me in the company of—what is your name, Madame?" turning to the woman.

" They call me La Chinoise," she said.

"Tell her that you left me in the company of La Chinoise. She will marry me still. You couldn't induce her to do anything else. I am not afraid, Crampton. At first I thought that Felicia wanted fame. She has told me herself that she will sacrifice everything for me. Ha! ha! ha! The situation is clearing itself. *Bon jour*, Crampton. *A demain*. Wait till you see me in the morning. And now, La Chinoise, we will get into a cab, and drive to your mansion in Mayfair. Not Mayfair? Well, Leicester Square. It is all the same to me, and it is equally London. Hey, cabby, go as fast as you can. There is no time to be lost."

Chapter XI

REGINALD'S strange exaltation—a condition that
to the pompous ego-maniac was a comparatively
novel one—wore off before he reached La Chinoise's
apartment in one of the sordid thoroughfares that
open into Leicester Square. As he sat beside her,
in the swiftly moving cab, he shut his eyes, and tried
to forget the odious events that linked Felicia Halstead with the dead Déjazet in his memory. The
task was an impossible one. His jangled brain
could not shut out the picture of the tallowy, yellow model that stood erect in the Marylebone Road,
staring with its cold glass eyes, and inert as to the
smooth and nailless hands. The torrent of his
faith was rushing him into a keen association with
Déjazet. His persistent attention to the hateful
model, far from having opened to him the joyous
jewelled gates of the humorous, had simply entangled him more deeply. And now—and now—
he sat in a whirling hansom in juxtaposition with a
woman whom Déjazet had loved. He smiled at
Crampton's serene advice to forget it all. Forget
it all! Every move that he made on the chess-
board of his career brought him into Déjazet's cir-

[167]

cle more surely.   He cursed the Marylebone Road,
and he cursed the girl whose departure from London had induced him into that bewildering resort.

La Chinoise was not talkative.   Her frivolous,
mendacious, Parisian nature had been genuinely
moved by her encounter with Rellerick.   She sat
still and rested, until her mercenary nature should
have recuperated itself, and she could face a situation that might prove profitable.   La Chinoise, like
most of her class, despised her *métier*.   She had
not visited Piccadilly Circus for fun, and she would
be a fool for her pains, if she allowed a sickly sen-
timentality to interfere with legitimate business.
She was a handsome woman, marred by the fatal art
of "make-up"—over-decorated, over-illuminated,
over-dyed, over-dressed, over-padded, over-every-
thing.   Nature unadorned was to her a myth.

They alighted at her apartment, and she led the
way carelessly to her sanctum sanctorum.   Her
usual moods were re-asserting themselves, and by
the time that Reginald had thrown his dejected
personality into a chair her impudent courtesanship
was on the surface again, and she was congratulating herself upon the accidental resemblance that
promised to make her day lucrative.

He sat there, helplessly oppressed and pensive,
and watched her as she removed her gown, and
threw over the nudity of her shoulders a *peignoir*
of thick pink silk and lace.   Then he saw her shake
the masses of her sultry hair into a flowing mass
that reached to the waist-line.   So had Déjazet sat
and looked.   He could not help wondering if there

was envy in the glassy eyes of the monster in the museum. There might be. He thought of that horrid watch among the waxen criminals. The semi-obscurity of La Chinoise's room angered him. Springing to his feet, he struck a match, and lighted every jet in the dust-clouded chandelier.

" Monsieur loves the light," said La Chinoise, smiling, as she kicked the boots from her feet, and ran her toes into a pair of pink-lined slippers bounded on the instep by whitest fur. " *Moi, aussi.* I am not like you Londoners, who are happy in gloom and darkness. *Il faut être gai, car demain nous mourons,*" she murmured.

Her smile was most attractive. It was the smile that—according to her words—had fascinated Déjazet. Strange that he should now be basking in its warmth. The very counterpart of the poor artist whose joys and sorrows and virtues and crimes had ended—in wax.

" Tell me, *chéri,*" said La Chinoise, coming to him, sinking at his feet, and looking up alluringly into his eyes as picturesquely as she was able to do it—for her lissome days were over—" Tell me if we had not better forget the unfortunate Déjazet. It is painful to me to talk of him. I should much prefer not to do so. You recall him to me. Does not that satisfy you ? Let poor Déjazet rest."

Reginald looked at the woman with a ruddy glow of anger in his eyes. Did she imagine that he, Reginald Rellerick, London's pet actor, fêted everywhere, a household word through the United Kingdom, had deliberately elected to visit her in

Leicester Square with any object other than that he had named? The man's ego-mania revived immediately, his expression changed, and he gazed at La Chinoise with the supercilious air that he usually vented upon Crampton, and Felicia Halstead, and the other satellites of his daily life. His inability to endure the *malaise* of being unknown prompted him to identification. He proceeded, in his arrant coxcombry, to " give himself away."

"You are mistaken, woman," he said imperiously, " if you imagine that you are dealing with an inebriated soldier or a Londoner out for the night. I am Reginald Rellerick, the actor. My name is undoubtedly familiar to you. I told you why I came. I promised you that I would pay you well. Tell me what you know of Déjazet, and let us finish this miserable evening. My resemblance to the man you loved has startled me as profoundly as it has astonished you. The model of Tussaud's has overwhelmed me, until I hardly know whether I am here with you, or there with him. They have called him a murderer. You insinuated that Geneviève was no martyr. Explain. Explain."

She stared at him, blankly amazed, forgetting her coquetries—the tricks of her hideous trade. Her round face rested on her elbows, and the lace of her sleeves fell back, revealing a white and rounded arm that an artist would scarcely have passed un. noticed. This was the rich actor of whom she had heard—whom indeed she had seen, although her days in London had been very few. Yes, she remembered that, in the disguise of the rôle she had seen him play, some vague lost souvenir of Déjazet had occurred to her.

She continued to look at him. He was nervous, unstrung, irresponsible. This was a richer prize than she had imagined. Cerisette had brought her luck. Cerisette should be her nocturnal partner henceforth. She had the deep-rooted superstitions of the luckless sisterhood.

"What shall I tell you?" she asked quickly. "What is it that you wish to know?"

"Tell me," he said pantingly, "that this man whose features I wear, and whose outward semblance I can never shake off, was not the vulgar, purposeless criminal that he has been painted. Tell me that he did not shed the blood of Geneviève Delaunay out of sheer brutality. Let me understand him, so that when I see his waxen image again, I may know the whole truth."

La Chinoise was awe-struck. The muddy depths of her character were stirred. This man was interesting her, in spite of herself. The larder was empty; she was hungry, thirsty, and tired, in her silks and laces, but this actor, with his high-falutin' sentences was impressing her.

"Listen," she said, " and perhaps you will understand. Déjazet and Geneviève Delaunay met in the Quartier Latin. They were both young. He was an artist fighting his way to fame. She was— well, I don't know what she was. The story of her illustrious name may be true, but I have my sus-

picions of Geneviève Delaunay. I never believed
that she was true to him."

"And you told him that?" asked Reginald,
eagerly.

"Let me continue. Their *ménage* endured for
a long time. They were popular in the Quartier.
Everybody liked them, and they kept open house.
His name at last became known. There was a rage
for Déjazet pictures. She was proud of him, jealous of him, and imperious with him. I don't
believe that he had ever loved her very keenly.
Many people told me that he had tried to break
with her, but had desisted, fearing a scandal. It
was in one of his weariest moments that he met
me. I would have gone through blood and fire for
him, for I grew to love him as I have never loved
anyone. He installed me in a little house in Passy,
and there he used to see me, guarding his secret as
carefully from Geneviève Delaunay as though she
had been his legitimate wife. Still, he lived for his
art. He was a maniac on the subject of his art.
His ambition was to be internatiorally famous—to
sell his pictures in England and America—"

"Go on," cried Reginald, as she paused, "and
come to the point. Never mind about art."

"I must," she said, "it is the whole point of the
story. He had grown, as I said, to be quite indif-
ferent to Geneviève Delaunay. His intercourse
with me fanned that indifference into hatred. He
used to tell me that to meet her day after day, and
live in her society week after week, was utterly repulsive to him. If it had not been for me he could

not have endured it. I helped him, he said, to find some consolation in living. He was a rather melancholy, morose sort of man."

La Chinoise stopped again and looked at Reginald's face. It was so much like that of the dead Déjazet that for the moment she seemed to be telling his story to himself.

"Well," she resumed, "you know something of what followed. Geneviève's relatives, who had been hunting for her, discovered her whereabouts. You read the story of their indignation, and remember that a duel was arranged between Déjazet and Geneviève's brother. If he won, Geneviève was to go back to her relatives near Lyons. If he lost, he would marry her. He lost. That day he came to me. 'Claire,' he said—I was Claire in those days, for my nickname had not been born—'I have lost everything. I must marry this girl, and you and I must end our relations. I will try and do my duty. Perhaps I have been a brute. I hate her now, but, possibly, when she is my wife, bearing my name, I may become, at any rate, more reconciled to my life.'"

La Chinoise wiped a tear from her eye, but she went on: "You cannot realize what all this meant to me. Never for one moment had I contemplated the possibility of his losing that duel. The very idea that Déjazet could marry Geneviève Delaunay was, to me, too utterly preposterous to even worry about. In fact, it had not caused me a moment's trouble. For a time, after he had convinced me that marriage was absolutely inevitable, I was dazed and dumbfounded.　Then I registered a vow that this marriage should never take place, if I could prevent it.　I determined to watch Geneviève.　She was away from home a great deal, and I hoped to discover that she had other lovers, and thus publish her infamy to her own relatives. Alas!　What I discovered was worse, and it led to the tragedy."

Reginald was all a-fever with excitement.　He almost fell upon the words as they escaped from the lips of La Chinoise.

"As I told you," she said, "Déjazet lived for his art.　Love was a secondary consideration.　It was a pastime.　Art swallowed up all the serious episodes of his years.　He had been annoyed for a long time by the sudden appearance of certain pictures in the market labelled 'Suire.'　The pictures were much praised, and their technique strongly resembled that of Déjazet himself.　He was unable to discover the identity of 'Suire,' who seemed to be a myth.　He was invariably told that an introduction would be forthcoming, but difficulties always ensued.　Poor Déjazet!　He was horribly jealous of the new pictures.　They were spoken of in the same way as his own.　Soon people began to talk of the Déjazet-Suire school of art.　It was a bitter blow to him.　He hated Suire without knowing him in the least.　And then came my fatal work.　As I told you, I determined to watch Geneviève Delaunay.　I did so, and discovered that her absence from home was easily accounted for.　She had a studio of her own.　She was an artist herself. She was the redoubtable Suire. If I had only known enough to keep this knowledge to myself! But I didn't. I was blinded by hatred, and a desire to prevent the marriage of Déjazet and Geneviève. I went straight to him, and told him that the precious girl, who was to be his wife, was his deadly rival in art, the unknown Suire."

Reginald gazed at the woman in wonder. A vast and surging sympathy for Déjazet took possession of him. Joy illumined his face, as he thought of the yellow, nailless thing in the Marylebone Road, and its complete justification. Here was a man, wrapped up in his art, carving a name for himself in the marble of posterity, living for the multitude only—suddenly confronted with the torture of rivalry. Before he heard any further, he was ready to pinnacle Déjazet, for was he not—Reginald could not finish his thought. His face grew gray in the brilliantly lighted room; the joy left his eyes; he saw the pink-clad courtesan still kneeling in confession before him. The hideous parallel that streaked him side by side with Déjazet, became blackly emphatic. He placed his hands before his eyes, and murmured, " I must not justify him. I dare not justify him. I will hear no more. Let me go."

He arose, and staggered towards the door. From his pocket he took his purse, and emptied twenty shining sovereigns into a vase on La Chinoise's table. The woman heard the chink of the falling money. It satisfied the mercenary direction of her character, but this actor had interested her so strongly, that she made an effort to detain him longer.

"I will finish," she cried, "I must finish. Listen for a few minutes more."

She forced him back to his seat, and fell again at his knees, the pink billows of her silken skirt enveloping him.

"Déjazet was insane when he heard that his rival was his own mistress," she continued, as calmly as she could. "He had hated her before. Now his hatred took the form of mania. 'She is robbing me of everything,' he said to me, 'and yet I am bound to marry her.' He taxed the girl with her perfidy. Her excuses may seem natural to you, but to him and to me they were forced and exaggerated. She told him that she had no love for art itself ; and no original ideas whatsoever. She had lived with him for years, and she had studied him carefully. It had occurred to her, she said, that the time might come when his resources would end. He had worked for so long that fatigue might set in at any time. Moreover, she wished to see him rich, and in a position to retire, if he cared to do so. So she determined to work herself, and save her money for him. She copied his style, and encroached upon his ideas. The success that came to her was welcome to her for his sake only. She cared nothing for what the critics said. In fact, she never bothered herself about their words. And as a proof of all this, she brought her savings to him —thousands of francs—and threw them into his lap. She gave them to him freely, she said, and only wished that there were more. And more there should be, for she would work, and work for his sake."

A groan from Reginald frightened La Chinoise. She poured some brandy from a decanter, and held it to his lips.

" He was intensely exasperated," she said. " Of course he declined to believe her words. They were plausible, but nothing more. I know of no woman on this earth who could snap her fingers at fame, and say to any one man, ' I prefer you.' Such a creature doesn't exist. She would be a curiosity if she did. I told him that. Was I not right ?"

The actor swallowed the brandy, and gasped : " You were right—you were right," he shouted. " Of course you were right. The woman who professes to look upon success as a secondary consideration, is a liar and a perjurer. Yes, you were right. And he believed you—did he not ?"

" He believed me," said La Chinoise. " He loved me as much as he hated her. He used to tell me that if I had been in her place originally it would have been different, for his love would never have changed. But he was not a bad man. Even after this terrible discovery—a discovery that nearly unhinged his reason, he thought of me, and of my empty life. He would have broken his promise for my sake, and have positively declined to tie himself for life to Geneviève Delaunay, had it not been for her relatives. They forced him literally at the

point of the sword to the marriage ceremony, and
—and—as you know, it took place."

"Yes," he muttered, "I know. It took place."

"The rest," she said, breaking into sobs, "it is
not necessary to dwell upon. Imagine the poor
fellow alone with the woman he hated—alone with
her, as his wife, for the first time. To a man of his
artistic temperament what must it have meant?
There she was, linked to him until death should
intervene. She had ruined his life in every way,
and the married career was calmly to begin. I
have not much imagination," inserted La Chinoise,
drying her eyes with a tiny lace handkerchief, "but
I can see that wedding-night before me—the bride
stupidly happy in her senseless, colourless, merciless
way ; the bridegroom writhing in agony at a fate
that compelled him to be at the beck and call of
the creature he detested, day after day, week after
week, year after year. I can understand it all—
the rebellion of his proud, artistic nature, the brave
determination to remove so fatal an obstacle, the
murder—"

La Chinoise sank back pale and shuddering.
Her callous nature had its sensitive spots, and her
sympathy for the criminal she had loved overcame
her. Reginald looked at her with a curious sensation of gratitude and of admiration, apparent even
in his eyes. She was a handsome woman and an
intelligent woman. She had never thrust herself
in the path of any man. Her calling was degrad-
ing, humiliating, beyond the pale of even Christian
charity, but she was a woman who understood the

tortures of the artist confronted with ingratitude and the terrors of rivalry.

She could understand and condone the fate of Déjazet. And he thought again of the silent, staring figure in the Tussaud exhibition, at which the ribald mob gazed all day, and of which the catalogues had told cruel lies in plausible prose.

"You understood him," murmured Reginald, bending forward to rouse her from the semi-swoon into which she had fallen, "you understood him so well. You have the artist's soul. You realize the agony of interrupted glory—the pain of knowing that an interloper is wresting your laurels away—that all your efforts will count for nothing—that the fickle public will tire of you and ring their praises in the ears of your successor. That was what he suffered, and what—"

"You suffer?" she asked, softly.

He bowed his head. She bent down and kissed it softly.

"Déjazet!" she said. "My own Déjazet once more!"

The name was uttered and it caused him no spasm of anguish. She had applied it to him, and he wondered why the sound was so soothing and so gracious.

"I will call you Déjazet," she said, "and my better days will return to me, with the sun and the happiness of Paris, instead of the clouds and the misery of London. And you will call me Claire. He used to call me Claire. La Chinoise is my nickname in Leicester Square, and I thought I should wear it for ever.   Will you call me Claire ?"

And the ego-maniac, subdued as he had never been before, intimidated, bewildered, hopeful, murmured, " Claire."

Chapter XII

JUSTIFYING CRIME.

THERE was little sleep for the mouldy Crampton after he had left Reginald Rellerick in the toils of La Chinoise. He returned to the actor's apartment, and went conventionally to bed, but he was apprehensive and ill at ease. Vivid pictures of a gross and disastrous scandal arose in his perplexed imagination. But the victim in the case was always Felicia Halstead—never Reginald Rellerick. He saw the little goddess of his middle-age rudely confronted with the horror of her idol's iniquity, and all his hopes were centred in a wild idea of helping her over the morass that was opening before her.

He was at his desk early, with his paste-pot and scissors. There was always something to scrap-book—clippings from sleepy, out-of-town papers that arrived weeks later. The press comments upon Rellerick and his doings were surprisingly numerous. No wonder that there are more ego-maniacs in the footlight calling than in any other walk of life. Men, better, worthier and honester in every way than the illuminated exponents of mimic passions, may live and die " unparagraphed " and unknown. Those who really love, and hate, and sin, and die, may escape unsmirched by printer's ink. It is for the people who pretend to do it all for so much per week, that the paragrapher exists in all his strength. The actor's road, leading to the goal known as " Household Words," is a swift and easy one. He is pushed toward it by the willing hand of the press. For the lawyer, the doctor, the clergyman, and the scholar it is harder. They are real and desperate, and " too much advertisement " would be bad for their souls. It is given gratuitously to the man of the stage, and in return he barks at the donor and envelopes himself in his own ego-mania.

Reginald Rellerick joined Crampton at noon, just as the feverish forebodings of the early morning hours were returning to the secretary. The actor was quieter than Crampton had seen him since the beginning of the Tussaud affair. His eyes were calmer and brighter. These symptoms gave the secretary no satisfaction. They were abnormal, and had been scandalously brought about.

The actor took his usual long chair, and waited for Crampton to speak. He waited in vain, and irritated by the silence—there is nothing more exasperating on earth—he took the initiative as amiably as possible.

"You will be glad to know," he said—and there was an undercurrent of satire in his tones—" that my evening was absolutely successful. I have heard Déjazet's justification. I told you that I believed there was much to be condoned. I am now satisfied that my double "—he emphasized the word with ferocity—" was less detestable than the world supposed."

Crampton shuffled uneasily. " In other words," he stammered, " you can excuse the man who murdered the girl that trusted him."

" There were extenuating circumstances," the actor murmured.

" Society does not admit of extenuating circumstances," retorted the secretary indignantly, shedding his coat of mould, and posing before his astonished master in the new light of accuser. " Society takes no heed of such excuses. The lunatic asylums are filled with the people who make them. Be careful, Mr. Rellerick. You have gone far— very far. I should advise you to stop. The papers are beginning to scent something unusual. Here is a paragraph that I clipped this morning from the *Weekly Squib*. Read it."

He handed a square cutting to the actor who read as follows : " Strange forces seem to be at work in the complicated personality of the actor, Reginald Rellerick. There are those who say that his recent failure in Pinerville's new play has seriously affected his mind. Although he announced his intention of taking a long-needed rest at the summer-resorts that he has always patronized, he is known to be in London. Mr. Rellerick has been seen at Madame Tussaud's wax-work exhibition in the Marylebone Road, eagerly studying the newly added model of Déjazet, the notorious criminal, recently guillotined in Paris. The figure is a speaking likeness of Rellerick, and they say that it has annoyed him considerably. We are suspicious of the theatrical profession. We are unwilling to cater to the rage for advertisement that afflicts the actor and actress. This paper tries to steer away from that sort of thing. In the present case, however, there is genuine apprehension for Mr. Rellerick's condition. We cannot afford to lose him yet."

"Dolts!" exclaimed Reginald, tearing the paper into atoms. "Dolts! What shall I do about it, Crampton? Shall I write one of my characteristic letters, full of sarcasm, and sparkle—a letter that will be read and commented upon everywhere? Or shall I confer with the Tussaud management with a view to having the figure removed from the Chamber of Horrors?"

Crampton turned and regarded him pitilessly. "I advise you," he said slowly, "to oust yourself from the web that is closing around you. It is due to your own irrevocable selfishness. Try and forget yourself and these matters entirely. This Déjazet incident has troubled you. Let it rest. Your efforts to justify the crime of a brute who resembles you—merely because he resembles you—is outrageous. My counsel to you is to forget Tussaud's, to leave London, to break off your engagement with Miss Halstead, and to start upon your next season like a man—ready for success, if success is possible ; prepared for failure, if failure must come."

Reginald winced at this unusual tone, but now, convinced that Crampton was in league against him with the rest of the world, he resolved to overlook their relative positions as master and servant, and see which way the wind was blowing.

"That is your advice," he said, sneeringly. "And pray what has Miss Halstead to do with the case? Why should I relinquish the woman I—I—love, merely because a weekly scandal-monger suggests that Madame Tussaud's exhibition has affected my reason?"

The frankness of the question perplexed the hopeless secretary. Crampton, however, decided that to voice his suspicions would perhaps be to fill the actor's fevered brain with new ideas. He took a radical course.

"You do not love Miss Halstead," he said. "Marriage with her would be an evil thing for both of you. The engagement must be broken off. Further scandal must be stopped. There is no middle course."

"And if I do not marry Felicia Halstead "—the actor made a frantic effort to be cool as he asked the question—" what will she do? She loves me. It is the object of her life to be my wife. Suppose I break off our engagement. What will happen?"

His pulses beat wildly. He hoped against hope that this quaint Oxonian Master of Arts, might also be master of the non-collegiate art of disposing of his detested rival without the infamy of the wedding. It seemed ages before Crampton answered. It was in reality one second.

"She will try to establish herself as an actress in London. She will accept the offers that she has

had. Yes, she has had them. But the difficulties that beset a woman alone and unprotected
are innumerable. She will succeed for a season,
and then—then you will have the coast to yourself."

Poor Felicia! As he uttered this callous pro-
phecy—this cruelty for the sake of kindness—
Crampton saw her once more as she sat in the cab
beside him, driving through the gray and early
London to an unspeakable destiny. He glared
mercilessly at the ego-maniac.

"You are too hopeful, Crampton," Reginald
said quietly, "too wickedly hopeful, I might add.
I should like to ask you your reasons for your evident belief that I am jealous of Miss Halstead's
professional prestige. You are quite mistaken. I
am not jealous. Her position on the stage to-day,
she owes entirely to me. Ask her, and she will tell
you so herself. To further advance her interests,
I am about to marry her. I shall not abandon my
plans. Perhaps, under the circumstances, it would
be advisable for you to seek another position,
Crampton. I am not accustomed to such words as
you have spoken. You are ungrateful. You forget that you came to me at a time when you were
making a niggardly pittance as tutor to an imbecile
boy. You can go. In fact I shall consider that
you are now free."

"You will consider nothing of the sort," replied
Crampton, quite as calmly as his master had
spoken, but with a light in his eyes that Reginald
had never seen there before. "If I go, I will have

your footsteps dogged by those whose work it is to prevent crime. I will tell every newspaper writer in London what I know of this fantastic evil story. It shall point the moral of ego-mania. You will never permit me to go. I shall stay, and watch you, in order that no harm may come to her. Take my advice, and let a sleeping dog lie. Do as I say—begin your next season as you began your last. Hope for the best. London does not forget its favourites easily. You have failed once. It will be to the interest of this loyal city to see that you do not fail again."

If he could only have yielded to the wisdom of these words! Rellerick was conscious of the yearning to be normal and self-oblivious. But ego-mania has roots that entwine themselves round the very entrails of the victim. Try as he would, he could see nothing but the insistently magnified image of himself. He had failed, and she had caused his failure. He could take no risks. He must marry her and remove her from his path. He would buy her a big house, and surround her by servants. She should have children to busy herself with—anything that would leave him free for a continuance of the adulation of the London mob, for which his soul hungered. Ego-mania is a gross physical appetite that grows by what it feeds upon. Reginald had fed well, and London had plied him with the food that he must have. He was no longer able to do without it. He thought voluntarily of Felicia and then—involuntarily, of the yellow image in the Marylebone Road. That reminded him ; he had an appointment that afternoon with La Chinoise. They were to go together to Madame Tussaud's, and look upon the waxen presentment of Déjazet. He quite forgot Crampton, who sat there watching him like a Nemesis. Recalling his utterances, Reginald came to the conclusion that the man was a trifle upset by his experience on the preceding night. Possibly, also, he was awed at the mere notion of leaving the actor's service. Reginald could understand this. A terrible situation it must be for any man, accustomed to minister day by day to his choice personality, to suddenly find himself cut away from it. Reginald felt quite sorry for Crampton.

"Your threats are silly, my man," he said. "I had really no intention of giving you your *congé*. Stay and watch me as you say. But for the future, we will drop all allusions to the unfortunate image at Madame Tussaud's, and also to my affianced wife, Felicia Halstead. I have been foolish enough to discuss these matters with you, and you have rewarded me by insolence and insult. I wish to see no more newspaper clippings referring to these events. I will take care of them later on. There are such things as libel laws in England, I am thankful to say."

The secretary, temporarily awed by Reginald's grandiloquent manner, into the subjection that was almost second nature to him, bowed submissively.

"One thing I would like to ask," he said. "It is this: Did the woman with whom I left you last night really know anything of the mur—of the artist who has interested you so much ?"

He waited anxiously. Reginald gave him a malignant look, as he answered, " We will discuss the subject no further. Please confine yourself literally to your duties as secretary. As a confidential adviser I find that you are a failure, Crampton. You might write a few lines to Miss Halstead from me. Say that I am very busy and as happy as it is possible for me to be during her absence. Add that I am hungering for her return, and can scarcely wait the day that brings her back to London. I will sign the letter when I return."

This parting shot completely satisfied him. He felt more like himself, and less like Déjazet, than he had done for days. He laughed to himself as he heard Crampton's melancholy acquiescence. After all, Crampton was bound to obey him. He might reason, and argue, and advise, and utter futile threats, but he was a paid satellite, doing the dutiful for so much per week. Reginald was reduced to further good humor by the knowledge that the morose Oxonian was undoubtedly interested in Felicia Halstead. He chuckled at the mere notion.

" If I could only utter a fond ' Bless you, my children,' " he thought, " and pack them off to a desert island ; it would be the best thing in the world that could happen to me. If Felicia would only take a fancy to Crampton ! How perverse women are. I suppose that no force on earth— nothing electrical, mechanical, or psychological—

would ever induce Felicia Halstead to see happiness in a career as Mrs. Crampton. They talk of hypnotism. I don't believe that Charcot himself could move that woman's affections from me."

He sighed. His ego-mania received no balm from the knowledge that poor Felicia loved him so devotedly. It was the obstacle in his path. He could not quite dismiss from his mind the notion that the union of Felicia and Crampton would be the complete simplification of all his difficulties.

He met La Chinoise in front of the Exhibition building in the Marylebone Road. The courtesan had risen to the occasion, and had garbed herself in a manner unlikely to offend the fastidious notions of the famous actor. The colour on her cheek was less flamboyant, and the carmine varnish that usually cracked upon her lips was omitted. She wore something black, elegantly designed ; and a *chic* little hat, of Parisian ingenuity, appealed pleasantly and ungaudily.

" *Mon petit Déjazet,*" she said, as she saw him approach, and ran girlishly to meet him with outstretched hands.

Reginald smiled upon her almost sunnily. She was assuredly a comely woman, but slightly tainted by the life that she led. He bought the admission tickets for the museum as cheerfully as though he were a light-hearted Lubin out for a half-holiday with his Dulcinea. Proximity to this woman was very pleasant. He felt a keen appreciation of Déjazet's artistic selection. They entered the building, and went at once to the Chamber of Hor-

rors. The doleful Hungarian band was twanging
out its dirge-like popularities in the other halls.
The usual mob of sight-seers was present—sight-
seers from Manchester, sight-seers from Liverpool,
sight-seers from Birmingham.   The absence of
Londoners was amazing.

The actor's spirits sank again as La Chinoise
steered him through the ranks of staring, tallowy
dolls—plastic monuments of human weakness,
there to teach no lesson, but merely to cater to a
sensational curiosity.   He shivered as he heard her
comments upon the horrors.   They were all the
same to her—the Lambeth poisoner, and the youth
that fired at Her Majesty in Constitution Hill ; the
Reading baby-farmer, and the Blackheath burglar ;
Henry Wainwright, and James Greenacre ; Maria
Manning, and Fouquier-Tinville.

"*Des misérable—tous,*" she said, but her voice
was frivolously light and she was enjoying it all.
The actor could not understand it.   He could not
comprehend the ease with which this woman flitted
from horror to horror with her catalogue open, and
her curiosity piqued.   The dread feeling that had
overwhelmed him at his first visit was with him
again.   He could scarcely breathe in the close,
contaminated air.   To him, the models standing
dimly in the semi-obscurity, were tangible ghosts.
He inhaled the odour of the frowsy stuffs they wore.
He shrank from their glassy eyes.   He shuddered
as he saw their yellow, smooth and polished fingers,
nailless and menacing.   His vitality was lowered,
and the mockery of it all overcame him.

"Let us go, Claire," he said, " I cannot stand it. Let us go."

She took his arm, and led him almost by force to the pedestal upon which Déjazet stood. The figure was still the centre of attraction. It was new enough to capture the attention of the crowd. Reginald stood among the people, and listened to their comments. An ancient clergyman, with white hair, had speared the opportunity to read a lesson on the sinfulness of illicit love, to the gaping youths.

" Behold," he said, " the end of it all. This man, with a famous career in his very grasp, was brought to ruin by his own untrammelled desires. Had he married Mademoiselle Delaunay in the first instance, and settled down like a Christian to the only association in which there is safety, the world might now have been ringing with his praises. Look at him as he stands there, a horrid example of the degradation of those that fail to conform with the laws that hold society together."

The youths continued to gape at Déjazet, but they heard the words of the old minister, and they were perhaps affected. Reginald laid one of his moist and tremulous hands upon the old man's shoulder.

" Suppose," he said, " that it was this desire to keep the world ringing with his praises that prompted Déjazet to kill Geneviève Delaunay. Suppose that she was not the innocent victim that the world presumes her to be—that she was ready, metaphorically, to cut his throat and rear her own fame upon the spot where his had stood? What then? Is not that a justification?"

" There is no justification," replied the old clergy-man, glancing in astonishment at the eager face half hidden by the soft felt hat that Reginald always wore when he came to see his double. "'Men the most infamous are fond of fame,' as Churchill said. He that can succeed only without competition is a poor specimen of manhood. But there are no records of any rival in this case of Déjazet. We have heard of nothing but simple unadulterated hatred of an unfortunate, misguided girl."

"No, there are no records," retorted Reginald, heaving a sigh of relief. "Circumstances, my reverend gentleman, alter cases. You nearly admitted it."

The crowd had turned curiously towards the speakers. Anything for a little sensation, with London sight-seers. The old clergymen, however, with a look of distrust at Reginald and his companion, moved quietly away.

"I cried yesterday when I saw this waxen Déjazet," said La Chinoise artlessly, " but to-day I can feel no sorrow. It seems to me that I am with him, that I hold him by my side once more. *Allons, mon petit Déjazet.* Let us go, as it seems to grieve you to be here. You are pale and trembling. Without doubt it must be terrifying to a man's nerves, to see himself in wax, and hear himself criticised by a mob. Let us go."

The actor's gaze was fixed imploringly upon his double. He felt that the figure was real and conscious, and could see his old love, La Chinoise, as she stood beside him. The wide-open, lashless eyes seemed to be looking directly at him. They hypnotised him. He felt powerless to move. He could have stood there all day, imagining the sentiments of the yellow monster. He was fascinated in spite of himself. The real woman, however, was asserting herself. She was swaying him, as she had swayed Déjazet. He fancied that he saw a gleam of satisfaction in the eyes of the model, as he finally listened to her voice, and was led away.

"I hate to hear those comments," he sighed, "now that I understand Déjazet's impulses. He was no more of a criminal than—than I am. Is it not so, Claire?"

"*Mon petit Déjazet*," she murmured, affectionately. It was the stock-in-trade of her remarks.

Reginald Rellerick installed La Chinoise in a little ornate villa situated in St. John's Wood. And before the week was over her *ménage* was firmly established. She had taken her place among the doubtful occupants of the locality. To her he confided the story of his theatrical *contretemps* though he was careful to keep from her the fact that he was pledged to marry Felicia. He listened to her bright, Parisian femininities, and a new charm came into his life—the charm that a frivolous, *taquinante* woman can always exert over a morbid and sinister nature.

La Chinoise was extravagant—as the woman rescued from the gutter usually is. Reginald catered to her extravagance recklessly. A brougham was placed in her stable, and she had carte blanche with the tradespeople of the vicinity. To Crampton he said nothing of this latest move. He started to live what novelists call "a dual life." The man who owns two houses invariably leads a dual life—in novels and on the stage.

LaChinoise understood the situation pretty thoroughly, and cleverly she endeavoured to illumine the life of her protector. That she had a genuine affection for him was questionable. There are few Felicia Halsteads in this world, willing to pour out their lives at the altar of a worthless egotist. The illusion, however, was complete. Reginald believed that she loved him, and for the first time in his life he felt an almost altruistic devotion to a woman.

And so events rushed on. To her, he was Déjazets. To him, she was Déjazet's selection. And the model in Madame Tussaud's was visited frequently. It stood yellow and ugly, on its pedestal, food for the sight-seers, at a cost of one-and-sixpence per sight-seer.

Chapter XIII

LONDON again ! Felicia Halstead alighted from the incoming train at the Euston terminus, and looked delightedly around. The dear old *brou-ha-ha*, the affable tumult, the pungent odour of an intense population, and the fascinating sense of bewilderment that comes from the multitude, appealed to her most agreeably. She shook her skirts free, drank in a long breath of the Euston air—as though it were health-giving and pure—and —remembered that she was alone. She had written to Mrs. Landington and to Reginald to tell them that she intended, at her mother's insistence, to prolong her stay in Liverpool. And then, whimsically, she had rebelled at her exile from what she called penny-dreadfully "life and love." She could endure ex-Londonization no longer. Family ties were very dear ; her native county possessed all those poetic associations that belong to native counties. London, however, was the only place in the world for her, and after having written that she should be absent for still two weeks, she came suddenly back. Perhaps there was another reason for her unexpected change of purpose.

[196]

Reginald's letters had ceased to reach her.   Before they ceased entirely they had been eminently un-satisfactory type-written affairs, engineered by Crampton, and signed crudely by the great actor himself.   Felicia felt pained at receiving, in reply to her diary-like effusions to Reginald, cold, me-chanical-looking, Crampton-made notes.   The prac-tical ingenuity that has done away with the mag-netic illegibility of handwriting was undoubtedly valuable, thought Felicia.   But after a pen-and-ink soul-outpouring it was not agreeable to get a violet-typed note beginning " Yours of yesterday to hand."   Felicia's soul rebelled at the labour-saving, poetry-exterminating sentiment of the age. She tried her luck again, and wrote eight crossed pages of frank confessions.   Another type-written letter came to her, bearing all the signs of Cramp-ton's work, with nothing of Reginald but the sig-nature.   To her plaintive remark about her mother's anxiety to keep her in Lancashire—she remem-bered she had worded it, " Ah, there is no love like a mother's.   It is the one unselfish passion "—the typewriter replied : " Your statements anent moth-er's love duly noted.   You are quite right."   Poor Crampton had tried to understand her letters. Alas ! he was lacking in sentiment.   Where was Reginald ?   Surely her letters deserved a fate other than that of being answered by a secretary.

Felicia's sensation of satisfaction on return to the metropolis, was soon confounded by a feeling of loneliness.   It was horrid to get back unwel-comed.   She had contemplated surprising Mrs.

Landington and Reginald, but she was inclined to wish that she had been less fantastic. She shivered a little as she saw the crowd pass her by unnoticed. She envied the girls who had travelled with her, as she saw them being embraced vehemently on the platform. She felt like a foreigner in a strange country, and as she hailed a hansom and ordered her luggage deposited upon it, her temporary exultation vanished, and she was singularly depressed.

The long ride to Notting Hill cheered her. She soon discovered, however, that it was not always advisable to "surprise" respectable widows who wear black alpaca dresses, and cameo brooches containing an extinct husband's hair. Mrs. Landington was unprepared for Felicia's advent. The actress found her asleep on a sofa in the "best parlour," clad in a rather ribald-looking cotton wrapper—too low at the neck, and too short at the edge—while by her side was a high tumbler, a bottle of " Scotch " that she had invariably saved for " medicinal purposes," and some soda-water ; very little soda-water.

"Landy," cried Felicia, disgusted, yet amused, " for Heaven's sake, what has happened ? Wake up—wake up—it is I—Felicia."

The respectable widow with the switchback *embonpoint*, sat up and endeavoured to collect her respectability. It is hard work for a plump widow to look distinctly proper in a tousled cotton toga, hair dishevelled, and *vis-à-vis* to what the world insists upon regarding as signs of revelry. Mrs. Landington rubbed her eyes, caught sight of her ankles, and of a certain red warmth of flannel petticoats not usually offered to the public, and instantly—as a matter of course—fell back upon the redeeming malady of the London lower classes.

"Miss 'Alstead," she said, with some asperity, "and without a word of warning. Really, miss, it is the custom for ladies " (she emphasized the last word) " to write to their 'omes, before they arrive. Not that I could ha' done much. I've 'ad the spasms awful. I was awake all night with 'em, and finally, I said to myself, that it was a case for Scotch whiskey. I 'ates it. It regularly goes against me, but 'ealth is 'ealth, and I'm 'appy to say that I feel better."

Mrs. Landington arose, looking such a ludicrous figure of respectability caught napping, that Felicia was obliged to turn aside her head and laugh. The housekeeper hastily removed various tell-tale signs —such as half-a-dozen high tumblers containing the dregs of whiskey and water, plates, cups and dishes. Felicia did not see them. Had she done so, she would have been tempted to believe that the Landington had been "at home" to her friends—scions of the nobility of the east end. She straightened out mats, the demoralization of which seemed to suggest that the housekeeper and her guests were not unfamiliar with the "light, fantastic toe." Then her cloak of respectability was ready, and she slipped it on without more ado.

"I'm glad to see you, my dear," she said, "for I've been as lonely as an 'ermit. 'Aven't seen a soul since you left. 'Aven't been outside the doors of the 'ouse. If you 'adn't come back, I should have gone melancholy, for by nature, I'm naturally lively, and fond of society."

Felicia was making herself slowly comfortable, and at the same time giving her housekeeper an opportunity to recover her equilibrium. Mrs. Landington put the whiskey on the sideboard, taking a final sip for the last of her " spasms." Then she asked to be excused, and went upstairs for the alpaca dress, and the cameo brooch, without which she was as a fort without defences.

There were a number of letters awaiting Felicia. She opened them slowly, and glanced at their contents. They all referred to her last successful appearance in Pinerville's new play. Verily that success, planted so recently, had ripened with great rapidity. The harvest seemed to be unlimited. Two letters contained offers of engagement in leading stock companies, with comfortable salary and iron-clad contract. She tossed them from her contemptuously and sighed. The last letter that she opened caused her to think. There comes a time in the life of many a man—likewise woman—when it is noble and poetic to eschew the mercenary, and scoff sensationally at the sordid inducements of pounds, shillings, and pence. But there also comes a moment when this sort of nobility is inclined to hide its diminished head ; when the man—likewise woman—feels for the first time that there is nothing particularly poetical in sneering at money, that means independence, emancipation, security for one'self and for one's dependents. Felicia allowed the last letter to drop to her feet. Her eyes rounded themselves. She had been offered by the principal theatrical dabbler of London's West End, a stellar engagement to last for three seasons, at a guaranteed salary of one hundred and fifty pounds per week. One hundred and fifty pounds! A fortune!

There was not the slightest change in Felicia's heart. But she had just come from her humble home in Lancashire, where her mother, had it not been for her help, would have been obliged to "make ends meet " on a yearly sum of money that was precisely the same as what this letter offered to her, per week. She made silly little calculations of what she could do with such wealth. She could afford to bestow a dowry upon Floss and Edna when her sisters married, and dowries, while not at all essential to a maiden's welfare—are inducements to the right man to come forward. Felicia felt that, in her heart of hearts. One hundred and fifty pounds per week, for perhaps thirty weeks of each of three years! How they economized at home! She recalled their teas, with seed-cake, shrimps and lettuce,—the luxuries of the impecunious middle classes in England. Floss and Edna "turned" their dresses when the original sides grew shabby, and her mother—well, she distinctly remembered her mother's black silk dress, still her " Sunday-go-to-meeting " gown, ten years ago. Felicia grew frightened at her thoughts ; she hid her face in her hands as though to shut them out. They were persistent.

"Of course, when I'm married to Reginald," she said to herself, "I can do a great deal for them. He is rich, and what he gains, I gain also. I shall be his leading lady, and I shall act, and—and—but I shall be his wife, and how could I accept a salary? Then, suppose a time comes when I cannot act. I want children that will bind me more closely to him. If he would only consent to let me accept this engagement, just for the sake of the money, I could come to him a rich woman, and I could have given my family enough to make them comfortable. How I should hate it! How I should loathe it! How I hope that he will never consent to it! But it does seem wicked to let such an opportunity slip through one's fingers. If Reginald had an unlucky season, how welcome my money would be to him, and how glad I should be to know that I had helped him. One hundred and fifty pounds a week. I wonder if Queen Victoria gets as much."

Felicia, whose knowledge of money was of a very limited nature, drew a mental picture of another Buckingham Palace that she could build for herself and Reginald, with a special wing in it for her mother and the girls. And she imagined them all rising up, and calling her blessed. She thought of Reginald's joy and gratitude. It was a tempting picture.

Mrs. Landington came back to the room, her seething chest respectably alpaca'd, and the cameo brooch resting comfortably at the top of the fleshy toboggan slide.   The white ruching fortified her neck, as usual.   She was herself again.

"You must 'ave luncheon," she said busily, "for there's nothing more fatiguing than a railway journey.   A nice bit of mutton stew, and a cup o' strong tea will make you as right as a trivet."

"Not yet, Landy," declared Felicia eagerly. "Sit down.   I want to talk to you."

"Oh, I know," said Mrs. Landington affably— the last glass of whiskey had been very kind to her —"You want to ask me about Mr. Rellerick. Well, my dear, I 'aven't seen anything of him, but they've got a new figure at Mrs. Tussor's waxworks, that's a speaking likeness.   I went to see it one day—by-the-bye, my dear, I did leave the 'ouse, but on that occasion only—and it quite upset me.   I went with Mrs. Jones, the 'ousekeeper next door, and if she hadn't had a brandy-flask with her I believe I should have fainted.   Such a likeness! It looked like Mr. Reginald's corpse.   I declare that it made me all of a tremble.   I 'aven't got many nerves about my constitootion, but if I saw a model of myself perched up there in that way, I believe I should go into a lunatic asylum."

"Yes, I heard of it," murmured Felicia, anxiously, "but I didn't know it looked like him.   I wonder if he has seen it.   I wrote him about it, for I read an account of it in a Liverpool paper.   I am sure he must be very annoyed at it.   But perhaps you only imagine the likeness, Landy.   Probably, if I saw it I should'nt detect any resemblance."

"I imagine nothing, Miss 'Alstead," declared the

housekeeper majestically, " I went to Mrs. Tussor's in my sober senses, and I tell you that the model of Deejazzy, as they call 'im, made me feel quite sick, knowing Mr. Rellerick as I do.   Whether he's seen it or not, I don't know, but he ought to stop it.   It can't be pleasant to look like a nasty person who killed the girl he had been keeping company with, and her a-waiting to marry him."

Felicia looked genuinely disturbed.   She knew Reginald's impressionable nature, and she felt convinced that this model must have exasperated him. And to make matters worse, she had playfully alluded to it in one of her letters.   Still, he was an exclusive person, was Reginald, and she couldn't quite imagine him wasting much time among the cheap wax-works of the Marylebone Road.

" What I wanted to talk to you about, Landy," said Felicia, trying to dismiss the Tussaud matter from her mind, " was this letter which I have just opened.   A manager has written to me to say that he hears I am not to be tempted by outside offers ; that I have been sought by a number of metropolitan gentlemen, and that they haven't got the courage to play their best cards.   He is resolved, he says, to offer me terms which no woman to-day could afford to refuse.   And," Felicia sighed helplessly, " he has promised me one hundred and fifty pounds a week, to accept his engagement."

Mrs. Landington gasped.   At first she was not sure that she had heard correctly.   Whiskey has a way of playing strange tricks, even with its accustomed patrons.   She repeated the amount incred-

ulously, and Felicia nodded her head, and con-
firmed it.

"One hundred and fifty pounds!" she exclaimed
melodramatically, "and you a mere chit of a child.
It's positively sinful to give such wages to theatre
people, when honest men with enormous families—
and the honester the man, the more enormous his
family, I've always found—work for a paltry thirty
shillings a week, every day but Sunday. It's extravagant. It's—well, I can't believe it. In a
week, you'll earn more than these honest men earn
in a year. You can thank your lucky stars."

"That's precisely it, Landy. I am not sure that
Reginald will allow me to accept the offer. We
are to be married very soon. That is settled.
And he is very peculiar about the theatre. He
knows that I hate it, and am delighted at the idea
of escaping it. But in this case, Landy, which has
come upon me so suddenly, it seems wicked to
refuse, when I can earn so much for him, and for
my mother and sisters. I've seen them trying to
make ends meet, and considering every sixpence
before they spend it, and here is a flood of money
almost flowing at my feet. Don't you think that
Reginald will see it in this light?"

The fat housekeeper simply stared at the young
actress in amazement. Her veins were all aglow
with what seemed to her a sort of Monte Cristo
story. It was a few seconds before she was able
to answer.

"You don't mean to tell me," she exclaimed,
stridently, "that you would consider this man.

He was afraid you'd set up in opposition to him, or he'd never have married you. We argued that out together, you and I. It suited your purpose then to marry him. It was safer and better. He proposed, as I said he'd do, and you accepted. But now, something new has happened. The best man on earth isn't worth a hundred and fifty pounds a week. You could buy a prince for less, if you cared for titles, which don't amount to much in my humble opinion. Let Mr. Rellerick go, my dear Miss 'Alstead, and if he wants to marry you, when you've made this fortune, all well and good. That's the way I look at it."

Poor Felicia! There was no consolation to be received from her own sex. That seemed certain.

"No," she said sadly, "that I would never do. He is dearer to me than any money could be. I only care for the money for his sake, and for that of my family. My only hope is that he will see how much better it would be for me to take this engagement, work for three years to come into the possession of several thousand pounds, make my people comfortable for life, and then give myself to him, not penniless. If he is sensible, he will think this. But if not—well, I will go to my dear, obstinate Reginald just as I am, and he will not begrudge me the money that his wife's relatives will undoubtedly need."

Mrs. Landington lost her patience, her politeness, and her usual sense of subservience. "Felicia 'Alstead," she said, angrily, "you're a fool, and you'll rue it to your dying day. There aren't many girls who get a chance to make a fortune in an easy and ladylike manner, without toadying to a man. You get the chance, and are willing to throw it away for an actor, who has been a good employer to you, but who won't pass his life trying to make you 'appy when you're his wife. One hundred and fifty pounds a week! And to think that you hesitate. I'm only sorry this offer didn't come before you met him in Euston Station, and jumped at his proposal."

Felicia caught her breath, in a sort of sob. " It would have made no difference," she said. "I don't care for money, and I don't care for fame. I am simply struggling between selfishness and unselfishness. It seems selfish to give this all up, when by a small sacrifice of my own heart's desire, I can do so much good, not only for my people, but for Reginald himself. I really ought, I suppose, to postpone my marriage indefinitely, and write him in the strain that ' 'tis best for you and best for me !' But I can't do it, Landy. I can't do it, and I shan't. I am pledged to him. He might think that I was trying to be his rival, and that I loved the theatre for the theatre's sake, as he does. I must ask his permission, and—oh ! I know I'm a fool, Landy—but I do hope that he will insist upon my marrying him."

The actress took up the letter that had caused her this riot of sensation, and read again the blackly traced words standing forth so unmistakably upon the white paper. There was no denying their significance.   The letter meant everything that she had understood it to mean.   It was a real stereotyped case of the penny-dreadful "strife between love and duty."   As Reginald's leading lady her salary had been a small one—just enough for her own wants, and for a few of those experienced by her dependents in Lancashire.   It seemed strange to her that any manager should be suddenly anxious to multiply her value by ten, when she had done so little to warrant the multiplication.   Why, if she were worth one hundred and fifty pounds to the manager, had Reginald thought so economically of her services?   Those are the questions that occur resentfully to every man who is confronted suddenly by the luminous vision of appreciation.   Felicia, being a woman, resented nothing.   She merely thought it all over, and pondered over the queries that she was unable to answer.   She was perfectly well aware that she had not even the faintest inclination to avail herself of this golden opportunity ; that it was as distasteful to her as it could possibly be ; that the idea of being Reginald's wife, safe in the harbour of her husband's affection, was as precious to her as ever. But she had just come from Lancashire, and she could not forget the picture of her mother struggling with gas-bills, and water-rates, and butchers' demands, and grocers' exactions, with two buxom girls on her hands, waiting to be launched upon the sea of life.

It made her feel detestably small and selfish. They were all making wedding-presents for her at home, rejoicing in her happiness, and thankful for the marriage that would give to her the man of her heart. And suddenly the golden bolt had fallen at her feet, and she was bound to admit that, for her mother and sisters, its value was unlimited. And for Reginald! He—good, unselfish soul (so she thought)—was perfectly willing to link himself with the penniless girl of his choice. How much better it would be for him, if she had money. He might at any time lose his health and his ability to induce public patronage. He was not wealthy. He lived extravagantly, and spent every farthing that he made. Would he not feel more comfortable if he knew that there was a cozy bank-account placed to the credit of his wife?

So she reasoned, and as each step in her logic showed her its pellucid, unquestionable quality, her spirits sank and her courage fell. She would frankly consult with Reginald, and she would try to influence him to her way of thinking. It was true that she and her housekeeper had ignobly foreseen his proposal of marriage, in his unwillingness to face competition. But she never really believed that any such thought occurred to him when he had met her on that cherished morning, in Euston Station, and they had plighted their troth. This was the one little blur upon her complete happiness, and she would tell him all about it some day—some day when she was his wife, and they were in a confidential mood. For Felicia believed that married life was one long and lovely vista of confidential moods.

In the meantime there was no use perplexing her soul about this merciless situation. She was pledged to her word, at any rate, and she liked to remember that. If he were willing to wait for three years, while she gathered in the golden shekels, well—she sighed, as she thought of it—she would be a martyr to duty. It would be a martyrdom at which her soul would ultimately rejoice. If on the other hand, he bade her give it all up, to be his wife immediately as had been arranged, well—she did not sigh this time—she would be blissfully obliged to bow to the force of inexorable circumstances.

How she hoped for those inexorable circumstances! It was not noble, perhaps, to hope for them, but she was thankful for the web that had been woven around her. She would go at once to Reginald's apartments. She would not sleep over her doubts and her fears.

Felicia sat down to Mrs. Landington's conventional dish of glutinous stew, with weak tea accompaniment. The housekeeper was highly displeased with her, and endeavoured between mouthfuls, to picturesquely display the criminality of her behaviour. But Felicia, tired of logic, declined further argument. When the meal was over she dressed herself, arranged her hair as Reginald liked to see it arranged, and called a cab.

Chapter XIV

SHE " INTERVIEWS " CRAMPTON

REGINALD'S irregular incomings and unex-
plained outgoings were at first unnoticed by his
secretary. His visits to St. John's Wood, deftly
arranged, with all the secret enjoyment of clan-
destine meetings, did not appeal to Crampton. The
secretary's mental opthalmia was, however, soon
dissipated. Tell-tale bills which he was bound to
open, came in; letters " confirming orders " reached
him; there were receipts to file away and other
documents, upon which the ego-maniac had scarcely
reckoned. The first of these papers caused Crampton to bound in his chair, as though he had been
suddenly syringed with electricity. It occurred to
him that his master had quietly married Felicia
Halstead, and ensconced her in a " nest " in St.
John's Wood. The absurdity of this conclusion
soon forced itself upon him. He was, nevertheless,
unable to rest without ocular proof that it was not
Felicia upon whom Rellerick lavished so much
attention. The ocular proof was easy to obtain.
A green bus to the " Angel " and a short walk
afterwards, settled Mr. Crampton's mind. He saw
the little ornate villa with his own eyes, and he

saw La Chinoise herself, clad in the sumptuousest of *parvenu* clothes, stepping from its veranda into her brougham. And Crampton went back, heaving sighs of relief upon the unresponsive air. Although this was a new complication, in an already unduly complicated case, the secretary was thankful for it. It meant breathing time ; a possible postponement of a dreaded *dénouement* Although, in his heart of hearts, he resented this fresh and dastardly insult to Felicia Halstead, he felt that it might militate in her favour. He had faith in the desperate measures of women like La Chinoise. A faint feeling of loyalty—the loyalty that comes to every Englishman from a long line of ancestors—compelled him to conceal Reginald's cheap and unromantic behaviour from the world. What a hit this story of the actor's new household would make in the weeklies ! How the paragraphers would gloat over the mendacity of the man who had once lectured upon " the beauty of the actor's life," and tried to convince a public that the real artist was happiest at home.

The day after his discovery Crampton sat alone, in a corner of Reginald's sanctum. He made no pretence of work. There were letters to answer, letters to file away, at least two articles for magazines to be written, and Mr. Rellerick's opinion on the influence of the Greek drama to be set forth for a well-known weekly. Crampton preferred to read. He was anxious to study his master's case scientifically. It was not a medical volume that he had selected, but a stout book by Nordau, and a chapter entitled " Ego-Mania." But from Nordau's generalization he could obtain no very particular comfort.

" The ego-maniac," he read, " must of necessity immensely over-estimate his own importance and the significance of all his actions, for he is only engrossed with himself, and but little, or not at all, with external things. He is, therefore, not in a position to comprehend his relation to other men and the universe, and to appreciate properly the part he has to play in the aggregate of social institutions."

Crampton was so absorbed in his book that he failed to hear the sudden stopping of a hansom cab at the outside door, and the subsequent peal of the door-bell. He read on and on, his parchment face bent over his book. It was not until the rustle of a dress, not a yard from his ear, diverted his attention from his metaphysical researches, that he looked up and saw—Felicia Halstead.

She had rushed up stairs in joyous juvenility, and she had bounded into the room like an elastic ball. Her features, always mobile, had expressed the emotions of the most adorably kaleidoscopic femininity. But now, as he looked up, he saw that her face was blanche and surprised, that her hands had fallen limply to her side. A grave disappointment wrenched the pleasure from her eyes. Crampton closed his book hastily.

" When did you return, Miss Halstead ?" he asked agitatedly. " In your last letter you said you would not be back for two weeks. I am quite sure of that. I—I—could not possibly be mistaken."

"You were not mistaken," she said with a little satirical laugh. "You are a good secretary, Crampton. "You know your master's letters by heart. You answer them so poetically that they might almost be addressed to you personally. Where—where—is Reginald? I felt sure that I should find him here."

Crampton indulged in his customary shuffle, but he determined to be as non-committal as possible. " Why should you expect to find Mr. Rellerick in his apartment," he queried, "when he could not possibly be aware of your return? Had you informed him of your plans, he might possibly have met you."

" Possibly !" exclaimed Felicia.

"As it is "—Crampton moistened his lips, which were dry and feverish—" as it is, I am sorry to tell you that Mr. Rellerick is out of town for a few days. He may be back to-day; he may be back to-morrow ; I cannot say. He was a little bit ' run down,' and felt that a change of scene would be beneficial. Had he known that you were to return——"

"Crampton," said Felicia slowly, " where has Reginald gone ? Tell me and I will send him a wire. I am sorry that I came home so suddenly. It has not been as pleasurable as I expected it to be. It shall teach me a lesson. Give me Reginald's address."

The mouldy secretary was nonplussed. A loyal

lie would do no good.   He sat silent, his heart oppressed with pity for this girl.   She stood before him, anxiety in every feature, and he felt that prevarication was powerless to help her.

"Tell me his address, Crampton," she cried impatiently ; "he was to remain in London until I returned.   Not in one of his letters did he speak to me of feeling out of sorts, or of going away for a holiday."

"Still "—Crampton decided to be on the safe side, "there is no use concealing from you the fact that Mr. Rellerick *is* out of sorts.   I have been much worried about him.   I—I—even now—I am trying to diagnose his case."

Felicia trembled.   This was an unexpected blow. Her return to London had not surprised Reginald. The surprise was all on her side.

"My poor Reginald !" she murmured.   "I knew nothing of this, Crampton?   Why don't you explain yourself ?   Why do you sit there, parrying all my questions, when you could tell me everything and set my mind at rest in a minute.   It is not like you.   It is cruel.   It is unkind."

Felicia's perplexity resolved itself into tears. She sat down and cried from sheer vexation and alarm.   The sight of Felicia's grief lacerated poor Crampton's heart.   He tried to think of some consoling remark.   He conjured his brain for balm. The more she cried the more perturbed he grew. Resentment at Rellerick's behaviour soon came uppermost in his mind.   Still he could think of nothing to say, and the more he tried to speak the more hopelessly tongue-tied he felt.

Felicia arose in stormy anger. "You watch me as though you enjoyed my sorrow," she said furiously. "I will not be treated in this way. You are keeping something from me, and I am determined that I will know everything. He is not seriously ill, is he, Crampton? Tell me at once. If you don't, I will scream and alarm the servants. Tell me. Tell me. Tell me."

She went to him and taking his arm, she squeezed it until he winced with pain. Crampton realized the fact that Felicia was growing hysterical. He had, as she said, parried her questions.

"Mr. Rellerick is not seriously ill," he said, walking to the other end of the room so as to avoid as much as possible the spectacle of her anxious face. "He has been very much upset. It is an imaginary ailment—one that it would be no use consulting a physician about. The truth is, Miss Halstead, that he has been foolish enough to worry himself about a figure in Madame Tussaud's exhibition that strongly resembles him. It is the figure of a murderer. He has been so much affected by it that he has even endeavoured to find excuses for this murderer, whose likeness he bears. I can't quite understand his sentiments. I have tried to do so. He seems to grow worse."

"Poor Reginald!" sighed Felicia, in keen distress. "I might have known that a man of his artistic temperament would be haunted by this singular coincidence. Can't something be done? Cannot he bring influence to bear upon these wax-work people, and induce them to withdraw the model ? It seems simple enough. They are not in existence to insult the public, but to amuse it."

Crampton shook his head. " Mr. Rellerick wouldn't call attention to his vexation," he said, " He feels it too keenly."

" And he has left London to—to—try and forget it ?"

Crampton jumped at the suggestion. It was a perfect fit for the occasion. He nodded in acquiescence.

" And where has he gone ?" she persisted.

" He did not tell me," the secretary replied, as though pleading for mercy. " I swear to you, Miss Halstead, that he did not tell me. Not by one word did he indicate his whereabouts. And I tell you that he may be back at any moment. Believe that I am speaking the truth."

Felicia's feminine intuition read Crampton like a book. She looked him through and through. She detected the grain of loyalty for his master, that still remained. This would have pleased her at any other time. It exasperated her under these circumstances.

" He did not tell you," she remarked furiously, " no, he did not tell you. But you know ! I am willing to swear that you know. He is not in a—" she hated to say it—" in a—" the word choked her —" sanitarium."

The secretary looked at her bewildered. The very question showed that she had analysed Regi-

nald's moods far more surely than he had done.
And he wished at that moment that he could have
answered her in the affirmative. It would have
been painful, but it would have been a relief.

"He is not in a sanitarium—as far as I know,"
Crampton responded. "Mr. Rellerick, as I told you,
may return at any moment. Miss Halstead," here
he changed his tone to one of extreme deference
and humble suggestion, "you are young and you
have a future. Be advised by me—and I am old
enough to be your father. Do not marry Reginald
Rellerick."

Felicia started up, enveloped in her indignation.
"You are going too far, Mr. Crampton," she said.
"Really the position of a secretary should be limited. I assure you that I shall inform Mr. Rellerick
of your behaviour. It is rank disloyalty."

"It is not," said Crampton. He was wound up
now. The winding up of Crampton was not a facile
task. "It is not rank disloyalty. You can tell him
what I say, Miss Halstead. I am perfectly willing
that you should do so. Mr. Rellerick knows my
views on the subject. I have already made them
quite clear to him. If you marry him, you will rue
it, and—" he thought this was a strong card to play
—"he will rue it as well."

This finale brought Felicia to tears again. She
sobbed so convulsively that the warm, womanly
heart of the secretary was crushed. He sat there
in agony looking at her. He longed to take her in
his arms—the arms that were old enough to belong
to her father—and comfort her. Why was he sere,

and why was he fifty, to still feel the outrageous blood of something-and-twenty still avalanching through his veins? Crampton was ashamed of himself, and his tortured brain asked him if it was really pure unselfishness that prompted him to warn this girl against a marriage with the ego-maniacal actor. And while his heart was still pumping the red torrent through his body, he could not answer the question satisfactorily. He felt that he was deceiving himself. When he had grown cool again, and had forced himself to look tamely at this woman in distress, he knew that it was genuine unselfishness. If he never saw her again, he would still love to warn her against a union with the ego-maniac. If he knew that she would give herself to the first man that passed in the street, he would still persist in trying to prevent her from wedding this actor who looked, and—he believed—felt, like Déjazet the murderer.

"I don't mind your saying that I shall rue it," fretted poor Felicia, "because you don't, and can't know me. But—but—why—why do you say that my Reginald will rue it? I never before thought you were so cruel, Mr. Crampton."

The secretary was touched. He wished that he was safely away from the whole unfortunate affair. It was a harsh fate that had mingled him with it.

He answered evasively: "He is a man of moods, which change like the colours of a chameleon. He is nervous, excitable, unstrung. You are not afraid, because you think that you can rectify all this. You will not succeed, Miss Halstead. Therefore I

say that you will be sparing yourself much wretch-
edness if you take my advice."

Felicia dried her eyes.   She felt weak and stupid.
Yet she reflected that circumstances were relentlessly pointing her out the path of duty.   She
would never give up Reginald.   Duty or no duty
she would be his wife.   Nothing should prevent
that.   But was not Reginald's apparent indisposi-
tion a very strong plea in favor of her acceptance
of the princely one hundred and fifty per week for
three years ?   Might he not have lived through his
sorrowful imaginings by that time ?   Surely his consent would not be withheld.

" Mr. Crampton," she said quietly, after a pause
of five minutes that seemed like five hours, " I will
confide in you.   You have been cruel, and insolent,
and merciless, but still you know Reginald, and
you appear at the present time to be prodigal of
advice.   When you suggest that I break off my
engagement, you talk futile nonsense.   I would
sooner die.   That sounds rather radical, doesn't it,
but I assure you that it is quite true.   I came here
to-day to see Reginald, and to ask him for counsel.
I have received an offer such as I never imagined
would have befallen me, had I been a Bernhardt or
a Duse.   I knew I was in demand, but that fact
scarcely interested me.   A manager has offered me
one hundred and fifty pounds per week for three
years, and I want—at least I intend to ask—Reginald to allow me to accept.   We can wait three
years, and then marry, when I shall have some
money, and my family will be provided for."

Crampton surveyed her curiously.   Her strange devotion to the ego-maniac puzzled him.   He knew all that philosophers had said about the eccentri-cities of woman, but try as he would he could not fathom Felicia's attachment to Reginald Rellerick. The actor was not particularly young ; his ego-mania had almost stamped itself upon his face, until his once regular features were simply a reflection of his unlovely nature ; he had none of the quali-ties that women were supposed to love.   And yet this girl, young, lovely, adorable, amiable, and gifted was willing to sacrifice herself, her fame, and her family, for his possession.   Crampton put her metaphorically beneath the microscope, and looked at her as though he were Grant Allen analysing an ichneumon fly or a Colorado beetle.

" My dear Miss Halstead," he said at last, and it seemed to him that he was listening to his own voice, reproduced by a phonograph, " Fame is a wonderful thing, and only foolish poets call it barren and ephemeral.   It appeals to men, because it brings not only empty glory, but substantial wealth.   I can quite understand that your real lover is dearer to you than mere glory.   But here is an offer that means a competence for you, with fame at the same time.   You cannot seriously hesitate. You must accept this offer.   If I were you, I would go back home and instantly notify your manager that you agree to his terms."

His voice squeaked phonographically.   He could almost hear a br-r-r as he spoke the final words.

" Then you think Reginald will agree to it ?"

Felicia said, and she could not suppress a mournful intonation as she thought how horribly easy it was, and how readily her suggestion could be carried out.

" Your Reginald will not consent," cried Crampton harshly. " Most assuredly he will not consent. He will hold you to your promise. At the end of three years when you are famous and wealthy he would not want you. He would not then marry you if you brought him a million. He refused the Countess of Dwight, who was rolling in wealth. She was deeply in love with him, and he would not listen to her."

Felicia clasped her hands rapturously, as a sixteen-year-old school-girl might do, when the gay cavalier upon whom her fancy has rested waves his hands to her, as he prances past the door of her seminary. Felicia heard Crampton's words with a sensation of voluptuous joy, that the poor secretary would have been fiercely unwilling to induce.

" Then," she said, " if he will not consent, that ends it. The offer is as good as though it had been unmade. What you tell me so angrily, Mr. Crampton, is the sweetest news I could hear. I shall put the question to him, for I am determined that I will do my duty. Surely Reginald will understand why I ask his advice !"

Crampton lost his patience, and seeing how vainly he had laboured, he resolved to pull down this insensate girl's hope with one mighty tug. "Mr. Rellerick," he said, " will never consent to this engagement, because he would fear you as a rival, and while your name was stamping itself upon the public, he would be gradually effaced. I am telling you the truth, Miss Halstead."

Felicia laughed. She felt light-hearted and almost gay. Perhaps Crampton spoke the truth, but it was a truth that brought no gloom to her heart. If Reginald were afraid of her as a rival, she felt glad that she had artistic qualities enough to induce such a sentiment. She thanked heaven for her gifts, if she had any, inasmuch as they were the means of linking her to the man she loved. Don't think that Felicia was a fool. She was merely ardently in love with a worthless object, and if you have never heard of the blindness that accompanies such a condition, then you have come across very few romantic, unreasoning women.

" You are telling me the truth, and I am satisfied with it," she murmured. "You have done what you perhaps consider you were called upon to do, Crampton. I shall not take your advice. I shall say to Reginald, ' Please let me accept this engagement. It will be best for you and best for me.' Oh, I shall urge it seriously, Crampton. I shall, indeed. My people at home are greatly in need of money, and it will be unpleasant for me to ask it of my husband—my husband," she repeated, savouring the cherished words. " But if he refuses, I shall marry him as soon as he likes, and not fear the result."

Crampton's head was bowed in anguish. He felt that he had clumsily muddled the whole affair. Had he possessed any eloquence he could surely have convinced this usually sane girl of her folly. But he had angered her, insulted her, spoken harshly to her, brought her to tears—he saw them now dripping from her eyes—and he had simply led her to her fate.

He was desperate. " I shall be near you, he said at last, inanely. " I shall be near you. No harm shall come to you. You will trust me, will you not, Felicia ?"

" Miss Halstead," she corrected, imperiously. " This interview has not changed our relations, Mr. Crampton. You will notice that I call you Mr. Crampton and not—"

She wondered what his name was. A slight smile twined around her lips as she reflected that it was probably Ebenezer, or Thomas, or, more likely still, James. He looked a James. He had James indelibly marked on his person. Cramoton, however, declined to come to her aid.

She continued : " Whatever your Christian name may be, I do not use it. As for your promise to stay near me, I am afraid that I shall not need your services. I imagine that no harm can come to me when I am the wife of the man I love. Should any harm come at that time I shall welcome it."

She tinkled with sarcastic laughter. He merely echoed the words " welcome it."

" In the meantime," said Felicia, surprised how easy, and how not unpleasant it is to be unkind and imperial (it is wonderful how quickly the sadistic taste for wounding other people's feelings is acquired) " in the meantime, I shall ask you to wire as soon as Regi—Mr. Rellerick, returns from this strange vacation, of which you decline to tell me anything. I shall expect to hear from you as soon as he appears.   Until then I shall not see you. Good-day, Mr. Crampton.   No, do not trouble," as he moved towards the door to accompany her down stairs. " I know the way.   I shall walk home. The weather is pleasant.   Good-morning, Mr. Crampton."

And Crampton, as soon as he had heard the closing of the outside door, did what he had not done for years—since the first of his old Oxford days, when he was young, and emotional, and easily impressed.   He wept.

Chapter XV

THE FLESH AND THE WAX

FELICIA HALSTEAD'S ingenuously uncultured mind had always revelled in Madame Tussaud's wax-works. She was one of those women who may be termed naturally uneducated. She had frequently enjoyed a contemplation of the yellow, inartistic mockeries that seem to parody and cheapen the noble art of sculpture. She appreciated the impudent figures in the Marylebone Road collection, for the sake of the gaudy clothes they wore. The more clothes she inspected, the more complete was her appreciation. She liked to wonder how much Isabella of Valois paid for her gown, and to picture Catherine of Arragon indulging in the vulgar modern pastime of " shopping." She was interested in the dresses of Bloody Mary and Queen Elizabeth, and she liked surreptitiously to lift the gowns of the models, in order to discover if Philippa of Hainault and Berengaria wore underclothes. The details of the multi-colored exhibition were what she liked, and what most of its patrons like. The high and mighty object of education which it professes, was totally ignored by Felicia. She had studied the lives of the Kings and Queens when at school. It was a satisfaction to see them modelled in wax. She believed implicitly in the portraits, and if anybody had told her that by boiling down Richard I, it would be possible to trot him forth as Gladstone or Disraeli, she would have laughed scornfully. It is lucky that the percentage of sceptics in the world is a small one—lucky for trade, lucky for art, lucky for the world itself. Felicia Halstead was one of the amiably ordinary women for whom the amusement caterers work. Such women simplify the labours of the entertainers. The success of Tussaud's is probably due to the fact that it appeals exclusively to the ordinary.

Felicia took Mrs. Landington with her to see the figure that had so strangely affected Reginald Rellerick, and she started for the exhibition in anything but a holiday frame of mind. It seemed odd to her to set out for her cherished wax-works in a mournful mood. The bag of chocolate creams that invariably accompanied her (for it is always pleasant to middle-class amusement-seekers to punctuate sensations with sweetmeats) was omitted. Felicia dragged Mrs. Landington from her household duties, and plunged with her into the wax-work abominations of the bus-riddled thoroughfare.

The young actress felt melancholy and oppressed. Her interview with Crampton had pained her, and his strange information that her actor was away from London, without plans, and without address, appealed to her as inexplicably ominous. Mrs. Landington had heard the news with a series of

" Well, I nevers !" that seemed to insinuate her black-alpaca incredulity. She hoped that everything would end well, but—she doubted it. The prospect of possible misery is always inexpressibly dear to women of Mrs. Landington's chaste and usual category.

Felicia paced through the various rooms, silently, but obviously distressed. Her Kings and Queens irritated her. She felt inclined to regard them as interlopers. Their aspect was corpsey, and she wondered how they could ever have entertained her. She knew them by heart, and they were quite unchanged, save that their clothes looked rustier and more dust-covered. John, who signed the Magna Charta, seemed to be running to seed, and Henry VIII. to be resting upon his sextuply conjugal laurels in a sort of mildewed atmosphere. She would not allow the buxom housekeeper, anxious to get the most for her shilling's-worth, to consult her catalogue. She tore her past the groups, until the cameo brooch at the top of the fleshly toboggan-slide heaved. They all vexed her. She was there to see one particular figure, and to get at it she had to wade through Geoffrey Chaucers and John Wycliffes and Cardinal Wolseys and Oliver Cromwells. They were all in the way—all blocking her path, there so placidly erect and so uncompromisingly rigid.

Yet when she reached the Chamber of Horrors, and was pushed into it by the crowd of hungry sensation-seekers, who had accepted the roomsful of good and illustrious folks as a *hors d'œuvre* to the delightful criminals, she was in no hurry to find Déjazet. She disliked the idea of viewing Reginald's alleged double before she had seen the actor himself. She had returned to him after a long absence. It seemed horrid to seek the wax before she had found the flesh. Felicia was slightly superstitious. Before she had been ten minutes in the Chamber of Horrors, she regretted her visit as thoroughly as Reginald had done, on the eventful morning when he had first looked upon Déjazet.

"We'll go, Landy," she said, quickly. "I don't want to see this model. The idea frightens me. I don't know why I came. Come. We will return."

But the housekeeper had been permitted to do scant justice to the crowned heads, and had not the slightest intention of ignoring the criminals. She said simply, but very decidedly : " I shall stay, my dear, now that I am here. If you don't wish to wait, I will not detain you."

Felicia, the unimaginative Felicia, had worked herself up into such an excitement that she was literally unable to return by herself. She dreaded repassing those quaint, immovable men and women on their pedestals. So she resolved to see the thing through to the bitter end, and taking a light hold of Mrs. Landington's cape, she followed that immaculate matron in childlike obedience.

The edge had worn off Déjazet's novelty, and the crowd had other enticements. The tide of sin had washed in new candidates for admiration. One cannot even be a pinnacled murderer, undisturbed for very long. The affable youths, the giggley girls, the boiled-mutton matrons, and the frolicsome fathers all edged for the latest inducements—a precocious child who had stabbed her baby brother, and a prominent physician, whose guilty practice in London's Mayfair region had won him notoriety. Felicia and Mrs. Landington left these titbits for future reference. The young actress had been forced by the mob to relinquish her grip upon the housekeeper's cape. She became separated from her, and unwilling to walk about alone, in her wrought-up condition, she sat upon the first bench she found, and determined to rest for a short time and recover the energy which she felt that she needed for an inspection of Déjazet.

There was a wax figure in front of her, but she felt too dejected to look at it. She leaned her head upon her hands, and only the feet of the model appeared to her. The crowd ebbed and flowed. Men and women drifted past her, chattering idly and volubly, dipping into paper bags containing the necessary sweets, and enjoying themselves in the stodgy and slouchy way peculiar to the English crowd. She thought of the vaunted "educational usefulness " of Tussaud's, and smiled. How the Londoners loved to furnish excuses for their eccentric pastimes ! Nothing but the lack of a semi-religious, semi-educational pretext, is responsible for the omission of the bull-ring from the ranks of metropolitan entertainments. Felicia felt better, as she sat there without looking at the " sights." The almost apoplectic effect of wading through those lines of rigid dolls wore gradually off.

She began to feel once more the desire to be confronted with Reginald's Rellerick's double—the object of her visit to Tussaud's. Her eyes which had listlessly rested upon the feet of the model before which she had cast herself, were energetically uplifted. Then Felicia arose, and unable to overcome her feelings, uttered a slight shrill cry of surprise. The feet at which she had gazed belonged to Reginald's double. She had been sitting apathetically in front of Déjazet. Felicia rubbed her eyes, and stared at the doll. A slight *frisson* ran through the roots of her hair. She felt as she used to feel when she read ghost stories, and anecdotes with a supernatural flavor.

It was Reginald—horribly and distinctly, but with an evil insinuation that alarmed her. The expression in Déjazet's face was bad, but it was an expression which she had seen—she must have seen it, for it seemed so familiar—in that of her lover. The glass eyes that stared at her so emptily, had nevertheless something of the look she had detected in Reginald's that morning when he had told her that she was trying to supplant him. Déjazet's mouth was slightly twisted with cruelty, and his lips were thick and sensual. Felicia drew a breath of shivering resentment, as in spite of herself, her brain recognized this ugly monster as the counterpart of her beloved actor. She wished that she had never seen it. She began to bitterly reproach herself for morbid, and wholly unnecessary curiosity.

Then her pliant feminine nature asserted itself,
and she began to think, in poignant distress, of the
agony that this sight must have given Reginald, in
the flesh.   Ah, she knew him and his temperament.
Could any man survive the horror of seeing himself
ceroplastically displayed as a murderer? She remembered Reginald's complete self-satisfaction.
How he had cherished his own personality! What
joy the flattering photographer had given him!
How he had revelled in the idealism of the crayon
artist! With what bliss the imaginings of the "im-
pressionist" had filled him! And now to see himself done in wax, as an assassin, for idle droves of
people to look at, must have been a bitter blow.
Felicia's sympathetic instincts gushed forth, and
she felt that she must go to Reginald at once, and
comfort him in his mortification. She recalled an
old legend that she had read somewhere—she
couldn't remember where—setting forth the fact
that the man who is permitted to look upon his own
double must shortly afterwards die. The legend
returned to her. It must have been years since she
had read it. It had remained, unremembered, on
one of the curious shelves of her memory. It came
forth, flavoured with her early enthusiasm. It had
appealed to her as so inordinately fantastic, years
ago.

She looked around for Mrs. Landington, feeling
a keen desire to hear her h'less talk again. An illiterate person is most refreshing in a crowdedly
sensational moment. An illiterate person is a sort
of relaxative, the value of which cannot be overesti-

mated.   But the housekeeper was not to be seen, and Felicia gave up all hopes of finding her in the turgid crowd that blocked the Chamber.

She made a solemn promise to herself not to look at Déjazet's face again.   She would try and forget that she had ever been guilty of recognizing the features of Reginald, in the jaundiced waxen cast of the model.   Her visit had seemed to open the door to disloyalty, and Heaven knew that she clung to the man who had asked her to be his wife.

She deliberately turned her back to Déjazet, and prepared to move away from the figure.   And then Felicia felt that her eerie sensations must have unhinged her mind.   Her face grew white, and she was suddenly seized with a fit of trembling, for—with her back to Déjazet, and her eyes resolutely fixed upon the group of people twenty yards away, she saw the horror again.   She knew that he was behind her, and yet in front of her, he stood gaunt, erect, and staring, among the sightseers.   It was an illusion, of course.   It must be. She turned and looked back.   Yes, Déjazet stood there, and she sanely realized that fact before glancing ahead.   Then, with the determination to be cool, in spite of everything, she gazed in front of her.   The other Déjazet had not stirred.

Perhaps it was a looking-glass effect—the result of curiously-disposed mirrors, destined to amaze the mob.   Felicia would not have been surprised if she had seen galaxies of Déjazet, to the north, to the south, to the east, and to the west.   The Déjazet in front of her, however, moved, and she watched him, fascinated, as one is fascinated by the horrors of a nightmare.

She saw him deliberately turn his head, and speak to a woman by his side. She remarked the woman —stout, magnificently dressed, and undoubtedly French—one of those women English girls hate as the possessor of a *chic* that is rarely acquired, and quite unpurchasable, in England. He smiled. She smiled. They both stared at the figure behind Felicia. He spoke. She spoke. They looked again, intently and silently. He linked his arm through hers as though for fleshly protection. She pressed it closely, in immediate response. Felicia winced at the ugly fact of possession that the woman made quite clear.

An instant later, and her faculties alertly returned to her. She realized the fact that the apparent Déjazet in front of her was the real Reginald Rellerick. There could be no doubt at all about that. This was not the resort of the fantastic and the imaginative. She was with cheap people, in a cheap place, in a cheap locality. Cheapness was branded upon everything. This was the abode of the ultra-ordinary. Her lover had returned to London and had determined to visit the wax-work exhibition once more. She stared at him, quietly and subtly anxious to explain everything reasonably and satisfactorily.

Who was the woman by his side? What did this companionship signify? Felicia moved from her position directly ahead of them and turned to the side, resolved to watch them. Her heart was beating violently. She felt it cannon against her ribs, in an irrepressible tumult. Reginald and his companion appeared to be studying Déjazet earnestly. There was no anger in his eyes. They shone with a sort of softened light. To Felicia it looked very much as though this horrid yellow monster was favorably considered by her lover. The woman merely appeared to acquiesce in everything he said. Yes, she was French. Felicia could detect the "*ouis*" forming themselves upon her red and humid lips. How horrid she was, and how audacious! Felicia called her "bold." It is the word invariably applied by the English girl to the *insouciant*, rebellious demeanour of the Frenchwoman. The mystery of her presence there was quite inexplicable. Reginald was so fastidious, so solitary, so uncommunicative, that the sight of him in familiar and agreeable intercourse with a person branded, even in Felicia's inexperienced eyes, with the stigma of the courtesan, amazed and stupefied her.

They stood there quite oblivious of the passing crowd. Men and women came and went; gazed and commented; chattered and laughed—but Reginald and this woman paid not the slightest heed to them. Felicia saw Mrs. Landington walking alone at the back of the crowd, moving towards the exit. She made no effort to rejoin her. She allowed her to pass from the Chamber of Horrors, preferring to meet Reginald unaccompanied.

If Felicia had seen the slightest symptom of horror upon the face of her lover—the horror she had imagined for him—she would have broken through the crowd instantly, and thrusting aside his comrade, have flung herself unconventionally in his arms. But there was not a tinge of distress visible upon his features. If he had been staring at a benefactor of the human race his look could not have been blander, or more benign. It puzzled and grieved her. Again she looked at the waxen Déjazet, and felt the tingling of disgust in her veins. Yet he, whom this monster suggested so strongly, appeared to be almost happy, and quite unmoved.

Felicia herself began to attract attention. Two rude boys approached her, and pretending to believe that she was a wax-work, as she stood there so silently and attitudinally, they pinched her arm. She reddened, but the action served to stimulate her. She went to the exit, and made up her mind to wait there until Reginald and the woman were ready to depart.

The time passed so slowly that Felicia could scarcely repress her impatience. She heard the outgoing crowds expressing their satisfaction at the sixpenny-worth of misery they had witnessed. She felt exasperated at their idle, unfeeling comments. How could she ever have revelled in this hideous array of ghosts, and have spent afternoons in their midst, with chocolate creams and catalogues ?

She saw Reginald and the woman slowly approaching. They seemed unable to tear themselves away from the place. Reginald turned frequently to gaze at the solitary figure that was no longer a *pièce de résistance* of the exhibition, but had settled down to a long catalogued career of common-or-garden criminality. Summoning all her pluck, she advanced and placed herself in their path.

The woman made some remark in French, expressing annoyance. Then Reginald saw her, and if she had ever doubted the inadvisability of returning to one's "loved ones" unannounced, she had no opportunity to doubt it now. His face grew marble in whiteness, and into his eyes came the very expression that she had seen in Déjazet's glassy counterfeits. It was the identical expression, and Felicia saw it for herself. Fortunately her own *amour propre* stepped in, and she preferred to believe that she was unstrung and imaginative. The actor dropped the arm of the woman, and it fell to her side, fat, and bulging through its silken sleeve.

The ego-maniac recovered himself almost immediately, long before Felicia had emerged from her emotion.

"Felicia!" he cried in astonishment. "I—I—had thought you were in Liverpool. You—you—have returned."

The banality of these remarks was obvious, but they gave him time for further machination. He spoke a few words in a very low tone to La Chinoise, who cast a semi-derisive look at the little actress.

"I—I—came back to surprise you," she said haltingly, "I—I seem to have succeeded."

"Of course I am surprised," Reginald remarked

"but"—sarcastically—"it is a very pleasant surprise. If you will permit me to take this lady to her carriage we will go to my apartments to luncheon." Then to La Chinoise, with a great display of solemn politeness, "Permit me, Madame."

La Chinoise smiled, and followed Reginald. Felicia trotted quickly behind them. In spite of herself, she felt glad. Reginald's tone to this woman was one of deference rather than familiarity. He had probably been in Paris, and had returned with some French artist, to whom he was displaying the "sights" of London. She hoped so. It was such an easy and pleasant thing to hope.

"Where shall I tell your coachman to drive you?" asked Reginald, as La Chinoise entered the brougham, and he stood waiting for her orders. And when Felicia heard the command to start for a well-known milliner's establishment in Bond Street she felt a still keener inclination to be satisfied.

They were alone—at last. Reginald tried hard to keep from his features the malignant hatred he felt for this girl. The very sight of her had aroused in him sensations that had been dormant since her absence. She was the cause of all his agony, and he was obliged to marry her in the far-fetched hope of thus removing her from one path to another. And the other seemed to him utterly detestable.

"Who was that woman, Reginald?" Felicia asked instantly, anxious to clear up that muddy point.

Reginald had his reply ready. "A costumer," he said. "I have engaged her to make my ward-

robe for next season.   They say she is very clever.
She was anxious to look at the clothes worn by our
kings and queens.   So I brought her here."

There was not a tremor in his voice, as he uttered this coagulation of lies.

"You have been in Paris?" queried Felicia, feeling the titillation of hope in her breast.

"In Paris!" echoed Reginald.   "Why, my dear
girl, I have never left London."

"Then Crampton lied," cried Felicia.   "I went
to your house and he told me that you were away
—out of town—he did not know where.   I felt that
the man was romancing.   I asked him to let me
know when you returned."

The ego-maniac shuddered.   Here was the beginning of the symptoms of obnoxious possession,
that the law was soon to sanction—that he was even
anxious to court, for the sake of his career.   How
ugly it looked—this affection of which poets prated,
and which novelists blazoned forth!

" My dear child," he said loftily.   " Crampton is
a fool.   A friend of mine in St. John's Wood has
written a play.   He is a very busy man, and could
not afford the time to come to me.   So I put myself in the position of Mahomet with respect to the
mountain, and went to him.   Don't listen to Crampton, Felicia,"—a shade of uneasiness crept into his
voice—" he is growing old and stupid.   I shall be
forced to dispense with his services very soon."

How easily it was all explained!   Felicia almost
laughed as she recalled the hideous hour she had
spent at Madame Tussaud's.   How useful all her

agony had been as a pleasant paving to the delightful way of Reginald's sunny mood.

"If you only knew how exquisite it is to see you again," she murmured, pressing his arm, and as she pressed it she quickly remembered La Chinoise's action and forgot it.

The actor could not reply. His aversion was so strong that poor Felicia's girlish pressure irritated him beyond expression.

"And I am so sorry," she went on, "that I wrote you about that horrid Déjazet. I came to see if he really looked like you, and "—she felt an almost voluptuous joy in the pretty lie—"I couldn't see any resemblance. Imagine Reginald Rellerick looking like a murderer. What an absurd idea."

"Déjazet," he said, bitterly resentful, " was perhaps what the world calls a murderer. But he was not as bad as silly people think he was. I know many worse people than Déjazet."

He said this so indignantly, that Felicia looked at him dumb with astonishment. But she reflected that this was probably his consolation for what was undoubtedly a most deplorable incident. It was an extremely plausible consolation. Felicia's sympathy for him gushed forth again, and she pressed his arm even more affectionately.

" Let us go," she said purringly, looking up into the face of the ego-maniac. "I have something to tell you, Reginald—some advice to ask you. I shall wait until we are alone, because I want to argue, and I don't feel in the mood for it just yet."

He looked at her suspiciously, but Felicia's glance

met his own so sweetly, that he was disarmed. He hated her very sweetness, in its lack of sophisticated quality. What a difference between this bread-and-butter girl, and the richly-caparisoned womanhood of La Chinoise! How could men run after the silly enigma of guilelessness, when it was possible to obtain the splendid authority of autumnal maturity?

He fretted in impatience, as they were whirled to his apartment.

Chapter XVI

"A WEEK FROM TO-DAY"

How dissimilar were the sensations of the two
as they sat in the suave juxtaposition of the vehicle!
Felicia almost forgot her own troubled individuality in Reginald's presence. The memory of her
impecunious mother and stagnating sisters faded
slowly away. She still recalled the "big offer"
that had appealed to her practical sense. It
loomed up occasionally, as she leaned on his arm,
and assumed the proportions of an ominous black
cloud. Suppose he should consent to her three
years' contract! As she reflected upon this faint
possibility, she was almost tempted to leave un-
mentioned the managerial inducement. It was so
pleasant to be by his side again ; to respire with
him the ambition-laden atmosphere of London ; to
know that she was the only creature privileged at
this particular moment to bask in his sunshine.
She lay there with her eyes half closed—a captiva-
ting picture of confidence.

Reginald felt suddenly weary and nervous. The
presence of this woman was hateful to him. The
fact that he was enduring this *malaise* for the sake
of his own ego-pedestal that she had endangered,

simply enfuriated him more thoroughly against her. He felt her head as it rested upon his coat sleeve, and physical contact—which is one of the most capricious, the most illogical, and the most potential of all human conditions—stung him into dismay. And the time was approaching rapidly, unerringly, irrevocably, when he must acknowledge her as his wife ; when he must sit with her at the breakfast-table, and watch her eating boiled eggs and kippered herrings ; when his dinner-hour must be hers, and his nights be passed by her side. Reginald, like most ego-maniacs, had no very grave respect for the institution of marriage. The very fact that Felicia, by this union, would share his name, and enjoy the reflection of his lustrous career, was melancholy enough. The ego-maniac wants everything for himself. He must be the one luminous object in a sky that is otherwise dark.

He thought almost tenderly of his yellow double in the Marylebone Road, alone and emancipated. The model had interested him strangely that morning. He wondered why he had considered it uncanny. It had his own classic and thought-loving profile, and every characteristic of his own personality that he had for years admired. Déjazet seemed to have stared at him sympathetically, as he stood in the museum with La Chinoise—the very woman whom the French artist had worshipped. After all, this waxen hereafter at Tussaud's was not so dreadful. Déjazet was surrounded by the ceroplastic emblems of men and women who had won notoriety, either by the extremes of virtue or of vice. His was not an ordinary position. The world—which is the ego-maniac's heaven—had marvelled at him, and the London crowds watched him day by day. Geneviève Delaunay slept in her grave, unremembered, and unmodelled. The man who, for the sake of his art, had removed her from his path, had a pedestal all to himself. To the ego-maniac (and the world is full of types less pronounced than Reginald Rellerick) there is danger in the contemplation of notoriety. The mental pervert, who would rather be an extraordinary criminal, than an ordinary nonentity, is not a stranger to the annals of crime. Morbid museums are much frequented. The tiny urchin, who reads penny-dreadfuls, and loves to imagine himself in the varied situations of their heroes, is the egg from which the ego-maniac is hatched.

Crampton's face was a study in perplexity, as he saw Felicia and Reginald drive up to the door. The actor looked at his secretary with an impudently satirical and quasi-triumphant air. Felicia tossed her stupid little head as she noticed the humble Oxonian, who had been guilty of the iniquity of offering advice to the headstrong girl. And the secretary knew that his cause was lost.

"Any letters, Crampton?" asked Reginald, loftily, proudly conscious that he was master of the occasion, now as ever.

Crampton was reckless and defiant. "A few bills from St. John's Wood," he said, pointedly. "I paid them, presuming that they were correct. There was an account of thirty pounds, and some odd shillings at—"

" That will do," Reginald interrupted, with a sinister glance at his mouldy factotum. " I do not wish to be worried with money affairs. I have never asked for such details, Crampton, and I do not intend to begin now. I am surprised at you."

" I thought "—began the secretary, with the sinking feeling of deference that Reginald's high-falutin way invariably induced.   But what he thought was, in the language of the law-court, "irrelevant and immaterial," and Reginald moved away to his sanctum, followed by Felicia. She closed the door quickly.

" Now," she said, standing at the portal, expectant and laughing. " You may kiss me."

The fact was so obvious, that the humor of the poor, clinging thing appealed to him, and he smiled in his ugly and *sournois* manner. Probably he would have appreciated her more, if she had displayed the tawdry coquetries of La Chinoise, the courtesan, who had studied the philosophy of the offensive and the defensive in matters of sexual companionship. Felicia was the foolish, unsophisticated English girl, redolent of strong tea, and lettuce, and she was not amusing. He summoned up his courage—for it was really a matter of courage—and kissed her. As he did so, the image of Déjazet, standing up at Tussaud's, with a smile on his pink wax lips, appeared before him, and gave him strength. He kissed her with a semblance of earnestness.

"And now," said Felicia, quivering with delight, "we'll have a nice long chat. Sit down and listen, Reginald, and be prepared to advise."

A vague and almost hopeless hope came to him. Perhaps some Lancashire squire with a rent-roll had proposed to her, and mamma had favored his suit! Possibly some domestic difficulty had occurred which urged her to settle for ever in the provinces. Reginald was conscious of a huge and overwhelming menace of magnanimity. He would not withhold his consent. He would—sorrowfully, of course—refuse to keep her to her engagement. He would dower her handsomely. He would give her his friendship for life—friendship was so nice and cheap. He would cause her to remember him gladly—for the adulation of Felicia at a safe and unsurpassable distance, would not be disagreeable. He would place a box in his theatre at the disposal of herself and husband, whenever she visited London. He sat there, dreaming of a swift and gorgeous release. And as this faint possibility of happiness flecked the darkness of his mind, he thought once more of Déjazet, and saw him this time, in all his frightful ostracism.

"Reginald," said Felicia, slowly and tentatively. "While I was at home in Lancashire, I could not help remembering that I am a horribly dependent girl. You know that mamma is poor, and my sisters—dear girls—are expensive. I have given them regularly half of my earnings" (and she did not think resentfully of the pittance he had allowed her), "and they have managed to jog along as cheerfully as possible. But—" sighing, " the girls are grown up. They need attractive gowns in order to keep up appearances, and—and—mamma's expenses seem to me to be larger than they were."

This sounded promising, and Reginald's almost hopeless hope flickered spasmodically.

" Of course," he said, nearly kindly. " Of course."

He felt more inclined to be magnanimous than ever—willing to give half his fortune to the Liverpool girls. He felt that they were ungainly, seed-cake-eating women, who wore white muslin, with blue sashes, and had large feet in buttoned boots.

" It would be humiliating to me, Reginald," she went on, almost pleadingly, " to ask for money, every time I needed to send some home. Of course I know that you are generosity personified, and would never refuse it, but—but—there is a way out of the difficulty, and perhaps—perhaps—you will consent to it."

Her heart sank, for an expression that distinctly resembled benevolence was woven into the texture of his features. Perhaps, after all, he was going to relinquish her for her own sake, and listen to the promptings that a sheer sense of duty induced her to make. Misericorde !

" You need not mind asking me for money, Felicia," he murmured, *vif* with a hope that seemed almost dazzling, still haunted by the vision of Déjazet sneering and deriding. " What I have is yours, now and always."

" Dear Reginald !" she said, and a tear trickled down her cheek. He was certainly going to see everything as she dreaded him to see it. " Then again," she went on. " I know that you, my dear boy, are not overburdened with riches, that you live extravagantly, that you make big productions which call for the expenditure of thousands of pounds, that your cherished profession is, at the best, but a game of speculation, and—and—I don't want to be an incubus." Then frightened at what appeared to her to be a veritable Niagara of irresistible logic she began to cry. Going up to him, she put her arms round his neck, and sobbed : " You know, dear, that I love you as much as ever."

For the first time, since the malevolence of fate had allowed her to supplant him, he felt that there were some redeeming features in poor Felicia Halstead. She was surely about to do the Marguerite Gautier act, and loving, relinquish him. She had undoubtedly been wooed in Lancashire. And he amused himself by imagining her lover—some sleek and well-fed business man, with glistening pomaded hair parted on the side, a respectable diagonal " tail-coat " and a nice silk hat, worn on Sundays only.

" Felicia," he said—and he made a pretense of being deeply moved, " I have your welfare always at heart. It has ever been my desire, as I think you will acknowledge, to see you happy and comfortable. Although it might wound me deeply to find our plans set aside "—the words seemed too sweet to utter with nonchalance—" you can be quite persuaded that I shall never do anything to interfere with your prospects."

The ego-maniac loves to " make sacrifices," because, by so doing, he seems to enhance his own
value.   But the sacrifices must naturally be inexpensive, and not calculated in any way to interfere
with his own voluptuous self-idolatry.

" But," said Felicia, drying her eyes and giving
her duty-cause a dig, " I don't want you to let me
go, if you really feel that it will be too hard for you.
Remember that.   Please remember that."

Reginald twitched with the excitement of an expectation that seemed to him to open the doors of
heaven—an expectation of freedom, of permission
to resume his career, non-confronted by the danger
of a dreaded and feminine rival.   He could scarcely
wait for her to continue.   He arose and placed his
trembling hand upon her shoulder.   "Go on, Felicia,
tell me all," he muttered.

Felicia scarcely knew how to begin.   She made
a supreme effort however, and started :   " You are
an actor, Reginald, for the sake of art and glory.
I told you truly, some time ago, that I could not
understand that.   It seems to me such a poor thing
to live for—the adulation of a crowd of people one
cares nothing whatsoever about.   I could never act
for laurels, my dear, but I could act for the sake of
the money that the work brings in.   When I got
back from Liverpool, I found a letter from Mortimer Branton—your old friend, Reginald—offering
me a three years' contract, at one hundred and fifty
pounds a week—a fortune, Reginald.   And—and—
it seemed to me—"

She stopped, terrified by the look upon his face

—a look oppressive, vindictive, deadly—the look that Déjazet at Madame Tussaud's wore in yellow wax. She paused for a moment, mortally afraid of that look, and then moistening her lips, upon which the crusts of fever were forming, went on : " It seemed to me that it would be sinful to set aside such an offer, unconsidered. One doesn't find such opportunities every day, dear. As I told you, I have no interest in the stage for itself, but if you consent, I—I will work hard, diligently, unceasingly for three years, and come to you then, as your wife, not—not quite penniless."

The reaction came swiftly to the actor. From the height of a golden promise that seemed to be the acme of exaltation, he was hurled headlong into the old pitiless and irremediable situation. The shock was so great, that the torrent of words which would have indicated his fury was fortunately stayed. The very pitfall that he had dreaded the morning after his failure had opened at his feet. Here, right before him, was the woman whom Lon_ don would rear up in his stead. He felt sick with disgust. Mortimer Branton, one of the wiliest and most infallible of the money-makers in the market of theatrical speculation, had seen the possibilities of Felicia Halstead, to the tune of a three years' contract, at an enormous salary. What he feared had come to pass, and in his ego-mania and dank selfishness he judged her by his own standard, and disregarded even the power of her love.

The torrent of anger that the sudden shock had dammed, broke loose at last. He grew apoplectically red in the face, trembled, and paced the room like a caged beast. " What did I tell you," he cried, " when you came to me with pretty pathetic stories of devotion?   What did I say when I accused you of trying to oust me from my position ?   Ah, I knew you, Felicia Halstead, I knew you.   What is a promise of marriage to you ?   With all your protestations, you succumb to the smallest tempta-tion.   I am tired of it.   I am weary, disgusted. Curse Pinerville.   Curse his play that brought me to this.   Bah !"

The room swam, and he almost fell, in the whirl-wind of his anger.   He forgot La Chinoise ; he for-got the last few days of his strange and threatening self-composure.   But he could see the waxen figure of Déjazet at Madame Tussaud's, and to his excited imagination, it seemed to be laughing in a waxen ecstasy of impossible mirth.

Felicia was afraid, but Felicia was a woman, wearing the opaque bandage of love.   Reginald's coarsely evident wrath was to her but the pardon-able fury of a baffled lover.   She sat and watched him, as though she were admiring the reckless grandeur of an electric storm.   Her feelings were hurt by the savagery of his words, but they daz-zled and stimulated her.

" You shall never accept this contract," he shouted, " Never.   I swear it.   You shall fulfil your promise.   You shall not mortify my soul by your vacillations and your disloyalty."

He ground his teeth in his rage.   She threw back her head in a little nervous way that was not unusual with her.   He saw her cool white throat, with its thin blue veins.   Once again the picture of Déjazet leaped into his mind.   The crowds were gazing at him now in the Marylebone Road, and recalling the details of his murder-crime.   For once Reginald was afraid of himself.   The effort to rid his mind of the Déjazet idea, was such a tremendous one that it exhausted his mental force.   He sat down, the perspiration dripping from his forehead.

" Why, my dear, dear Reginald," cried Felicia in alarm, " I did not mean to vex you like this.   I merely suggested to you my own idea—an idea that had you in view just as much as myself.   I told you that I wanted your advice.   I was afraid that you would tell me to sign the contract and go ahead.   Your manner a few minutes ago seemed to indicate your willingness.   You frighten me when you behave like this.   I have done nothing at all.   I have signed no contract.   We are in precisely the same position now, as we were when you spoke to me at Euston Station."

He stared at her, and tried to penetrate the significance of her words.   The ego-maniac always looks for a " significance," even when a blessing is bestowed upon him.   He would suspect an angel of mercy of ulterior motives.   His hatred of this woman surely exceeded the limits of mortal hatred. It was like a sirocco and it seared him.   He had been buoyed up by the fantastic hope that she would pass out of his life, surely and for ever, only to find that she was more irrevocably tangled up than ever with his career.

“You will fulfil your promise?” he asked harshly, and it seemed to him that a roomful of people looked at him, and called him No. 37, and commented upon the expression of his face, and declared that he looked the criminal, from head to foot.

“Of course I will,” she answered, gladly, still alarmed at the storm she had called forth, and trembling slightly. “ I love you, and my life has but one object. I hate the stage. I purposed resuming work simply for the reasons that you already know.”

Suspicion filmed his eyes, and he looked at her, darkly questioning. Her earnestness, the sincerity that had not swerved at the tirade that would have driven away a practical, unclinging woman seemed to convince him. He had made a mistake. She had not intended to compete with his stage career, unless he himself had advised it. She was still his, to hunt from the eyes of men, and fetter with the chains of an eternal domesticity. He had hated her before this, and now he dreaded her. She was a rival in imagination before this hour. Now she appeared before him as an actual combatant, selected as worthy to cope with him, by one of the shrewdest theatrical men in London—by the very man, in fact, whose championship he had himself sought in vain. Poor Felicia's unselfishness had operated cruelly against herself. Unselfishness frequently does this, for it is less vulgarly spectacular than ego-mania, and it is generally misconstrued.

There was no time to be lost, however. He realized that. She was still his, and the nauseating task of rebinding her to him confronted him eagerly.

"You frightened me, Felicia," he gasped. "I had relied upon—upon our marriage, and—and—you seemed so desperate."

Felicia went to him, and with her handkerchief—a pretty little lace affair that she wore at her waist—wiped the perspiration from his brow. Then she stroked his hair and kissed him as though he had been a spoiled child. And Felicia belonged to a sex that has taken to wearing trousers and inveighing against the tyranny of man—a sex that can never accomplish this new mission, until the Felicias of the world have been stamped out. And they are being born every day.

An inkling of sense crept into her mind. She said, simply: "I don't believe you love me, Reginald."

It was so quietly spoken, and there was such apparent resignation in it, that the ego-maniac felt another qualm of fear. In spite of all, she might never marry him, if she even suspected a fraction of the unlovely truth.

"I love you, Felicia," he said, with a force of will that astonished him, "else why should I have troubled to quarrel with you? We are angry only with those whom it is worth while to reproach. I talked nonsense about your supplanting me, but it was an excuse—you will admit that it was a plausible excuse, Felicia."

He seemed self-reproachful, and Felicia's ready sympathies came forth as usual. "Yes, yes, I know," she remarked, soothingly. " It is all understood. You were a wicked, spiteful boy, and you are sorry for it."

"Do you "—he put the question uneasily—"do you believe that I love you ?"

" If you say it," she replied, ingenuously, " I believe it. Say it."

He still felt the eyes of a roomful of people upon him. He seemed to be standing erect before them, awaiting their comments. In his ears rang such phrases as " Look at his expression," "See that queer compression of the lips," and " Can't you notice the lines about his mouth ?" His feet appeared to be stiff, and his legs without sensation. The clothes he wore pressed uncomfortably against his flesh. He experienced a strange inclination to laugh, but he was unable to coax a smile to his lips. Above the voices of the roomful of people he heard Felicia's words—" If you say it, I believe it. Say it."

" I say it," he murmured. " I love you."

He took her hand and held it in his own. It was pink, and plump, and pretty. His own fingers struck him as looking yellow and nailless, like those of the model at Tussaud's.

Felicia stood on tiptoe and kissed him. He was about to shrink from the embrace that gave him a sensation of something akin to pain, but too much was at stake. For the present, at any rate, he must dissemble. Later on, perhaps—He remembered La Chinoise, and the very different feeling of her warm, ripe and enthusiastic lips. Ah, he had met very few women like La Chinoise. How easy it would have been to follow the decrees of a fate that compelled him to marry La Chinoise !

" We will be married a week from to-day," said Felicia. " And then my poor boy will have no further occasion to fear the desertion of his sweetheart. Will a week from to-day suit you, Reginald ?"

" A week from to-day ?" he echoed. " Yes, a week from to-day."

They passed from the room, almost stumbling against Crampton at the head of the staircase. The secretary looked at them helplessly. He followed them downstairs. Reginald went first, and entered the dining-room. Felicia, a few yards behind, was on the threshold of that apartment. Crampton came forward, and she heard him say, in her ear : " A week from to-day. Do not be afraid. Remember my words."

Chapter XVII

SHRIMPS AND WATERCRESS

THE die was cast, and the denouement must work itself out to its very knots. The web into which fate had pushed him was closing around him. He could still wriggle a little, and feel the freedom of his wings, but there was no ultimate hope. He had made his bed, and it was there yawning for him. Felicia left him shortly after the naming of the "glad day," and went back to Notting Hill, on the condition that she should see him again that evening. She had reached the position when she was able to make "conditions," and he ground his teeth as he thought of it. His callous selfishness never suggested to him that poor Felicia's eagerness was due to a desire to take him away from himself, and from the odious souvenirs of his waxen counterpart.

He was to go to Notting Hill that night. He sat in a sort of stupor—in a veritable mental *cul-de-sac*. His thoughts flew to St. John's Wood and La Chinoise. He would not give her up. He could afford two households, and he could render life endurable in that way. It was an arrangement with which London was extremely familiar. The rule in the metropolis was external monogamy, internal polygamy. Who would care ? Possibly not even Felicia, as the bloom wore off the love-apple, and sentiment resolved itself into boiled mutton and caper-sauce.

He shut his eyes and thought. Before his mental vision arose the omnipresent Déjazet, still erect on his pedestal, yellow and menacing. And he remembered La Chinoise's story with a shudder. "Claire," Déjazet had said, on the eve of marriage with Geneviève, " I have lost everything. I must marry this girl, and you and I must end our relations. I will try and do my duty. Perhaps I have been a brute. I hate her now, but possibly when she is my wife, bearing my name, I may become, at any rate, more reconciled to my life."

Was he more infamous than the dead artist who had reached Madame Tussaud's, branded as a " murderer ?" Even this sinister thing, at which the ribald mob stared, had possessed the decency that holds the civilized world in its clasp. Even this murderer had contemplated abandoning the woman he loved, for the sake of the woman he married. Reginald hated to think contemptuously of himself. The ego-maniac is frequently virtuous, not in order to please society, but in order to please himself. He dislikes to damage the symmetry of his own picture. So Rellerick made up his mind that he would, for his own sake, inform La Chinoise of his contemplated marriage, and rupture their relations.

It would be a bitter blow to her, of course, for

she loved him as she had loved Déjazet. There would be a scene of agony that would be horrid, yet pleasant. And she would swear, as she had sworn before, that this marriage should not take place. He never doubted the affection of the Frenchwoman. It seemed to be such an exceedingly tangible affair and so absolutely reasonable. Moreover, he felt impelled to love her. She appeared to be knitted into the texture of his life. So had Déjazet felt, but Déjazet had said: "You and I must end our relations. I will try and do my duty." He would do the same. The grinning effigy in the Marylebone Road should be allowed no advantages. He would not be inferior to one whom the world called criminal.

Crampton came into the room, noiselessly, more mildewed than ever. The stoop of his shoulders seemed to have emphasized itself, and his rusty coat shone. The secretary was nervous and unable to settle to his usual tasks. He hovered around Reginald, as though he were trying to make up his mind to speak, and were unable to bring himself to it. He "pottered" about, and his parchment face was more bloodless than ever. Finally, he nerved himself to his effort, and his phonographic voice emerged from its silence.

He stood in front of the comatose actor, and said : "Shall you leave London after your marriage ? Shall you take your—your wife away ? It is usual, I know, but—is it not useless ?"

Reginald looked up, and pondered over the words before he quite understood what they meant.

Their import came upon him with a rush and aroused him to impatience.

"What has that to do with you?" he cried. "What does it matter to you whether we stay in London or go to Jamaica? I have no plans. What is your interest in the matter? Perhaps"—sarcastically—"you have some advice to offer in your latest rôle of confidence-dispenser."

Crampton had no illusions, and sarcasm was quite lost upon him. He was grappling with a tragedy, and his own skin mattered very little. "I have advice," he said earnestly. "Stay in London. You would be miserable away from it. It is your life, and the atmosphere that you love. Remain in London, with the crowd. It is the wisest thing to do."

Reginald laughed harshly. "You can't picture us cooing on a mountain," he said, "or billing by the side of some dirty stream that the poets call pellucid? You can't imagine us as twin souls with but one single thought—and that thought a purple mountain, or an orange sunset? Ha! Ha! Ha! I am afraid that you know me, Crampton. You think it more reasonable that we should stay in the metropolis, and start our *ménage* in the tumult—begin as we mean to go on. Ha! Ha! Ha!"

But even as he laughed—the prospect grew hateful and black. He must indeed begin his wedded life as he meant to end it. It was not his plan to establish Felicia Halstead in the crowd—to supply the Londoners with a Mrs. Reginald Rellerick. Her establishment should be everything that was seemly and luxurious. But it should be where she could languish, unknown and unsuspected. Yes, he had already settled that point in his mind. Her London life should end when the wedding-ring was on her finger. There could be no regrets, and no false hopes.

"Your advice is useless, Crampton," he said, lightly. " We shall go away—as every respectable married couple should do. While I may not care to join the throng of picnicking Benedicts, and do the stereotyped visit to Paris, or the conventional trip to Switzerland, we shall go away. And "—with a sudden impulse—" I will give to you the task of discovering for me a honeymoon resort. Let it be some secluded hotel—not too secluded—in some seaside place where there are not too many tourists, so that we shall not have to pick our way through gingerbeer bottles, and confectionery bags. Don't worry yourself about pasting any more clippings in my scrap-book, Crampton. Just busy yourself with my honeymoon resort, where I must go "—he tried to repress the look that came into his eyes—" a week from to-day."

"A week from to-day!" echoed Crampton again. " A week from to-day."

Presently he said slowly, " Mr. Rellerick, what am I to do while you are away?"

While he was away! Reginald was unable to realize the real meaning of the words. While he was away, honeymooning with Felicia Halstead! What was Crampton to do while he was away? What would he do himself? He could not see so

far into the future, and yet—he would begin being
" away " in a week. Eight days from now he
would be " away."   It seemed ridiculously improbable.   Yet it was nothing of the sort.   He would be
" away " as surely as he was now in London.   He
could not help smiling at the ludicrous audacity of
Crampton's question.

"You will do as you please," he answered.
" There is still a week to decide."

" I suppose— " the secretary's voice faltered, and
he seemed to be whipping himself to the question
—" I suppose that you will not want me to accompany you ?"

The actor stared at him in amazement. He
wondered if Crampton were taking leave of his
senses. " No," he said, " I shall not want you. Although they say that a *solitude à deux* becomes
very tiresome —personally, I know nothing about
it, though I suspect that ' they ' are right—I do not
look upon you, Crampton, as the right sort of person to cheer us up. With the best of intentions,
one could not call you lively. And I shall have no
duties for you to undertake. There will be no
letters to write or to answer. You can remain in
London until you hear from me. Or, if you care
to end your services in my behalf when I leave, I
will release you."

He spoke lightly, but it was an effort, He hated
Crampton, and was half afraid of the distrustful
eyes that stared at him so pitilessly. With this
taciturn person to greet him when he resumed his
career, he would always feel uncomfortable.

There would invariably be references to Mrs. Rellerick, and a tender solicitude for her welfare. He would prefer a myrmidon to whom his past was unknown. Crampton had been very valuable to him. All his most famous " addresses," and his most widely discussed magazine articles had been the work of Crampton. But he was sacrificing so much for the sake of his career, that he could well afford to include Crampton in the sacrifice. He feared his secretary. He did not dare to discharge him pointedly.

" I will wait for you," said Crampton slowly. " I will be in London when you return."

He shuffled away, with ambling, awkward steps, each long arm a pendulum swaying at his side. He had grown singularly non-acquiescent, Reginald thought. But he soon forgot Crampton. Crampton was a mere detail—just a spot on the web, and nothing more.

That evening he went to Notting Hill, determined to do his duty—the duty that the dead Déjazet had emphazised so strongly. It was a nauseous pill to swallow, but there would be others more nauseous, before his interrupted career could hope to reassert itself ? Would he ever again be the idol of London, his doings the pet themes of the newspapers, and his words the directions for the multitude ? He tried to peer into the future, as he sat jolted in a tight omnibus, on his way to Mrs. Landington's retreat. But the haze was thick and impenetrable. He could not pierce it. Looming up in the blackness, he could always detect Déjazet.

It was invariably Déjazet. He struggled vainly against this eternal obsession.

Reginald could scarcely induce himself to ring the respectable brass door-bell that decorated the side of Felicia's bower. He looked impudently at the house which held the woman whose tentacles were fastened upon his life. How relentlessly matter-of-fact it all was! No wonder people clamoured for romance and excitement at the theatre, when their daily life was so ugly and colourless. He was going to see fair Rosamund. He had dashed up to the bower in a twopenny bus, sandwiched between two fat women with shopping bags. And the bower was a cheap suburban house, with eight rooms and a bath, and a back door, and a yard. It was all so *kif-kif*—and yet he was a great actor, upon whom the public had relied for entertainment and self-oblivion. The bell rang lustily as he pulled it. He gazed into the bower through a " frosted " pane of glass in the front door. The steps of the bower had been " whitened " by a London slavey, at twelve pounds a year and the kitchen fat, and in the window at the top of the bower he could see the looking-glass, at which the slavey brushed her hair, and removed the smuts from her face—if, indeed, she ever removed them. This was Felicia's bower, and a very good bower he had thought it, when it had served his purposes unobtrusively. But now, she was about to enter his life as the only means of saving that life, and he sniffed contemptuously at the bower, and hated himself for being so close to it.

" Why, it's Mr. Rellerick," said Mrs. Landington joyously, as she opened the door, and wiped her mouth upon her apron—not because she needed to do it, but because lower-class London matrons always wipe their mouths upon their aprons, in emotional moments. " I do declare it's Mr. Rellerick," she continued. " I've 'eard the good news, sir, and I congratulate you, from the bottom of my 'eart. She's a good, dear girl is Miss 'Alstead. And she's a lucky girl, too, I say, for you've been a kind employer, sir, and you'll be a good 'usband."

Reginald felt sick at heart, as he was ushered into the parlour. Why had he come? This was surely an unnecessary torture. But it was part of his duty, the " duty " of which Déjazet had prated to La Chinoise. The ugly farce must proceed. Felicia was taking tea with a couple of friends. They were girls of the neighbourhood, who had " dropped in." In cities one has to live in " neighbourhoods," and they mean " neighbours." She sat there a radiant picture, her lovely face illumined, and her features wreathed in animation. It was a picture that all London would have loved to see, with its insipid suburban framing, and its odd contrast of cheap respectability. But to the ego-maniac it was loathsome. He looked at the tea, instead of at the divinely sympathetic face of the girl who presided at it. Alas ! that face was powerless to affect him, as it would have affected others.

And the tea ! He saw shrimps in a glass dish, and water-cress, with drops of freshness on it, on a plate. His eye took in hunks of soggy seed-cake, and mounds of plebeian bread-and-butter. She was pouring tea from a dark brown teapot, into ugly cups with red flowers on them, and on the plate by her side was half a muffin, with a large semicircle bitten out of it. This was his affianced wife—to be his in one week. And this was the woman whom London was willing to raise up in his stead —a woman with no soul, but with a soulless ability to act. At least that is what he thought. Mortimer Branton had offered one hundred and fifty pounds a week to this unfledged girl, who bit semicircles out of muffins, and poured out tea for the spinsters of the neighbourhood. His heart was filled with bitterness. Of what use is a reputation when it can be intruded upon by such a substitute?

"Reginald!" she cried, putting down the teapot, and rushing up to kiss him. He could almost taste the buttered muffin on her lips. "You dear good boy to come. I had almost given you up. You have never had a meal here before, and I'm sorry that Landy didn't provide anything nicer. I know you would sooner have seventeen courses, beginning at oysters, and ending at coffee, but—well, this will be a new experience to you. Sit down, and pretend you are at home."

She knew that he hated it, and she was secretly angry at those stupid girls for being present. She should have been " out " to them, or have dismissed them early. But Felicia had longed to pour the story of her happiness into feminine ears, and she had hailed her visiting neighbours. What did it matter to her that they were merely Miss Robinson and Miss Smithson ? But now—she felt thoroughly vexed about it. The introductions were made, and the great actor bowed to the suburban nobodies. The nobodies were delighted. Miss Robinson insisted that Mr. Rellerick must sit by Felicia, because they were ·engaged. And Miss Smithson playfully asked if they should withdraw, and leave the lovers alone. Miss Robinson thought that it must be lovely to be engaged, and Miss Smithson asked pointed questions about true lovers' knots and " Mizpah " rings. There was no need for either Reginald or Felicia to utter a word. The nobodies kept up an endless chatter, anent the pomp and ceremony of marriage.

" To think," said the one, " that it will take place a week from to-day. I shall have to buy Felicia a ready-made present instead of working her a table-centre, as I should like to have done."

" You are impetuous people," chirruped the other, " but I suppose that true love knows no reason. Oh Felicia, if I were you, I should beg Mr. Rellerick to take you for your honeymoon to Ramsgate. The hotels there are always full of newly married people. It's such fun looking at them. If you go to Ramsgate I shall really be tempted to follow."

Simple, unsophisticated, suburban maidens ! Felicia sighed as she realized their discordant notes. Yes, she could have found it in her heart to wish that the lordly actor, trying to separate a shrimp from its shell (and failing) was nothing but a " young man," with none of the exotic qualities that in her heart she despised. If the fatiguing parade in front of other people had only ended for him when the final curtain fell! If he could have rushed from the gilded salons of the playhouse and found pleasure in the simple comfort of the suburbs, how much easier it would have been for them. But the actor becomes absorbed by the scenes that he mimics, and she knew that only too well. Still—and she cleared away her sighs—she would not like him if he were different. He was her ideal—just as he was Perhaps if he enjoyed shrimps and seed-cake he would lose the glamour that surrounded him.

Reginald felt more at his ease when the nobodies told him how they doted upon him as an actor; how they had waited at the pit-doors for hours, every time that he produced a new play; how they saw him a dozen times in every rôle that he essayed. This was more pleasing to his ears than the senseless orange-blossom cackle that brought him so close to his agony.

"But in your last play," said Miss Robinson, with a coy finger raised, "I will frankly confess that I was more interested in this dear, good girl, Felicia. It would have been dreadful for you, Mr. Rellerick, if you had married a novice. Fancy the two of you, always being able to play opposite parts, and each adored by the audience."

"It isn't often that stage honors are divided so charmingly," chirped Miss Smithson. "It is like Irving and Ellen Terry. But I often think that Miss Terry could get along very nicely without

Irving, but that he would be useless without her."

"You are silly girls," said Felicia—she did not dare to look at the face of her lover. "I shall never be a great actress, because I don't care about acting. It wouldn't vex me in the least if I never appeared again, and I shall coax Reginald, in all probability, to give me a long holiday for life."

She looked at him, when she had finished. His face was stern and set. There were crows' feet around his eyes, and even at that squalid little tea-table, amid the shrimps and water-cresses, he looked yellow and unreal and heavy—like the waxen Déjazet in the Marylebone Road. He tried to shake it off. The time had not yet come when he could dare to assert himself. He assumed a light mood, but it was more difficult to assume than that of any rôle he had ever played.

It was a melancholy evening—but it was the first step on the awful ladder that he was to mount before he could see his cherished career again. He might possibly be able to climb the rest of the ladder. He felt quite sure that he would be able to do so. He intended to do his duty ; he was quite sure of that. The bitter pill must be swallowed, and it was just as well for him to get some idea of what it was going to taste like. It was going to taste very nasty indeed, but there was everything at stake. He cursed her, as she sat there with her spinsters, and he cursed the day when he had first seen her. But it was waste of time. Everything was arranged. The loophole through which he would emerge was open. He had opened it, and he must try to feel thankful for its possibilities. Perhaps he would live to laugh at this watercress tea, and to look back upon all these agonies as a nightmare that would never be resumed.

He arose to go before the nobodies had attempted to depart. He was not anxious for another *tête-à-tête* with Felicia. That which was to begin in one short week was all that ..e could endure. It was easy to see that the nobodies were disappointed in him. All girls love a lover, and Reginald Rellerick had not played his rôle convincingly. There is no such thing as originality in love-making. The good old fever must take its course in the good old way. The "*ars amatoria*" of Ovid's day has reached the twentieth century, without suffering the vestige of a change.

As he left the house, he swore 'that he would see La Chinoise the next day. He would see her, if only to tell her that everything must be at an end between them. And he thought—as a gourmand thinks of an epicurean dish—of her tears— all for him ; of her agony—all for him ; and of her certain determination not to relinquish her second Déjazet—all for him. Yes, there was a whiff of pleasure in store for him, before he allowed his career to swallow everything. But he would do his duty ; he really would. So far, he felt rather pleased with himself.

Chapter XVIII

As Reginald Rellerick entered La Chinoise's ornate villa in St. John's Wood from the front, Cerisette left it surreptitiously from the back. La Chinoise had not abandoned her old friends—there wasn't a man in London good enough to induce her to do it, she often said—but she knew extremely well that the fastidious actor would not admit the feminine souvenirs of her Piccadilly Circusdom, and she could not afford to take risks. She was a wise woman in her generation. Moreover, she was no longer young, and maturity is obliged to look before it leaps. So the interchange of confidences between La Chinoise and Cerisette ceased, as the former, peering through the curtains, saw her protector approach, and Cerisette went out at the back as Reginald came in at the front.

She received her "*petit Déjazet*" with a charming affectation of nonchalance, and Reginald contrasted this entrance with that which he had made the day before in the Notting Hill house. Here it was warm, luxurious, unstudied, and tinted. Felicia in her "tidy" gown, with an immaculate bodice, neat collar and cuffs, and generally middle-class atmosphere, had repelled him. La Chinoise, in an indescribable *peignoir*, all lace and little jig-gly bows, her tiny feet pushed into a pair of em-broidered Persian slippers, was a pleasing spectacle to enjoy. She might be an exotic, and Reginaid told himself that, when a man attains his fourth de-cade, the watercress damsel palls. Felicia sug-gested long walks before breakfast, cold baths and absolute health. La Chinoise told of the orna-mental, pictorial femininity that some natures pre-fer. He heaved a sigh of relief as she greeted him. Like Felicia, she was also pouring out tea—but the tea service sat daintily on an absurd little table, and it was " egg-shell " china, furnished with curi-ous little handles.

" I did not expect you," she said coquettishly, as he embraced her (and there was no buttered muffin on her lips), " and I did not particularly want you to-day. Why did you come ?"

This was what he liked, and she probably knew it. He hated to be jumped at with words of wel-come, and kissed smackingly on each cheek. He preferred the senseless coquetries of the diplomatic woman, as warped men usually prefer such coquet-ries.

" I came to see you," he said, " because I have something very important to tell you—something," he sank his voice to a mournful whisper—" that it will pain you to hear."

The women belonging to La Chinoise's class are always prepared for the worst. They expect it, and are surprised when it doesn't come. La Chinoise was not in the least affected. She arose, and poured boiling water from the gypsy kettle into the fragile teapot.

"You must drink some tea," she said, "before you make yourself unpleasant. I know what you are going to tell me. You have discovered that this dear little place is too expensive. Of course, I know that. That is why I like it. I can survive that, *mon Déjazet*, as long as you love me—and as long as you do not cast me off."

She handed him a cup of tea, and sat at his feet on the white rug, as he tried to drink it. Her face was lighted with what seemed to be the most undiluted sort of affection. She sank into involuntary silence. There was no anxiety to hear what he had to say. Her pose was that of a woman simply exuding unselfish affection. Reginald sipped his tea in slow epicureanism. How delightful it was to rest amid such surroundings! Even the knowledge that, in a few short moments, he must virtuously push her aside, and shatter her hopes, was a sort of melancholy pleasure. Poor thing! How horrible for one solitary woman to find her life intruded upon by a brace of Déjazets. She had lived through the misery of her first disaster. Would she survive the second? Could she survive the second, when he was the second?

And he sipped his tea, as though it were nectar, gazing all the time upon the top of her head. A man never feels so puissant, so masterful, so absolutely one of the sterner sex, and so unconsciously noble, as when he is looking at the top of a woman's head. Possibly she had sat thus with Déjazet when the artist had told her of his contemplated marriage with Geneviève Delaunay. But the surroundings were different. Here it was a hothouse in the hothouse quarter of London. There it was the cold, Bohemian, Latin region, all students, and bread crusts, and poverty. Yes, he had advantages. The original Déjazet was less fortunate. Women loved comfort and opulence. What he had to tell her would be a bitter blow to her. Would she faint? Would she seize the Japanese sharply-pointed paper-knife that lay upon a table, and stab herself *à la* Bernhardt? The idea was not displeasing to him, but still, from a sense of duty, he would prevent it if possible. He reached out to the table, and taking up the knife, felt its edge, and quietly put it in his pocket.

"What are you doing, *mon petit ?*" she asked, lifting her fluffy head from his knee. "Why do you take my knife? Are you afraid that I am going to commit suicide? Alas! my poor little Déjazet, I am not that kind of woman. If I were, I should have done the deed long ago. There have been many 'situations' in my life, that could have led up to it."

He was conscious of a slight sense of disappointment. It would have been a distinct satisfaction to the ego-maniac, to see the woman whom he loved, and whom Déjazet had loved, in the throes of a suicidal determination. Every actor loves a dash of melodrama, and to Reginald this would have added to the sorrowful piquancy of the occasion.

" You would not do anything so foolish, I feel sure," he said reluctantly. "You are sensible, Claire, and as you say, your life has not been a very radiant one. I only wish I could have made it so, at this late day, but—circumstances forbid it."

She was curious, at last, for she felt the beginning of the end. Her keen eyes took in the sumptuous apartment she occupied. She noted the richly embroidered stuffs that hung from the doors, the oddly fashioned furniture, the magnificent carpet, the ornaments that decorated the cabinets, the mantel, and the numerous shelves. Still, she told herself that this was a peculiar man, filled with peculiar ideas, and she steeled her heart. In her face, there was nothing but complete confidence in him. She took a chair opposite to him, and gazed gravely at his face. It was very dark and grief-worn. She began to fear the worst, and it was hard work to be tranquil and *insouciante*, as she took his empty cup away from him, folded her hands, and waited for her doom. She had known so many of these dooms, but each seemed worse than its predecessor. It is impossible to grow accustomed to a continuous performance of disappointments.

He cleared his throat, and began : " You saw that little girl we met at Madame Tussaud's, Claire, when we were looking at Déjazet, and enjoying our first happiness."

La Chinoise remembered her extremely well

It was her business to do so. "That little English miss, with the Christmas-card face, and the badly-fitting clothes. The girl with features like an angel, and the outfit of a rubbish-basket. Yes, I saw her. How could I forget her, when you sent me away from you, to join her? She was your leading lady, you said."

"Yes," he assented dully. "She was my leading lady."

He could not continue. There was a clot in his throat that choked him. He felt like a coward, about to dash the happiness from a woman who adored him. He put himself in her place perpetually. He could imagine no worse fate for a woman, than that of being suddenly cut off from association with himself. His ego-maniacal instinct almost rendered him unselfish.

"Well?" said La Chinoise expectantly. "What of it? She looks like a harmless poor thing."

"I hate her," he cried vehemently, rising and steering himself through the alleys of chairs and tables and palms. "I hate her. I am sick of her. She is nauseating to me. I cannot endure her baby ways, and her incessant exactions. She is the one force in my life that I abominate. The idea of meeting her day after day is horrible to me, and yet——"

La Chinoise was silent in thought. Then she said laughingly—for it seemed too impossible to believe: "One would think that this was the story of Déjazet all over again; that irate parents insisted upon your marrying her, and that you would he led to the altar almost at the sword's point. But this is chilly, cloudy, foggy, unromantic England, *n'est-ce-pas ?*"

He would be brave. He must do it. There was no use prolonging the agony any more. Agony it was, of course, but it had a silver coating, and he would not have abandoned this hour, if he could have done it.

" It is the story of Déjazet," he said slowly, and he almost felt the glass eyes of the image in the Marylebone Road looking at him through the distance. " There are no parents in the case. There is no duel to be fought, but I am going to marry that girl, and I have come here to-day to tell you so."

He looked round to see if she were prostrate upon the carpet. But she was not. She sat idly playing with the lace of her *peignoir*, her brows knitted in thought. You or I—who are inclined to think that there are other people in the world besides ourselves—might have regarded that meditation as something with clammy calculation in it. The actor could see no calculation. She was distraught, and he waited in keenest anxiety for her mind to arrange itself.

" Well," she said, slowly—and her extreme effort to be seemly, and to avoid all false steps was not apparent to him. " It is certainly droll that there should be two Déjazets in my life. But this case is different. It is quite dissimilar. If you marry this girl, whom you hate, why need it make any difference to us ? I can stay here in St. John's

Wood, and I will still look upon you as my dearest friend and champion."

This was tentative, but he did not know it. " I came here to-day," he continued, " to tell you that our relations must end. I love you, Claire. It will be one of the cruellest blows dealt me, to separate from you. But it must be done. My duty is clear, is it not ?"

Claire forgot herself for the moment. " Why is it clear ?" she asked angrily. " It was clear in Déjazet's case, but he was a different man. He was an artist, with a chivalrous nature, and he gave me up, filled with a sort of Quixotic notion that he was unable to carry out. With you, it is otherwise."

" With me it is otherwise," cried the ego-maniac, roused to self-defense, in a bitter effort to be as symmetrical as his counterpart. " Am I indeed worse than this man who poses in a Chamber of Horrors, as the newest of the horrors ? He was so chivalrous ! He was so Quixotic ! It was noble for him to give up the woman he loved, and tie himself to the woman he married. But with me it is different. I am not chivalrous ! I am not Quixotic ! I can easily do what this criminal scorned to do. You can think of Déjazet tenderly, as a martyr. But I am different. And, pray, what has induced you to think that I am different ?"

He stopped in front of her, furiously wrestling for his own cause. He looked upon the woman with much of the anger that he usually vented upon Felicia Halstead. She was unable to credit him with the decent motives that had actuated the dead

Déjazet, and his indignation knew no bounds. She saw that she had made a mistake—that her calculations had miscarried. That the evil was irremediable, she did not believe. That he would leave her was tolerably certain, for his miserable competition with the dead original was clear to her. But the cases were different. They were certainly different. Déjazet was a struggler and a Bohemian of the old-fashioned type. This man in front of her, with the exotic ideas, was a Bohemian of the new-fashioned type—a Bohemian who could "rough it" only on quilted silken couches, with costly accessories. The cause was not at all hopeless.

La Chinoise, with a sudden impulse, threw herself upon a sofa and sobbed. She had carefully removed the pins from her hair, and it fell in a mass over her shoulders. Her attitude was that of absolute abandonment to an almost masterful grief. She knew that he was watching her, and that she made an artistic picture. It was not all assumed. She was genuinely distressed at the unexpected turn that things had taken. It seemed that the fates were against her. She could never make any headway against the turbulent seas of her life. Tantalus-like, the cup was always snatched from her lips, as she was about to drink. She wept for herself, but the effect upon him was agreeable. His sarcasms died upon his lips, and he saw only the woman, prone, and tear-drenched, bewailing his loss.

"Forgive me," she said presently, drying her eyes, "and do not reproach me. Déjazet was lost

to me, and I dread a repetition of that misery.
Forgive me for ever suggesting that you would do
what he disdained. If he was good, you are better" (she might have added "because you are
richer," but didn't), "and I apologize to you for my
unworthy ideas. Oh, *mon petit, je suis désolée*. I
would say, as I said to him, 'You shall not marry
this girl,' and I would search London for proofs of
her infamy. But—oh! how well I remember it—
it was that very search of mine in Déjazet's case,
that brought about the disaster. I would not do it
again. I discovered that she was his rival. It could
not be, in your case, and I would not tell you, if I
knew that it was. I have reproached myself ever
since."

There was the ring of sincerity in these last
words, but to him the false and the sincere sounded
alike, inasmuch as they both catered to his own
vanity. The maggots of his endless self-love fed
easily upon everything that she said. But he
started as she spoke of the "disaster" that her
work had hastened. He started, and trembled,
and as he stood before her, erect and immobile, he
felt that she was a mob of women, gazing at him,
and commenting upon him. Once more he seemed
to be No. 37 in the catalogue—yellow and sinister.

"You could discover nothing about Felicia," he
said at last, resolutely pushing aside these ideas.
"You could not tell me that she is my rival. I
know that she is. I discovered it for myself."

La Chinoise sat up, and her eyes looked like
those of an owl, in their solemnity and darkness.

"Then," she said falteringly, "You hate her—quite as he hated her. It is impossible. It is beyond the natural. *Grand ciel! Quel horreur!*"

He might have been a somnambulist, a man in a hypnotic condition, as he sang dreamily: "I have lost everything. I must marry this girl, and you and I must end our relations. I will try and do my duty. Perhaps I have been a brute. I hate her now, but, possibly, when she is my wife, bearing my name, I may become at any rate more reconciled to my life."

Claire heard him, as though dazed. It sounded like an echo of the past, translated into English. The real woman in her nature leaped into life for an instant, and forgetful of herself, oblivious of the ruin of her prospects, she sprang from her chair, and cried out, "You shall not marry this woman. I will prevent it. It shall not be permitted. I swear it."

The ego-maniac was satisfied. Unable to realize the intensity of the words she uttered, and the reason for their utterance, he accepted them blindly as proof that she loved him as she had loved Déjazet. A dulcet self-complacency crept into his face. He was reinstated in his own self-affection. The rest was easy.

"Claire," he said peacefully, "It is all over. I must marry, and you shall not prevent it. Be reasonable, my dear one. He left you to the fate that brought you to the painted atrocities of Piccadilly Circus. I shall do nothing of the sort. You have told me that in reality I am better than Déjazet.

I will show you that you were right. I am not what the world calls rich, but I shall do what I can. Before coming here to-day, I instructed my lawyers to buy this house for you. Within a week, it will be yours for life, and you will be beyond the clutches of immediate want. The furniture I have already presented to you. I hate to make the gift. It seems like a bargain, but, my dear, it will be some relief to me to know that you are provided for, and although it will not compensate you for my loss—it will—"

He broke down, touched by the harrowing picture of his own magnanimity. How splendidly he had behaved. What quiet force, and resolute self-sacrifice there were in his words. He had never been fonder of himself than he was at this moment. But he had not reckoned upon such a result as came almost immediately, and he could scarcely credit it. The courtesan, suddenly reared up by his words, took the place of the woman who had threatened to prevent his marriage. The cosy little house in St. John's Wood, thrown into her lap, as it were, banished forever the heroic dregs that had struggled to the top for one moment, in the outcast's nature. The house, the furniture, were hers for life, without the incubus of an exacting protector. La Chinoise struggled to her feet, and hurled thanks at his head—thanks that proclaimed her in her true colours—thanks that overwhelmed him with humiliation.

And when the effervescence of her gratitude had subsided, she said quietly, " You were right, *mon*

Déjazet. It is an odious thing to separate, but it must be done. And in time, my darling Reginald, you will grow to love this girl. She will bear you children, and she will be true to you. That much of her character I could read when we met her at the wax-works. I shall grieve for you always, Reginald. I shall never forget you. Your gifts will not compensate me for your love, but, as you say, it is something to be provided for, and I must be satisfied."

She smiled, and although she tried to inject a wistful expression into her features, it was not possible. She was plainly radiant, and at peace. She threw herself into his arms, and tried to sob, but even as she did so, he could see her in the mirror opposite, looking at the pictures, the furniture, and the hangings, and mentally saying a gratified " All mine."

He shook her from him in a rage of despair and disenchantment, which she did not understand. He was horribly in earnest, this poor *petit Déjazet*, who was richer, and consequently more generous than the other. And as she tried to soothe him, her words stung him, and her glad reconciliation to life without him, stabbed him in the tender region of self.

He was deserted—deserted by the woman who had loved the thing in the Marylebone Road— deserted because he had cast his gifts in her lap, and because with her, and her ilk, it was all a question of gifts. It was complete humiliation, that drove him, even more furiously than anything else had done, into the web spun by Felicia.

"One last kiss," said the siren, grateful for her competence. "You cannot refuse me that."

But he flung her rudely aside upon the quilted sofa that would help to extinguish the tragedy of his loss. He stalked from the house, more completely crushed than he had ever been, and as he banged the front door, he knew that he had banged from his life a parody of love that would have been apparent to the merest youth. And La Chinoise, peering through the curtains, saw him go. She laughed quietly, and threw herself luxuriously into a chair.

"I can't afford to interfere now," she thought. "I am settled for life. And he will probably live happily with that girl for ever. Those two Déjazet stories, similar up to the present, must separate at some time. Ah, *mon Déjazet*, you have brought me peace at last."

Chapter XIX

THE MARRIAGE PRELUDE

IN a few hours the wedding-day would dawn.
Reginald, tossing about on his big, blue, bed—his
his big, blue, solitary bed, for the last time—tried
vainly to sleep. It was out of the question. His
brain was alert and busy, and the shadows in the
room might have been alive, as they bumped themselves against him—absolute obstacles in the way
of his self-forgetfulness. The night was interminable. He could not drive from his mind the picture
of his double—also alone with the shadows. Before another sun had set Reginald would be miles
away from London—miles away from his waxen
counterpart. An almost frantic desire to look
upon the yellow Déjazet, for the last time, took
possession of him. It would be for the last time.
When he returned to London, with all his troubles
in the background, Madame Tussaud's would be to
him but the husk of a hideous memory. But he
longed to see how he looked in the eyes of the mob
once more, and then cut himself resolutely away
from his obsession forever. He would like to gaze
at the wax, and cry "Criminal! Criminal!" before
it. He wished to see if he could hurl this epithet

at his double, without wrenching his heart-strings.
It was the final effort of the ego-maniac to be normal. In the life of every such man there is one
fierce struggle to be as his fellows are.

Reginald arose, and threw on his clothes. He
was not quite sure what he was going to do, but
he was desperate and unreasoning. All around
him he saw the preparations for his departure.
There was his portmanteau, labelled "Windermere." It was at Windermere that he was to spend
his honeymoon. Crampton had suggested Windermere. He could not imagine why. It was a long
way off—so many tearing, merciless miles from
London. Reginald looked at the clock on the
mantel-piece. It struck two o'clock. He would be
alone—alone with Felicia—with Felicia, his wife—
that very night. He shuddered as he thought of
the relentless rush of events. It was cold. The
unlived hours of the morning are usually chilly and
devitalizing. He could not stand the horror of this
silent, almost reproachful house, and acting on the
impulse that had prompted him to throw on his
clothes, he rushed out into the street.

He trod the weary, dreary way to the Marylebone Road, but it seemed to him a quick and
almost invigorating route. How often had he
walked there before! And what had he gained by
it? Nothing but the inspiration to justify a man
whom the world abhorred. If he could be normal
again! He almost envied the poor homeless
wretches—the sediment of metropolitan life—who
passed him on his way. They were not duplicated

in wax for the public to gaze upon. They existed and they died, and nobody cared. For an instant he wondered if fame were really worth while—if it were human—if it were not a struggle for the abnormal, for no other reason than to be abnormal.

When he reached the hateful building in the Marylebone Road, the fever of its colour seemed to have disappeared. It looked gray, and sombre, as such a resort for ghosts should look. The desire to enter simply overwhelmed him. Why should this museum be closed at its most interesting moment? Fantastic ideas of a carnival of criminals in the Chamber of Horrors occurred to him. If he could only detect his Déjazet in undignified orgies. Possibly the wax that stood so turgid during the day relaxed at night. Perhaps Déjazet came down from his pedestal at night, and laid siege to the waxen hearts of Maria Manning and Elizabeth Gibbons. Perchance the luckless hounded artist leaped from his thraldom in the cavern of criminals, and aspired to higher things, in other rooms, with the kings and queens. What if the " horrors " revolted, in the dead hours of the morning, forced the monarchs and celebrities to abdicate their positions, and sat, high and mighty, in the haunts of the lucky ones ?

There was a dim light perceptible through one of the windows. Prosaically, Reginald told himself that workmen were making repairs. Even in the world of wax, things went wrong occasionally. The actor watched the light as though it were his last hope. It seemed to beckon to him to come in and make himself at home. As he looked at it, it was suddenly extinguished, and a little old man, in an overcoat turned up at the collar, let himself out of a tiny door at the side, and locked it. The workmen had gone, and the watchman had made his rounds.

The watchman saw the eager, fevered actor, and frowned. "I've seen you here before," he said. "It's a strange hour for honest folks to be out in. I must ask you to move on, or I shall call a policeman."

"No," murmured Reginald in low tones. "It is not necessary. I am an actor studying a part. I should like to enter for a few minutes, and see how the waxworks look at this hour of the morning."

"Impossible." was the stern retort. "You had better go away. There's a bobby at the corner."

"Look here," said Reginald, with the diplomacy of desperation, "this is a very serious matter to me, my man. If you let me in, I swear to you that nobody shall be any the wiser. I promise you that I will stay five minutes only, and—and—here's a five-pound note for your kindness. That means a pound a minute. You don't often get such good pay, I imagine."

The obduracy of the watchman gave way. A five-pound was a five-pound note, and—actors were strange people. The man probably spoke the truth. He had heard of Bernhardt sleeping in her coffin, for the sake of the experience, and he had been told of several ladies who had visited consumptive patients in hospitals, in order to study the symptoms. In any case, a five-pound note was a five-pound note.

He turned slowly, and unlocked the door. The five-pound note crackled in his fingers—there is no other paper money that crackles so musically—and he beckoned to the actor to follow him.

"Five minutes," he said. "I am breaking the rules, sir, but you are paying me well for it. Five minutes, and no more."

He lighted a gas-jet in each room, and led the way to the Chamber of Horrors, at the instigation of Rellerick.

"In five minutes I shall be back," he said. "I will leave you until then."

The actor's footsteps clanked over the deserted floors. As soon as he was alone, a dreadful desire to shriek out aloud, seized him. He seemed to feel the obscurity of the horrible cavern. The waxen figures in their draperies, looked like corpses in winding-sheets. If they had been silent and unfathomable in the day-time, they were incomparably more oppressively taciturn at this unexplored hour. In the gloom he could see the sere outlines of their faces, and the dark cavities that held their glassy eyes. It was like a visit to a sepulchre, and the actor's blood seemed to coagulate in his veins. This was the hall that echoed the cockneyism of the 'Arries and 'Arriets of the metropolis. Now, there was not a sound alive through its length and breadth. Reginald could almost hear himself breathe.   The noise of his pumping pulses was the only real issue he encountered.

Déjazet stood there with the others, just as lugubrious as ever.   There was not the least indication of illicit revelry, or of nocturnal resurrection. The figure maintained the same attitude that Reginald had noted previously.   It looked darker, more deathlike, more uncanny, in these watches of the night, than during the picnicking hours of daylight.   An unoccupied pedestal stood by the side of Déjazet.   They were preparing a new horror, culled from the sensationalism of the day.

Before he knew what he was doing, Reginald leaped upon the deserted pedestal, and stood by the side of his counterpart, his limbs seeking the same attitude, the terror of his expression sinking into the unsightly yellow nothingness of the double.   And as he stood there, his own identity seemed to wither and vanish.   He was Déjazet, indubitably.   It seemed to him that he understood every motive that had actuated the poor artist, as he had never understood before.   He wished that the doors at the end of the hall would suddenly frame the sight-seeing mob that he knew so well. He longed to be on exhibition by the side of his double, and to hear the ribald comments of the multitude.

Then he recalled his intention to hurl the epithet of " Criminal !" at the helpless wax, but the word burned his lips.   He could not give it utterance. Instead, he would have liked to cry " Martyr !" so that every image in the room could hear it; so that he might pose as the champion of this yellow, bloodless thing, that could no longer defend itself.

There was no more terror for him in his surroundings.   He would prefer to stay where he was, and be catalogued with the criminals.   They were at rest, any way.   There was no further contest to worry them.   The rapt attention of the mob was theirs by day and by night.   Their deeds had been sifted and classified.   Perhaps the watchman would forget him, and when Felicia went to the church to claim him as her own, she would not find him. And in the days to come, she would visit Tussaud's, and perhaps see him there, far beyond her reach, in the dismal, but imperishable ranks of what she would call " atrocities."

`His position on the pedestal tired' him.   His pulsating blood could not endure the perpetual pose, and he alighted from the standing-place, so that Déjazet towered above him once more, in his yellow, waxen superiority.   Then the spell was broken, and the cold, dark hall caused him to shiver.   The watchman appeared suddenly—a curious contrast, in his little, old, sordid life, to the majesty of the silent wax-works.

"Time's up," he said—and his voice echoed through the hall, until the very wax-works seemed to ring with it.

" I'm ready," whispered Reginald—for he could not permit his own voice to journey through the cavern.   Then he turned to Déjazet, and his lips formed the word " good-bye."   He looked to see if his double heeded his departure, and it seemed to him that the features of the model were contracted as though in anguish.

"Good-bye," he murmured again.

Then he followed the silent watchman, anxious to save his vitality from further depression. The little old man heaved a sigh of relief as he locked his unusual visitor from the exhibition. He had taken risks, for the sake of five pounds—risks of dynamite and other explosive possibilities. Thank heavens, that it had all ended so satisfactorily, and that he was five pounds the richer, without grave results.

Reginald was back in his own apartments before the day dawned, and for a couple of hours he slept a dream-ridden, uneasy sleep. He was with the wax-works again, this time "assisting" at the wedding of Déjazet and Marie Antoinette's head. The dream was so gruesome, yet vivid, that he awoke with the perspiration streaming from the pores of his skin, and was thankful for the light that came into his room through the blinds.

It was his wedding day—a black, forbidding morning. The day had dawned reluctantly, as though it were scarcely worth while, and more for the sake of keeping up the old battered routine, than to confer any new comforts on mankind. It was to be a quiet wedding, and none of the actor's friends had been bidden to it. Reginald Rellerick had never been able to understand the theory of inviting crowds of people to watch two mortal atoms linking themselves in conventional bonds.

Crampton was abroad early. He seemed to have

grown older within the last few days. Reginald almost pitied him, as he saw the old shoulders stooping over their self-imposed work, and noted the haggard, dessicated face that scarcely looked at him.

"You will start from Euston," said Crampton, in rough, gritty tones, "and you will reach Windermere late. Rooms have been secured for you, and a four-wheeler will meet you at the station."

It sounded as though Crampton were parcelling him off to eternity. How thoroughly the machine had worked! The wheels had gone round and round, and in a few more evolutions they would have whizzed him to Windermere, where he would find a four-wheeler awaiting him at the station, and rooms that had been secured for him, in advance. Nothing had been left to chance. The wheels had done their work well. There was not the slightest possibility that he would lose his way at Windermere, and wander into the lake. There was no hope of rooflessness and houselessness. It had all been cut and dried. Everything was cut and dried. Even the clothes that he was to wear had been pre-arranged. They lay on the big, blue bed—the limp trousers waiting for his chaste limbs; the sprawling coat clamouring for the support of his arms. His collar, his tie, his boots were there before his eyes. Even the chrysanthemum that was to adorn his buttonhole spread its starry white petals on the dressing-table.

He dressed himself slowly, and surveyed his form carefully in the long mirror. Yes, he looked yellow and dry, and there was a sinister twist to his features. He had once thought himself beautiful. Now, he was unable to detect any grace in his face or figure. He had aged. Possibly he would be rejuvenated. When he came back to London, his prospects brilliant, all the impediments in his path rigorously removed, then. . . . But he could not see himself back in London. He tried to imagine the old playhouse, in its glow of electricity, and with its crowd of eager faces—but it looked dark and distant. He could see nothing but the present that was jostling his vision ferociously.

The news of the marriage had " leaked out," and Crampton, for reasons best known to himself, had supplied the leak. The little ivy-covered church was well filled with the Bohemian element of the metropolis. Each newspaper had a reporter on hand, and there were artists, actors, managers, stage-hands, and a few of the "*flaneurs*" who live for the world behind the scenes. It was all informal; but it was none the less pictorial for that. Reginald had anticipated a deserted church. A few "witnesses"—there must always be "witnesses" to the deed of marriage—had been suggested to him, and he had easily consented to the names submitted. But the marriage of a great actor is scarcely less interesting than his death, and a few subtle paragraphs, in a few subtle journals, had sufficed to fill the little church.

Reginald went there as in a dream. It was a torture that must be endured, and if he could dream through it, it would be all the better for him. It was a simple and unadorned wedding, as far as the spectators were concerned. They saw the great actor in conventional morning attire, with a face set and stolid. Their eyes rested upon a radiant little bride, in a gray walking-dress of unobtrusive fashion. The witnesses were equally subdued in appearance. Crampton, Mrs. Landington, the two "nobodies" of the Notting Hill tea-party; and half a dozen other selected acquaintances, stood beside the bride and bridegroom at the altar rails.

Reginald heard the dull, drab tones of the minister with a smile upon his face. As the reverend gentleman took up the book, it seemed to the actor that it was a catalogue he held, and instead of the marriage service, he would not have been surprised to hear: "This is Déjazet, the self-confessed murderer of the beautiful Geneviève Delaunay. On their wedding night he strangled her to death, and——"

It was a ridiculous idea, but all these witnesses and acquaintances might have been wax-works—the relics of his former days, Tussauded around him. The funny little person over there was Pinerville, a man who had written very bright plays. Watch his smile, and study his features. There was Winkle, the dramatic critic, who praised everybody so highly that he had been driven to drink. See how red his nose was. There was a group from the club to which he belonged. Note the dark, unlaughing faces of the men. And beside him was Crampton. Crampton was the secretary of a famous actor, who had taught him to be reticent. Was he not a funny, mouldy thing? That fat woman with the cameo brooch over the toboggan of her bust, was Mrs. Landington, a fat housekeeper of Notting Hill, and the girl by his side was Felicia Halstead, an actress whom all London——

Reginald awoke, and heard the final words of the minister. It was the riot of his emotions as he read the imaginary catalogue over Felicia Halstead, that woke him. She might have been a famous actress. She would have been a famous actress. Now it was impossible. He had torn her from the grasp of the insatiable London public. She was his wife.

The clergyman was ending his service :—" and have pledged their troth, each to the other, and have declared the same by giving and receiving a ring, and by joining hands. I pronounce that they are man and wife, in the name of the Father, and of the Son, and of the Holy Ghost. Amen."

He laughed aloud as the final words were spoken. The people around him thought it was the eccentricity of glee. They were man and wife. He had plucked her from his path, as an obstacle, and she was his to do with as he chose. He looked at the fair and luminous face of the bride in disgust. How could he go on looking at that face which he detested until death released one of them? He heard the hum of the people, and he knew that some were shaking his hand, and that others were expressing impossible hopes to him. It was a tragedy-farce, but this was the last act. The curtain would be rung down shortly, and the play consigned to the critics.

What they were all saying he never quite knew. Pinerville, after his congratulations, seemed to murmur something about a comedy. He rather fancied that Winkle informed him of the birth of No. 10, to be named Reginald Rellerick Winkle. Mrs. Landington, he thought, was crying. He wondered why. What reason on earth had Mrs. Landington to cry? The club-men threw phrases with " old fellow," and " old boy," and " old chappie," and " old pal,"—always something old—at him. They were apparently the chorus, and they were singing the " old boy " song instead of the usual " tra-la-la."

Felicia took his arm, and they walked to the vestry, and thence into the dark, threatening morning. Mortimer Branton, whom he had noticed in the crowd, approached, and wrung Felicia's hand.

" You slighted my offer," he said, " but I am persistent. It is still open."

" Oh, Mr. Branton," laughed Felicia in her irrepressible delight; " don't you see that I am married? Doesn't that settle it forever?"

The manager shrugged his shoulders. " No," he answered, " You will have your month of honeymoon. You can think it over, then. I leave the offer open for one month."

Reginald scowled upon Branton, and would have insulted him at the church door, if the manager had remained. As it was, Branton stole quickly away, casting one amused look at Felicia's perplexed and indignant face.

An elegant brougham stood in the street, just behind the carriage assigned to the bride and bridegroom. Felicia had already stepped into the vehicle, and Reginald was about to reluctantly join her when the owner of the brougham came down the path, and called to the coachman. She cast a look at the bridegroom and he recognized her instantly. It was La Chinoise. She made a quick step forward and took his hand.

"I wish you luck," she said, nervously, "*Mon petit—mon petit* Reginald."

He started. It was not her usual mode of addressing him. "Have you forgotten Déjazet?" he asked.

Through her carmine tints she paled. "I will forget him," she replied, hurriedly, "if you will. Forget him. He belongs to the past. Be happy, *mon petit bonhomme. Je te le souhaite.*"

She pressed his cold, limp fingers in her own, stepped into the brougham, and was driven away. Reginald stood still for a moment, and watched the receding carriage. Then, with a sigh, he jumped into the conveyance that held Felicia, the driver whipped up his horses, and the marriage prelude had been played.

Chapter XX

HIS NEMESIS

REGINALD sat alone in the black, horsehair smoking room of the little hotel at Windermere. They had arrived late, after a taciturn journey from London ; they had supped in the dining-room with half-a-dozen belated travellers, and then Felicia had gone to their room, collapsing from the strain of the last few days. Her joy had been gradually checked, during the miserable journey from Euston —the fateful, melancholy Euston—and as she had left Reginald for the cruellest parody of a bridal chamber that had ever been imagined, she had looked almost apathetically at his rigid, tallowy face, unenlivened by a solitary human sentiment. She had murmured a weary " *Au revoir*," and had pressed his damp and unresponsive hand.

And now he sat alone, listening to the wooden ticking of an odious grandfather's clock, and to the tumult of the weather outside. It was a noisy vehement night. A raging wind almost shook the foundations of the slender hotel, and the rain was blown against the windows in showers. The large drops tapped electrically at the panes, and his wrought-up imagination tried to read a message in the din of the storm.

The smoking-room was deserted. One solitary man from London had arrived by the same train as the bride and bridegroom, and apparently he was as restless as Reginald himself. The actor could hear his footsteps upon the veranda outside, and he wondered if this was another bridegroom at Windermere for the sake of sweet communion. The man made him nervous, with his insistent footsteps. Yet he was interested in him, for the landlord had told him that he hailed from London. A metropolitan unit in this God-forsaken silent spot, seemed like the last link that bound him to his other life.

The grandfather's clock seemed anxious to tick away the minutes. The noise of the pendulum was like that of the tramp, tramp of soldiers, and combined with the swishing wind and the electric rain outside, it made Reginald feel that his ears were filled with sound. Here he was, sitting alone in this hideous country room, miles away from the vivid life of the metropolis, a prey to the keenest agony of dread and misery, and for what? For the sake of a woman who had clambered into his life, and who had perched herself upon his hopes and his prospects. The noose was around his neck, and she held the ropes. And she was upstairs, in white and lace, awaiting his advent, and probably listening to this dreadful *fracas* of the elements, that threatened to lift up the hotel and fling it away.

A horrible sense of helplessness took possession of him.   His blood seemed to engorge itself in his veins, and his breath came stertorously.   Then he was calm and reflective again, and the tapping of the rain at the window was distinctly audible.

" Lights out at twelve, sir," said a voice at the door.   " We close at midnight."

Lights out at twelve !   He looked at the grandfather's clock.   It was half-past eleven.   He had still half an hour in which to reconcile himself to his fate.   Still, if he chose, he could stay there even when the lights were out, as Déjazet stayed in the darkness of the Tussaud Exhibition of the Marylebone Road.   What would he give if he could look upon Déjazet at the present moment ?

He reached over to the tiny marble table at his side, and poured out, with a hand that shook, a goblet of brandy.   He swallowed it greedily, but the life that it caused to rush through his veins was not what he had thought.   The grandfather's clock ticked louder ; the wind howled its gusty requiem more vociferously ; and the torrents of rain beat against the window as though rhythmically crying, " Let me in !   Let me in !"

Again that engorgement of blood and that stertorous spasm made themselves felt, and he was conscious of waiting until the crowd in his brain had passed away.   He felt red, but as he glanced in the fly-spotted mirror opposite he looked yellow—as yellow as his double, now so far away from him ; as waxenly jaundiced as his poor Déjazet, who had suffered as he now suffered.

"Unable to overcome his loathing"—he was reading from the catalogue of Tussaud's Exhibition the plaintive story of the French artist's life and death. Perhaps Déjazet had sat in a smoking-room, and listened to a grandfather's clock ticking him towards his Geneviève. Reginald tried to calmly consider the sequence of events that had led him to this moment, for of course there was a sequence, and a logical sequence at that. His mind was incapable of logical reasoning. The moment itself stood forth, black and threatening, like a jet star, in a clouded sky, and the moment was all he could perceive.

She had wrecked his life, and ruined his career. And he had married her for the sake of that career. Could he ever resume his old life with this millstone of hatred around his neck? Would future generations ever remember the name of Reginald Rellerick? Would he ever go down to posterity? Everything seemed far away from him. There was nothing in this baleful place that suggested the glittering intoxication of London, and the luminous clot of fame that had been his before his Nemesis appeared.

His Nemesis! Yes, she was his Nemesis—this pale, languid, and clinging woman, who was at this moment breathing his name and forgetting the raging storm outside. She was his Nemesis—the infernal daughter of Nox; the goddess of vengeance; one of the Parcæ with a helm and a wheel by her side. And she was waiting for him to crush his ambition in her embrace. It was she who had dragged him to Windermere. If anybody had told him a year ago that he would be sitting alone in a squalid hotel, miles away from London, the unwilling bridegroom of a detested bride, he would have laughed derisively. He laughed hysterically even now. It seemed so utterly ridiculous. His life had been one long and emphatic worship of self. He had exclusively followed the dictates of his own will. And what had it all signified? Merely that at the prime of his life and of his hopes, he was sitting alone in a deserted hotel, listening to an old-fashioned clock that teemed towards midnight, when the lights would be put out.

The man on the veranda outside irritated him, and hurt his nerves. Why was that man parading his heels outside the hotel on such a merciless night? Perhaps it was the waxen Déjazet who had followed him from London to whisper advice in his ear, and to hurl an "*Et tu Brute!*" at him. His lips formed the word "Déjazet." He spoke it aloud, and the sound in the empty, horsehair smoking-room was dismal enough.

He was a weak fool after all. Men with wills of their own—men who went down into history—had not tamely submitted to a fate such as his. Even Déjazet had fought for the sake of posterity, and had won a yellow waxen notoriety in the eyes of the English middle-classes. Better that, than nothing at all. By all the silly, unstable laws of man, he was bound in a few minutes to rush joyfully to his wife, and fling himself into her unreluctant arms. His mind recoiled from the idea. He hated her very name ; he detested her personality ; he loathed the obstacles that she had thrown in his path. Why should he lie to himself for her sake, and for the sake of the world ?

And at that moment there came upon him, like a shock, the certain knowledge that he would never see London again ; never again hold rapt multitudes in the splendid enthusiasm of the theatre ; never again look upon the metropolis that had pinnacled and fêted him ; never again pose before admiring crowds as a hero and an idol ; never again live the glorious, selfish life that had pampered his ego, and raised him in his own eyes above the common herd. He would never see London again. He knew it. This was a new world to which he had been rushed by relentless steam. This was a world that some natures might prefer, but that was to him far inferior to death.

It was five minutes to twelve, and the woman who was the cause of it all, lay awaiting him on her pillow. He ground his teeth, and pressed his hands to his head, that seemed as though it would burst with the pent-up atrocities of his imagination. And when he recovered, he could have sworn that at the end of the room—there—there by the curtains that framed the entrance—there by the door that scarcely shut out the storm—he saw Déjazet on his pedestal—Déjazet, the man, the hero, who had taken fate into his own hands, and determined to submit to nothing.

He arose unsteadily, and staggered to his feet. He could afford no further thoughts. Those that had come from his brain seemed to have seared and pressed it. The grandfather's clock struck twelve. The last stroke died away unwillingly, as though it were a pity to end so brilliant a day—his wedding-day. A menial came in, and approached the dingy chandelier.

"Good-night, sir," said the menial firmly but obsequiously. A moment later the lights were extinguished, and he was groping his way up the stairs to his room. Even at that moment, with his brain whizzing, he was conscious of feeling the threadbare stair-carpet, and wondering how many weary feet it took to wear out the carpet path from the smoking room to the bridal chamber. And he knew that the man from the veranda had also come in, and was likewise going to his bed-room. It could not be very far removed from the bridal chamber—judging from the adjacent footsteps.

A resentment that seemed like an electric shock tugged at his heart, as in the dimly lighted corridor, he saw the door of the bridal chamber marked "No. 37." No. 37! It was Déjazet's number in the Tussaud catalogue, and he realized it with a smile that seemed to twist his features. Here at last he would be brought face to face with his Nemesis—the woman that had dragged him from the metropolis that he would never see again. . . .

He opened the door, which was unlocked, and turning quickly, as soon as he had entered, he tried the key in the lock to shut out the world. The key resisted his efforts. He could not lock the door. It might have been tampered with, so powerless

was he to bolt himself in.   What did it matter any.
way? Nobody would disturb them.   This was a
deserted hotel in Windermere, and who would dare
to force a way into his bridal chamber?

"Reginald!" said Felicia in a low tone, raising
her head from the pillow, and looking at him from
her recumbent position. He stood still by the
door, and his eyes fell upon his wife, in her white
linen and lace. If he could only be calm. . . .

The blood rushed through his veins, and then
engorged itself in his brain. The swollen red current shut out all external noise. The grandfather's
clock ticked no longer; the wind outside had suc-
cumbed to the concert within him; the rain tapping
at the window-panes seemed suddenly to have
stopped.

"Reginald," she murmured—this poor little
bride, in one vain woman-effort to be coy.

He opened his eyes and saw her. She was as
white as the dimity counterpane that covered the
bed. The lace fell from her neck, and he saw her
blanche blue-veined throat, a throat as slender as
that of Lady Jane Grey, that had been severed by
the axe of the executioner.

"The body was found with four black finger-
marks on its throat," he muttered to himself, closing his eyes, while the blood swished no longer, but
seemed to coagulate in his head.

"Reginald!" For the third time the little bride
called to him, extending her arms as though to welcome him to her bosom.

He opened his eyes, but he could see her no

longer.   A red mist arose and interposed itself between him and her.   A horrible bloody curtain
spread itself before his view.   His Nemesis was
calling to him, and beckoning to him.

" Unable to overcome his loathing. . . .

He rushed at her like a maniac.   He knew where
she lay, white and quivering, although he could no
longer see her.   It was but a step to the bed.
He bounded over the intervening space, agile as a
panther, although blinded by the curtain that
darkened his brain.   The iron of the bedstead
struck him in the chest.   It was a guiding blow.
A moment later he had found her.   He felt the
lace upon her gown.   It brushed against his fingers,
and in his rage he pulled it and tore it from her
throat.   His fingers had reached her warm white
flesh.   He pressed the four tips against her
throat, . . .

There was a scream that rose loudly above the
noise of the storm, drowning the whirling wind and
rain, in its acute penetrating agony.   The maniac
paused for a moment, stayed by the affrighted voice
of his bride.   Then it seemed to give him fresh
nerve.   He was avenging his wrongs ; he was
championing his career ; he was struggling for the
sake of posterity as Déjazet had done.   Again he
saw her throat, and lifted her violently from her
pillow. . . .

There were steps outside ; a hand taking possession of the door-knob, and in an instant he realized
that they were no longer alone.   Into the chamber
burst Crampton, the secretary, mouldy no longer ;

the stoop in his shoulders vanished, a man alert, erect and resolute. He lost no time. He saw the poor little bride, with the veins standing blue in her face, as the fingers of the bridegroom tried to force the life from her body.

He grappled with the maniac, seizing him from the back. Reginald, in his mental revolution, knew that he was to be balked of his victim. He turned his murderous hand upon the intruder, and tried to find his throat. As he did so, the climax to his fate came swiftiy. For an instant he knew everything ; the next instant the clot in his brain seemed to break. He fell heavily to the floor, the blood pouring from his mouth and ears, and staining the carpet with a red halo.

Crampton looked down upon him, tumultuously thankful for one moment, that his own hand had been spared the horror of shedding this blood— this blood that oozed so slowly but so certainly.

Felicia, half fainting, raised herself from the bed, and saw the prostrate form of her hero. She motioned to Crampton to take her to him, and the secretary lifted her in his arms, and placed her tenderly in a chair by the side of the awful, swollen ego-maniac.

" He would have killed you," said Crampton softly. " He was Déjazet, wreaking Déjazet's vengeance on the helpless Geneviève. And "—he added this as a consolation—" he was not responsible for what he did. I knew it. I tried to avert it, and—and——"

Crampton broke down ; the tensity of his nervous strain gave way, and he sobbed helplessly, like an overgrown schoolboy, in the presence of a sudden catastrophe. But Felicia was dazed. She had not yet quite recovered from the frenzied clutch of those murderous fingers. The four marks on her throat were distinctly visible. Crampton saw them and shuddered. The lace of her gown hung in strips from her body, and as she sat there, mute in her chair, the ends of the lace fell into the pool of Reginald's blood and were dyed carmine. She remained there, comatose, and stupid, for a half hour. The grandfather's clock below had resumed its noisy sway. The wind and the rain had taken a new lease of din, and filled the room with a swirl and a patter. Crampton was thankful for Felicia's semi-swoon. He stood there and watched, as she sat silent by the side of the man to whom she had given her girlish, illogical life.

Then he felt that the spell must be broken. He lifted her in his arms, motioned to the people outside the bridal chamber to open another room for him, and carried her in. He listened to the doctor, who declared that she was suffering from shock rather than from strangulation, and prepared to stay in Windermere, until she was ready to be conveyed to London.

      *   *   *   *   *

Great was the sensation, in the London papers, as the news of Reginald Rellerick's death was flashed to the metropolis. The real facts were suppressed by the reverent Crampton, who perhaps alone knew them. Death from apoplexy on his

wedding-night was, however, quite dramatic enough
to satisfy the Londoners. The papers teemed with
columns of obituary, and eulogies that the dead
ego-maniac would have gloried in. He was the
greatest, the best, the most artistic, the most en-
lightened. Everything was superlative in death,
as is generally the case, when the positive and com-
parative have been the rule during life.

A few of the Londoners, his friends, noticed a
strange coincidence. Pushed away in an obscure
part of the papers, far removed from the magnificent obituary notice and the sensational headlines,
was a tiny paragraph that read as follows :

STRANGE ACCIDENT AT TUSSAUD'S : Just before midnight yesterday, as the watchman was making his first rounds
among the wax-works at Madame Tussaud's, a remarkable
thing happened. Without any warning whatsoever, and
without the slightest apparent reason, the large artistic figure
representing the murderer Déjazet, in the Chamber of Horrors, fell from its pedestal. It was comparately new, which
makes the event peculiarly odd. Nothing of the kind seems
to have ever happened before. The waxen Déjazet was
smashed to atoms. The watchman was quite upset, and has,
it is understood, resigned his position.

THE END.

www.ingramcontent.com/pod-product-compliance
Lightning Source LLC
Chambersburg PA
CBHW020923120726
47905CB00008B/2350